PRAISE FOR
HOWARD WALDROP AND
STRANGE MONSTERS
OF THE RECENT PAST . . .

"UNIQUE, ADDICTIVE . . . IF THIS IS YOUR FIRST
TASTE OF WALDROP, I ENVY YOU."
—George R.R. Martin

"THE RESULT OF WALDROP'S BIZARRELY ECLEC-
TIC IMAGINATION AND GONZO SENSE OF HU-
MOR IS MAGIC . . . EXCELLENT."
—Gardner Dozois

"WALDROP SUBTLY MUTATES THE PAST, EXTRAP-
OLATING THE CHANGES INTO SOME OF THE
MOST INSIGHTFUL, AND FREQUENTLY AMUS-
ING, STORIES BEING WRITTEN TODAY, IN OR
OUT OF THE SCIENCE FICTION GENRE."
—*The Houston Post/Sun*

"PRICELESS, IRREPLACEABLE WALDROP STO-
RIES. TREASURE THEM."
—from the foreword by Lewis Shiner

Ace Books by Howard Waldrop

STRANGE MONSTERS OF THE RECENT PAST
NIGHT OF THE COOTERS

NIGHT OF THE COOTERS

HOWARD WALDROP

ACE BOOKS, NEW YORK

All persons, places, and organizations in this book—except those clearly in the public domain—are fictitious, and any resemblance that may seem to exist to actual persons, places, or organizations living, dead, or defunct, is purely coincidental. With the exception of the introductory essays of non-fiction, clearly labeled as such, these are works of fiction.

This Ace Book contains the complete text of the original hardcover edition. It has been completely reset in a typeface designed for easy reading, and was printed from new film.

NIGHT OF THE COOTERS

An Ace Book/published by arrangement with
the author

PRINTING HISTORY
Ursus Imprints edition published 1990
Ace edition/July 1993

All rights reserved.
Copyright © 1990 by Howard Waldrop.
Cover art by Don Ivan Punchatz.
This book may not be reproduced in whole or in part,
by mimeograph or any other means, without permission.
For information address:
The Berkley Publishing Group,
200 Madison Avenue, New York, NY 10016.

ISBN: 0-441-57473-4

Ace Books are published by The Berkley Publishing Group,
200 Madison Avenue, New York, NY 10016.
The name "ACE" and the "A" logo
are trademarks belonging to Charter Communications, Inc.

PRINTED IN THE UNITED STATES OF AMERICA

10 9 8 7 6 5 4 3 2 1

Some very old debts: Hi, Mom! Hi, Mary! Hi, Aunt Ethel! Ms. Katherine C. Long and Ms. Eileen Gunn of the various Washingtons. And George R. R. Martin, who will find himself on these pages much more than he wants . . .

CONTENTS

HOWARD

by Chad Oliver

I suppose that we have all known people, sometimes for many years, who defy description. They may be pleasant enough, sort of like peanut butter or medium-aged wallpaper, but they are so bland that there is simply nothing of interest to say about them.

Howard Waldrop is not like that.

Howard does indeed defy description, but for the opposite reason. His personality is so strong, so distinctive, so unlike any other, human or alien, that he swamps (Howard likes swamps and spends much time in them) and tramples anything as mundane as a character sketch. Howard is Howard, and no matter where you grab him (as Bubbles LaTour used to say) you've more than got your hands full.

Since we have to begin somewhere, suppose we try a few straightforward declarative sentences that are neither more nor less than the exact literal truth.

1. On more than one occasion, I have trusted Howard with my life and I tend to be somewhat selective in those situations.

2. I have been unable to get Howard off a trout stream at midnight, exposing us both to possible drowning, death from hypothermia, starvation, and other unpleasant conditions.

3. I have been around writers for most of my years on this mudball Earth, and I have never known a writer who was *anything* like Howard—in his work habits (and he does work, you know; those stories don't just float in out of the sky), in his quality, or in the sheer maddening originality of his mind.

4. Howard is one of those annoying people who can fix anything and knows everything, but there is an unassuming

charm about him that renders all this palatable. He may just possibly be the least pretentious man in the world.

So what happened to all the simple declarative sentences?

That's Howard for you, damn him. He has a way of confounding all conventional good intentions.

"Here is Howard Waldrop, coming downstairs now, bump, bump, bump, on the back of his head, behind Christopher Robin."

There are a lot of people who know Howard, or at least know about Howard. Almost invariably, when you mention his name to them, people smile. It is not the smile of a remembered joke, the snicker inspired by a buffoon, or the well-what-can-you-say smile of superiority. It is the smile that wells up in you when someone or something makes you feel good. That's what Howard does. There is an aura about him that is overwhelmingly positive, even when Howard is in one of his usual seemingly hopeless situations. Howard is like one of his beloved cartoon characters—drop an anvil on him, plug him with an Acme harpoon, slam him into a granite wall until he is flat as a pancake and rolls around like a dime, no problem. You *know* Howard will emerge unscathed, at least on the outside. Howard is one of those guys who strolls through minefields every day of his life. The mines somehow never go off—quite.

Is the man perfect? Is there no other side to Howard Waldrop? I must confess that I have told only part of the story. This is because so much has already been written about Howard, and the standard works are readily available. The classic sources, as everyone knows, are:

The Hidden Waldrop, by Cuthbert McJung Adler. 1985. Vienna: Cerebral Ethnobotany Press.

Howard Waldrop: Highway Assassin, by Sgt. Jim Bob Hackamore. 1987. College Station: Texas A & M University Police Publications.

The Mississippi Roots of Howard Waldrop, by Edna Mae Luckett. 1984. Vicksburg: Confederate Garden Club Brochure #77.

"Be Quiet, Howard!" The Art of Getting A Word in Edgewise, by Chum Frink. 1990. San Francisco: Semiotics Publishing Company.

A Mammal's Revenge on the Fishes That Spawned Him, by

S. Orbital Ridges. 1989. Stackpole, Pennsylvania: Rod and Stream Press.

I am often asked (well, one time a bewhiskered, croak-voiced, slime-encrusted character did ask me) about Howard as a fisherman. Fisherman! Howard is no more a fisherman than Captain Ahab was mildly curious about whales.

Howard is consumed by fly fishing, absorbed in it, lost in it. It is on a river with line hissing in the frozen air and imagination working overtime that the true Howard lives. This is where Howard is pure Howard, making not even minimal concessions to such nonsense as Society. (He is, by the way, the most considerate and generous of fishing companions, and this despite his desperate psychological problems.) I would find his devotion to fly fishing an addiction bordering on madness except for one tiny fact: I've been there. I understand. I've got the disease too, the severe trout inflammation. The only difference is that I no longer have Howard's incredible endurance and energy. (No longer? Let's face it: I was not that full of beans on the best day I ever had, which was March 30, 1934.) It is also true that Howard's range is greater than mine. Trout or bass, suckers or gar, it's all the same to Howard if it swims in the water.

I do not need to tell you how fine a writer Howard is. You have his book in your hands. Read it. I will tell you that one of Howard's major talents is his ability as a story doctor. Ask any of the folks who lived through Turkey City. Howard can take another person's story and dissect it with uncanny precision. He does it with unfailing courtesy, too, even when he tells the truth.

You really cannot measure friendship. I am talking about true friends, not just folks who happen to be part of your life for one reason or another. A person either is a friend or is not.

But if you had to measure it, surely ("Don't call me Shirley!") the tests would be two:

Has it weathered the years?

It has.

Was that friend there when you needed a friend the most?

Howard was there.

Austin, Texas
March, 1990

INTRODUCTION TO

NIGHT OF THE COOTERS

THIS is what comes of not paying attention to your fly when it's on the water.

August 1985. I'd been thinking for a couple of years about a story about a county sheriff, orgone boxes, a time paradox and a car that runs on orgone accumulators.

This isn't it, but I'm coming to that.

Chad Oliver had been in Colorado fishing when his mother passed away after a long illness. He'd returned to take care of all that that entails. Later, there was still time left on the fishing cabin rent, but Chad was threatening not to go back. So Bobby Newman and I piled him into the Ford F-150 pickup his wife uses to pull horse trailers with and took off 1000 miles for the last ten days of August. I'm forgetting to mention here that the North American SF Convention (held in a U.S. city when the World SF Convention is out of the States, as it was that year in Australia, in some antipodal hellhole) was to be in Austin, and that Chad was the Toastmaster, and I had to read a new story I hadn't written yet; all this was to happen the day *after* we got back from Colorado.

Enough of that. The only book I took with me was Frank McConnell's *Critical Edition of H. G. Wells' War of the Worlds*, with the usual scholarly apparatus.

Well, there I was, reading the book at night, fishing 18 hours a day, losing one giant rainbow or brown trout after another, because I'd run across a line in the book that made me remember something I'd noticed Wells had done way back when I read the book when I was a mere smolt . . .

Slowly the story of the county sheriff was becoming *this* story in my mind . . . let's see, that lip water next to that rock looks good, let's put this #12 Joe's Hopper next to it—splat—

nice drift—hmmm, then the sheriff will go home and—shit! missed another fish!

(A year or two later I was fishing the same waters while the Bork nomination hearings were being held. "Bork?" I said to Chad. "*Bork* is the sound a trout makes when it takes a fly.")

I wasn't doing much reeling but my mind was. We drove back at the end of the ten days, I got to Chad's house at 3 in the P.M., called everybody in town to find that 1) my house-mate's old dog had died that morning; 2) Leigh Kennedy, with whom, in the Eighties phrase, I had shared my life for 4-½ of the past 5 years, was going into the hospital for some fairly complicated surgery; 3) the woman friend of mine from California would be arriving for the NASFIC that next night.

I'm a tough guy, but not that tough. I went home and got some sleep. Next morning at 7 I got up and started writing "Night of the Cooters." I wrote till 7 P.M., finishing all but one scene. Then I went to see Leigh in the hospital (she was coming out from under the Damnitall or whatever drug they'd given her; she had me call her then-boyfriend, now husband and father of her twins)—she was okay. (Later, when people came to see her during the course of the con, she had to make Gardner Dozois leave the room—he was making her laugh so much, and every time she'd laugh she'd rip a stitch, she felt like.) Then I went to the airport and picked up my lady friend.

Next morning we go to the con. I had to read the story at like 1 P.M. I sat down behind a potted plant up on the mezzanine, finished the missing scene about two minutes before showtime, walked in and read it. After all the glorious fun of the convention, I typed it up and sent it to Ellen Datlow. She bought it. It was in Dozois' *Best SF of the Year* the next year, and up for the Nebula and Hugo, and so forth and so on, as the Wizard of Oz says.

The next part of this introduction could go *here*, or before "French Scenes," but since I want to talk about other stuff there, I'll put it here. I call it *The Old Guys and Gals*.

Ever watched a real dog of a movie made in the Thirties or Forties or Fifties? I mean, like *nothing's* going on there, then the supposed star goes into a store or gets lost in the woods, or falls off her horse, and runs into someone, female or male, who blows the movie wide open, picks the sonofabitch film up and walks away with it for the three or four, or if we're lucky, ten minutes they're on screen?

These are called character actors. There are now several books about them (*Who Was That?* is one, where you look them up not by their names but by Judges, Maids, Mayors, Prospectors, etc.) and one is called what they really were, *The Dependables*. When these people come on the screen, you realize just how *bad* some of the leading actors and actresses of the time were; these people weren't acting, they were *real*.

Who can keep their eye on Jeff Chandler trying to act his way out of some paper bag of a western while Arthur Hunnicutt's over there scratching his beard? Who wants *any* other woman when Eve Arden's on the screen? Ever tried to watch an ingénue pout while Marjorie Main, as the household cook, spoon in one hand, wearing a nightmare of a checked dress and a hat that looks like a hostage window planter, terrorizes the area? How many eccentric Russians did Mischa Auer play? (Conversely, as Chad once said, he thought in the late Forties if he saw one more movie with S. Z. "Cuddles" Sakall in it, he'd *never* stop throwing up.) William Frawley could make anything—crooked cop, wise guy, lawyer, Broadway producer—happen up on the screen just by opening his mouth. Watch Margaret Hamilton sometime other than in *The Wizard of Oz*; she's waiting for some klutz of an actor to finish a line so perfectly that whatever she says seems like it's written in big letters on the screen itself.

The ones we love, the old ones, are all going away. There are character actors and actresses coming up—John Mahoney, Paul Dooley, Ned Beatty, Joan Cusack, Annie Potts, Clint Howard, Daniel Stern, and a whole bunch of others we always hope will be with us for a zillion years.

The new ones still don't light up the screen enough (*we* don't appreciate them enough yet) like Kate Freeman or Jack Elam or Dub Taylor, Dick Miller, Royal Dano, Henry Jones or Parley Baer still can. (They have that mythic aura of being the Last of the Breed, like longhorn cattle or buffalo kept on some rich rancher's place, even though the guy made all his money off some Zebu-Hereford miracle-science hybrid chock full of multi-vitamins that never saw soto grass—excuse my

nostalgia—in the vast mythic rangeland that is the movies . . .)

I'll miss them all when they go; I hope you can see that in
the other stories I've written through the years, and in this
book's "French Scenes"—especially here in "Night of the
Cooters." Of all the Franklin Pangborns, Percy Heltons,
Grady Suttons and Minerva Urecals, there's one I miss more
than the others. He was always the county sheriff in the story
that became "Night of the Cooters"; only the locale and time
and plot changed around him, as is fitting. I would have liked
to have been able, in another time and place, to write a movie
he could have played the lead in (as I would have for everybody else I've mentioned—just one role where they could
have done everything they were capable of, for people to see
how acting *really* works) but he checked out about 18 months
before I hit the Lake Fork of the Gunnison with Chad. I wish
he could have seen the story—I wish more than that he was
still around to act in the goddam thing, if somebody would
film it . . .

It's dedicated to him.

And, believe your butt, since that 10-day aberration while
I was thinking out this story, I've *always* had my mind on the
trout when I'm on the river.

NIGHT OF THE COOTERS

This story is in memory of Slim Pickens (1919–1983)

SHERIFF Lindley was asleep on the toilet in the Pachuco County courthouse when someone started pounding on the door.

"Bert! Bert!" the voice yelled as the sheriff jerked awake.

"Gol Dang!" said the lawman. The Waco newspaper slid off his lap onto the floor.

He pulled his pants up with one hand and the toilet chain on the waterbox overhead with the other. He opened the door. Chief Deputy Sweets stood before him, a complaint slip in his hand.

"Dang it, Sweets!" said the sheriff. "I told you never to bother me in there. It's the hottest Thursday in the history of Texas! You woke me up out of a hell of a dream!"

The deputy waited, wiping sweat from his forehead. There were two big circles, like half-moons, under the arms of his blue chambray shirt.

"I was fourteen, maybe fifteen years old, and I was a Aztec or a Mixtec or somethin'," said the sheriff. "Anyways, I was buck-naked, and I was standin' on one of them ball courts with the little-bitty stone rings twenty foot up one wall, and they was presentin' me to Moctezuma. I was real proud, and the sun was shinin', but it was real still and cool down there in the Valley of the Mexico. I looks up at the grandstand, and there's Moctezuma and all his high muckety-mucks with feathers and stuff hangin' off 'em, and more gold than a circus wagon. And there was these other guys, conquistadors and stuff, with beards and rusty helmets, and I-talian priests with crosses you coulda barred a livery-stable door with. One

5

of Moctezuma's men was explainin' how we was fixin' to
play ball for the gods and things.

"I knew in my dream I was captain of my team. I had a
name that sounded like a bird fart in Aztec talk, and they mentioned it and the name of the captain of the other team, too.
Well, everything was goin' all right, and I was prouder and
prouder, until the guy doing the talkin' let slip that whichever team won was gonna be paraded around Tenochtitlán and
given women and food and stuff like that, and then tomorrow
A.M. they was gonna be cut up and simmered real slow and
served up with chilis and onions and tomatoes.

"Well, you never seed such a fight as broke out then! They
was a-yellin', and a priest was swingin' a cross, and spears
and axes were flyin' around like it was an Irish funeral.   ·

"Next thing I know, you're a-bangin' on the door and
wakin' me up and bringin' me back to Pachuco County! What
the hell do you want?"

"Mr. De Spain wants you to come over to his place right
away."

"He does, huh?"

"That's right, Sheriff. He says he's got some miscreants he
wants you to arrest."

"Everybody else around here has desperadoes. De Spain
has miscreants. I'll be so danged glad when the town council
gets around to movin' the city limits fifty foot the other side
of his place, I won't know what to do! Every time anybody
farts too loud, he calls me."

Lindley and Sweets walked back to the office at the other
end of the courthouse. Four deputies sat around with their feet
propped up on desks. They rocked forward respectfully and
watched as the sheriff went to the hat pegs.

On one of the dowels was a sweat-stained hat with turned-
down points at front and back. The sidebrims were twisted in
curves. The hat angled up to end in a crown that looked like
the business end of a Phillips screwdriver. Under the hat was
a holster with a Navy Colt .41 that looked like someone had
used it to drive railroad spikes all the way to the Continental
Divide. Leaning under them was a 10-gauge pump shotgun
with the barrel sawed off just in front of the foregrip.

On the other peg was an immaculate new round-top Stetson

of brown felt with a snakeskin band half as wide as a finger-nail running around it.

The deputies stared.

Lindley picked up the Stetson.

The deputies rocked back in their chairs and resumed yak-king.

"Hey, Sweets!" said the sheriff at the door. "Change that damn calendar on your desk. It ain't Wednesday, August seventeenth; it's Thursday, August eighteenth."

"Sure thing, Sheriff."

"And you boys try not to play checkers so loud you wake the judge up, okay?"

"Sure thing, Sheriff."

Lindley went down the courthouse steps onto the rock walk. He passed the two courthouse cannons he and the deputies fired off three times a year—March second, July Fourth and Robert E. Lee's birthday. Each cannon had a pyramid of orna-mental cannonballs in front of it.

Waves of heat came off the cannons, the ammunition, the telegraph wires overhead, and, in the distance, the rails of the twice-a-day spur line from Waxahachie.

The town was still as a rusty shovel. The 45-star United States flag hung like an old, dried dishrag from its stanchion. From looking at the town you couldn't tell the nation was about to go to war with Spain over Cuba, that China was full of unrest, and that five thousand miles away a crazy German count was making airships.

Lindley had seen enough changes in his sixty-eight years. He had been born in the bottom of an Ohio keelboat in 1830; was in Bloody Kansas when John Brown came through; fought for the Confederacy, first as a corporal, then a sergeant major, from Chickamauga to the Wilderness; and had seen more skir-mishes with hostile tribes than most people would ever read about in a dozen Wide-Awake Library novels.

It was as hot as under an upside-down washpot on a tin shed roof. The sheriff's wagon horse seemed asleep as it trot-ted, head down, puffs hanging in the still air like brown shrubs made of dust around its hooves.

There were ten, maybe a dozen people in sight in the whole town. Those few on the street moved like molasses, only as far as they had to, from shade to shade. Anybody with sense

was asleep at home with wet towels hung over the windows,
or sitting as still as possible with a funeral-parlor fan in their
hands.

The sheriff licked his big droopy mustache and hoped nobody nodded to him. He was already too hot and tired to tip
his hat. He leaned back in the wagon seat and straightened his
bad leg (a Yankee souvenir) against the boot board. His grey
suit was like a boiling shroud. He was too hot to reach up and
flick the dust off his new hat.

He had become sheriff in the special election three years
ago, to fill out Sanderson's term when the governor had ap-
pointed the former sheriff attorney general. Nothing much had
happened in the county since then.

"Gee-hup," he said.

The horse trotted three steps before going back into its
walking trance.

Sheriff Lindley didn't bother her again until he pulled up at
De Spain's big place and said, "Whoa, there."

The black man who did everything for De Spain opened
the gate.

"Sheriff," he said.

"Luther," said Lindley, nodding his head.

"Around back, Mr. Lindley."

There were two boys—raggedy town kids, the Strother boy
and one of the poor Chisums—sitting on the edge of the well.
The Chisum kid had been crying.

De Spain was hot and bothered. He was only half dressed,
with suit pants, white shirt, vest and stockings on but no
shoes or coat. He hadn't macassared his hair yet. He was
pointing a rifle with a barrel big as a drainpipe at the two
boys.

"Here they are, Sheriff. Luther saw them down in the orchard. I'm sure he saw them stealing my peaches, but he
wouldn't tell me. I knew something was up when he didn't
put my clothes in the usual place next to the window where
I like to dress. So I looked out and saw them. They had half
a potato sack full by the time I crept around the house and
caught them. I want to charge them with trespass and thiev-
ery."

"Well, well," said the sheriff, looking down at the sackful
of evidence. He turned and pointed toward the black man.

"You want me to charge Luther here with collusion and abetting a crime?" Neither Lindley's nor Luther's faces betrayed any emotion.

"Of course not," said De Spain. "I've told him time and time again he's too soft on filchers. If this keeps happening, I'll hire another boy who'll enforce my orchard with buckshot, if need be."

De Spain was a young man with eyes like a weimaraner's. As Deputy Sweets said, he had the kind of face you couldn't hit just once. He owned half the town of Pachuco City. The other half paid him rent.

"Get in the wagon," said the sheriff.

"Aren't you going to cover them with your weapon?" asked De Spain.

"You should know by now, Mr. De Spain, that when I wear this suit I ain't got nothin' but a three-shot pocket pistol on me. Besides"—he looked at the two boys in the wagon bed—"they know if they give me any guff, I'll jerk a bowknot in one of 'em and bite the other'n's ass off."

"I don't think there's a need for profanity," said De Spain.

"It's too damn hot for anything else," said Lindley. "I'll clamp 'em in the *juzgado* and have Sweets run the papers over to your office tomorrow mornin'."

"I wish you'd take them out one of the rural roads somewhere and flail the tar out of them to teach them about property rights," said De Spain.

The sheriff tipped his hat back and looked up at De Spain's three-story house with the parlor so big you could hold a rodeo in it. Then he looked back at the businessman, who'd finally lowered the rifle.

"Well, I know you'd like that," said Lindley. "I seem to remember that most of the fellers who wrote the Constitution were pretty well off, but some of the other rich people thought they had funny ideas. But they were really pretty smart. One of the things they were smart about was the Bill of Rights. You know, Mr. De Spain, the reason they put in the Bill of Rights wasn't to give all the little people without jobs or money a lot of breaks with the law. Why they put that in there was for if the people without jobs or money ever got upset and turned on *them*, they could ask for the same justice everybody else got."

De Spain looked at him with disgust. "I've never liked your homespun parables, and I don't like the way you sheriff this county."

"I don't doubt that," said Lindley. "You've got sixteen months, three weeks and two days to find somebody to run against me. Good evening, Mr. De Spain."

He climbed onto the wagon seat.

"Luther."

"Sheriff."

He turned the horse around as De Spain and the black man took the sack of peaches through the kitchen door into the house.

The sheriff stopped the wagon near the railroad tracks where the houses began to deviate from the vertical.

"Jody. Billy Roy." He looked at them with eyes like chips of flint. "You're the dumbest pair of squirts that *ever* lived in Pachuco City! First off, half those peaches were still green. You'd have got bellyaches, and your mothers would have beaten you within an inch of your lives and given you so many doses of Black Draught you'd shit over ten-rail fences all week.

"Now listen to what I'm sayin', 'cause I'm only gonna say it once. If I ever hear of *either* of you stealing anything, anywhere in this county, I'm going to put you *both* in school."

"No, sheriff, please, no!" Their eyes were wide as horses'.

"I'll put you in there every morning and come and get you out seven long hours later, and I'll have the judge issue a writ keeping you there till you're *twelve years old*. And if you try to run away, I'll follow you to the ends of the earth with Joe Sweeper's bloodhounds, and I'll bring you back."

They were crying now.

"You git home."

They were running before they left the wagon.

Somewhere between the second piece of cornbread and the third helping of snap beans, a loud rumble shook the ground.

"Goodness' Sakes!" said Elsie, his wife of twenty-three years. "What can that be?"

"I expect that's Elmer, out by the creek. He came in last week and asked if he could blast on the place. I told him it didn't matter to me as long as he did it between sunup and sundown and didn't blow his whole family of rug-rats and yard-apes up.

"Jake, down at the mercantile, said Elmer bought enough dynamite to blow up Fort Worth if he'd a mind to—all but the last three sticks in the store. Jake had to reorder for stump-blowin' time."

"Whatever could he want with all that much?"

"Oh, that damn fool has the idea the vein in that old mine what played out in '83 might start up again on his property. He got to talking with the Smith boy, oh, hell, what's his name—?"

"Leo?"

"Yeah, Leo, the one that studies down in Austin, learns about stars and rocks and all that shit . . ."

"Watch your language, Bertram!"

"Oh, hell! Anyway, that boy must have put a bug up Elmer's butt about that—"

"Bertram!" said Elsie, putting down her knife and fork.

"Oh, hell, anyway. I guess Elmer'll blow the side off his hill and bury his house before he's through."

The sheriff was reading a week-old copy of the *Waco Herald* while Elsie washed up the dishes. He sure missed *Brann's Iconoclast*, the paper he used to read, which had ceased publication when the editor was gunned down on a Waco street by an irate Baptist four months before.

The Waco paper had a little squib from London, England, about there having been explosions on Mars ten nights in a row last month, and whether it was a sign of life on that planet or some unusual volcanic activity.

Sheriff Lindley had never given volcanoes (except those in the Valley of the Mexico) or the planet Mars much thought.

Hooves came pounding down the road. He put down his paper. *"Sheriff, sheriff!"* he said in a high, mocking voice.

"What?" asked Elsie. Then she heard the hooves and began to dry her hands on the towel on the nail above the sink.

The horse stopped out front; bare feet slapped up to the porch; small fists pounded on the door.

"Sheriff! Sheriff!" yelled a voice Lindley recognized as belonging to either Tommy or Jimmy Atkinson.

He strode to the door and opened it.

"Tommy, what's all the hooraw?"

"Jimmy. Sheriff, something fell on our pasture, tore it all to hell, knocked down *the tree*, killed some of our cattle, Tommy can't find his dog, Mother sent—"

"Hold on! Something fell on your place? Like what?"

"I don't know! Like a big rock, only sparks was flyin' off it, and it roared and blew up! It's at the north end of the place, and—"

"Elsie, run over and get Sweets and the boys. Have them go get Leo Smith if he ain't gone back to college yet. Sounds to me like Pachuco County's got its first shootin' star. Hold on, Jimmy, I'm comin' right along. We'll take my wagon; you can leave your pony here."

"Oh, hurry, Sheriff! It's big! It killed our cattle and tore up the fences—"

"Well, I can't arrest it for *that*." said Lindley. He put on his Stetson. "And I thought Elmer'd blowed hisself up. My, my, ain't never seen a shooting star before . . ."

"Damn if it don't look like somebody threw a locomotive through here," said the sheriff.

The Atkinson place used to have a sizable hill and the tallest tree in the county on it. Now it had half a hill and a big stump and beyond, a huge crater. Dirt had been thrown up in a ten-foot-high pile around it.

There was a huge, rounded, grey object buried in the dirt and torn caliche at the bottom. Waves of heat rose from it, and grey ash, like old charcoal, fell off it into the shimmering pit.

Half the town was riding out in wagons and on horseback as the news spread. The closest neighbors were walking over in the twilight, wearing their go-visiting clothes.

"Well, well," said the sheriff, looking down. "So that's what a meteor looks like."

Leo Smith was already in the pit, walking around.

"I figured you'd be here sooner or later," said Lindley.

"Hello, Sheriff," said Leo. "It's still too hot to touch. Part of a cow's buried under the back end."

The sheriff looked over at the Atkinson family. "You folks

is danged lucky. That thing coulda come down smack on your
house or, what's worse, your barn. What time it fall?"

"Straight up and down six o'clock," said Mrs. Atkinson.
"We was settin' down to supper. I saw it out of the corner of
my eye; then all tarnation came down. Rocks must have been
falling for ten minutes!"

"It's pretty spectacular, Sheriff," said Leo. "I'm going into
town to telegraph off to the professors at the University.
They'll sure want to look at this."

"Any reason other than general curiosity?" asked Lindley.

"I've only seen pictures and handled little bitty parts of
one," said Leo, "but it doesn't look usual. They're generally
like big rocks, all stone or iron. The outside of this one's soft
and crumbly. Ashy, too."

There was a slight pop and a stove-cooling noise from the
thing.

"Well, you can come back into town with me if you want
to. Hey, Sweets!"

The chief deputy came over.

"A couple of you boys better stay here tonight, keep people
from falling in the hole. I guess if Leo's gonna wire the University, you better keep anybody from knockin' chunks off it.
It'll probably get pretty crowded. If I was the Atkinsons, I'd
start chargin' a nickel a look."

"Sure thing, Sheriff."

Kerosene lanterns and carriage lights were moving toward
the Atkinsons' in the coming darkness.

"I'll be out here early tomorrow mornin' to take another
gander. I gotta serve a process paper on old Theobald before
he lights out for his chores. If I sent one o' you boys, he'd as
soon shoot you as say howdy."

"Sure thing, Sheriff."

He and Leo and Jimmy Atkinson got in the wagon and
rode off toward the quiet lights of town far away.

There was a new smell in the air.

The sheriff noticed it as he rode toward the Atkinson ranch
by the south road early the next morning. There was an odor
like when something goes wrong at the telegraph office.

Smoke was curling up from the pasture. Maybe there was
a scrub fire started from the heat of the falling star.

He topped the last rise. Before him lay devastation the likes of which he hadn't seen since the retreat from Atlanta.

"Great Gawd Ahmighty!" he said.

There were dead horses and charred wagons all around. The ranch house was untouched, but the barn was burned to the ground. There were crisscrossed lines of burnt grass that looked like they'd been painted with a tarbrush.

He saw no bodies anywhere. Where was Sweets? Where was Luke, the other deputy? Where had the people from the wagons gone? What had happened?

Lindley looked at the crater. There was a shiny rod sticking out of it, with something round on the end. From here it looked like one of those carnival acts where a guy spins a plate on the end of a dowel rod, only this glinted like metal in the early sun. As he watched, a small cloud of green steam rose above it from the pit.

He saw a motion behind an old tree uprooted by a storm twelve years ago. It was Sweets. He was yelling and waving the sheriff back.

Lindley rode his horse into a small draw, then came up into the open.

There was movement over at the crater. He thought he saw something. Reflected sunlight flashed by his eyes, and he thought he saw a rounded silhouette. He heard a noise like sometimes gets in bobwire on a windy day.

He heard a humming sound then, smelled the electric smell real strong. Fire started a few feet from him, out of nowhere, and moved toward him.

Then his horse exploded.

The air was an inferno, he was thrown spinning—

He must have blacked out. He had no memory of what went next. When he came to, he was running as fast as he ever had toward the uprooted tree.

Fire jumped all around. Luke was shooting over the tree roots with his pistol. He ducked. A long section of the trunk was washed over with flames and sparks.

Lindley dove behind the root tangle.

"What the ding-dong is goin' on?" he asked as he tried to catch his breath. He still had his new hat on, but his britches and coat were singed and smoking.

"God damn, Bert! I don't know," said Sweets, leaning

around Luke. "We was out here all night; it was a regular party; most of the time we was up on the lip up there. Maybe thirty or forty people comin' and goin' all the time. We was all talking and hoorawing, and then we heard something about an hour ago. We looked down, and I'll be damned if the whole top of that thing didn't come off like a Mason jar!

"We was watching, and these damn things started coming out—they looked like big old leather balls, big as horses, with snakes all out the front—"

"What?"

"Snakes. Yeah, tentacles Leo called them, like an octypuss. Leo'd come back from town and was here when them boogers came out. Martians he said they was, things from Mars. They had big old eyes, big as your head! Everybody was pushing and shoving; then one of them pulled out one of them gun things, real slow like, and he just started burning up everything in sight.

"We all ran back for whatever cover we could find—it took 'em a while to get up the dirt pile. They killed horses, dogs, anything they could see. Fire was everywhere. They use that thing just like the volunteer firemen use them water hoses in Waco!"

"Where's Leo?"

Sweets pointed to the draw that ran diagonally to the west. "We watched awhile, finally figured they couldn't line up on the ditch all the way to the rise. Leo and the others got away up the draw—he was gonna telegraph the University about it. The bunch that got away was supposed to send people out to the town road to warn people. You probably would have run into them if you hadn't been coming from Theobald's place.

"Anyway, soon as them things saw people were gettin' away, they got mad as hornets. That's when they lit up the Atkinsons' barn."

A flash of fire leapt in the roots of the tree, jumped back thirty feet into the burnt grass behind them, then moved back and forth in a curtain of sparks.

"Man, that's what I call a real smoke pole," said Luke.

"Well," Lindley said. "This just won't do. These things done attacked citizens in my jurisdiction, and they killed my horse."

He turned to Luke.

"Be real careful, and get back to town, get the posse up. Telegraph the Rangers and tell 'em to burn leather gettin' here. Then get ahold of Skip Whitworth and have him bring out The Gun."

Skip Whitworth sat behind the tree trunk and pulled the cover from the six-foot rifle at his side. Skip was in his late fifties. He had been a sniper in the War for Southern Independence when he had been in his twenties. He had once shot at a Yankee general just as the officer was bringing a forkful of beans up to his mouth. When the fork got there, there was only some shoulders and a gullet for the beans to drop into.

That had been from a mile and a half away, from sixty feet up a pine tree.

The rifle was an .80-caliber octagonal-barrel breechloader that used two and a half ounces of powder and a percussion cap the size of a jawbreaker for each shot. It had a telescopic sight running the entire length of the barrel.

"They're using that thing on the end of that stick to watch us," said Lindley. "I had Sweets jump around, and every time he did, one of those cooters would come up with that fire gun and give us what-for."

Skip said nothing. He loaded his rifle, which had a breech-block lever the size of a crowbar on it, then placed another round—cap, paper cartridge, ball—next to him.

He drew a bead and pulled the trigger. It sounded like dynamite had gone off in their ears.

The wobbling pole snapped in two halfway up. The top end flopped around back into the pit.

There was a scrabbling noise above the whirring from the earthen lip. Something round came up.

Skip had smoothly opened the breech, put in the ball, torn the cartridge with his teeth, put in the cap, closed the action, pulled back the hammer, and sighted before the shape reached the top of the dirt.

Metal glinted in the middle of the dark thing.

Skip fired.

There was a *squeech*; the whole top of the round thing opened up; it spun around and backward, things in its front working like a daddy longlegs thrown on a roaring stove.

Skip loaded again. There were flashes of light from the crater. Something came up shooting, fire leaping like hot sparks from a blacksmith's anvil, the air full of flames and smoke.

Skip fired again.

The fire gun flew up in the air. Snakes twisted, writhed, disappeared.

It was very quiet for a few seconds.

Then there was the renewed whining of machinery and noises like a pile driver, the sounds of filing and banging. Steam came up over the crater lip.

"Sounds like a steel foundry in there," said Sweets.

"I don't like it one bit," said Bert. "Be danged if I'm gonna let 'em get the drop on us. Can you keep them down?"

"How many are there?" asked Skip.

"Luke and Sweets saw four or five before all hell broke loose this morning. Probably more of 'em than that was inside."

"I've got three more shots. If they poke up, I'll get 'em."

"I'm going to town, then out to Elmer's. Sweets'll stay with you awhile. If you run outta bullets, light up out the draw. I don't want nobody killed. Sweets, keep an eye out for the posse. I'm telegraphing the Rangers again, then goin' to get Elmer and his dynamite. We're gonna fix their little red wagon for certain."

"Sure thing, Sheriff."

The sun had just passed noon.

Leo looked haggard. He had been up all night, then at the telegraph office sending off messages to the University. Inquiries had begun to come in from as far east as Baton Rouge. Leo had another, from Percival Lowell out in Flagstaff, Arizona Territory.

"Everybody at the University thinks it's wonderful," said Leo.

"People in Austin would," said the sheriff.

"They're sure these things are connected with Mars and those bright flashes of gas last month. Seems something's happened in England, starting about a week ago. No one's been able to get through to London for two or three days."

"You tell me Mars is attacking London, England, and Pachuco City, Texas?" asked the sheriff.

"It seems so," said Leo. He took off his glasses and rubbed his eyes.

"'Scuse me, Leo," said Lindley. "I got to get another telegram off to the Texas Rangers."

"That's funny," said Argyle, the telegraph operator. "The line was working just a second ago." He kept tapping his key and fiddling with his coil box.

Leo peered out the window. "Hey!" he said. "Where's the 3:14?" He looked at the railroad clock. It was 3:25.

In sixteen years of rail service, the train had been four minutes late, and that was after a mud slide in the storm twelve years ago.

"Uh-oh," said the sheriff.

They were turning out of Elmer's yard with a wagonload of dynamite. The wife and eleven of the kids were watching.

"Easy, Sheriff," said Elmer, who, with two of his boys and most of their guns, was riding in back with the explosives. "Jake sold me everything he had. I just didn't notice till we got back here with that stuff that some of it was already sweating."

"Holy shit!" said Lindley. "You mean we gotta go a mile an hour out there? Let's get out and throw the bad stuff off."

"Well, it's all mixed in," said Elmer. "I was sorta gonna set it all up on the hill and put one blasting cap in the whole load."

"Jesus. You woulda blowed up your house and Pachuco City, too."

"I was in a hurry," said Elmer, hanging his head.

"Well, can't be helped, then. We'll take it slow."

Lindley looked at his watch. It was six o'clock. He heard a high-up, fluttering sound. They looked at the sky. Coming down was a large, round, glowing object throwing off sparks in all directions. It was curved with points, like the thing in the crater at the Atkinson place. A long, thin trail of smoke from the back end hung in the air behind it.

They watched in awe as it sailed down. It went into the horizon to the north of Pachuco City.

"One," said one of the kids in the wagon, "two, three—"

Silently they took up the count. At twenty-seven there was a roaring boom, just like the night before.

"Five and a half miles," said the sheriff. "That puts it eight miles from the other one. Leo said the ones in London came down twenty-four hours apart, regular as clockwork."

They started off as fast as they could under the circumstances.

There were flashes of light beyond the Atkinson place in the near dusk. The lights moved off toward the north where the other thing had plowed in.

It was the time of evening when your eyes can fool you. Sheriff Lindley thought he saw something that shouldn't have been there sticking above the horizon. It glinted like metal in the dim light. He thought it moved, but it might have been the motion of the wagon as they lurched down a gully. When they came up, it was gone.

Skip was gone. His rifle was still there. It wasn't melted but had been crushed, as had the three-foot-thick tree trunk in front of it. All the caps and cartridges were gone.

There was a monstrous series of footprints leading from the crater down to the tree, then off into the distance to the north where Lindley thought he had seen something. There were three footprints in each series.

Sweets' hat had been mashed along with Skip's gun. Clanging and banging still came from the crater.

The four of them made their plans. Lindley had his shotgun and pistol, which Luke had brought out with him that morning, though he was still wearing his burnt suit and his untouched Stetson.

He tied together the fifteen sweatiest sticks of dynamite he could find.

They crept up, then rushed the crater.

"Hurry up!" yelled the sheriff to the men at the courthouse. "Get that cannon up those stairs!"

"He's still coming this way!" yelled Luke from up above.

They had been watching the giant machine from the courthouse since it had come up out of the Atkinson place, before the sheriff and Elmer and his boys made it into town after their sortie.

It had come across to the north, gone to the site of the sec-

ond crash, and stood motionless there for quite a while. When
it got dark, the deputies brought out the night binoculars. Everybody in town saw the flash of dynamite from the Atkinson
place.

A few moments after that, the machine had moved back toward there. It looked like a giant water tower with three legs.
It had a thing like a teacher's desk bell on top of it, and something that looked like a Kodak roll-film camera in front of
that. As the moon rose, they saw the thing had tentacles like
thick wires hanging from between the three giant legs.

The sheriff, Elmer, and his boys made it to town just as the
machine found the destruction they had caused at the first
landing site. It had turned toward town and was coming at a
pace of twenty miles an hour.

"Hurry the hell up!" yelled Luke. "Oh, shit—!" he ducked.
There was a flash of light overhead. The building shook. "That
heat gun comes out of the box on the front!" he said. "Look
out!" The building glared and shook again. Something down
the street caught fire.

"Load that sonofabitch," said Lindley. "Bob! Some of you
men make sure everybody's in the cyclone cellars or where
they won't burn. Cut out all the damn lights!"

"Hell, Sheriff. They know we're here!" yelled a deputy.

Lindley hit him with his hat, then followed the cannon up
to the top of the clock-tower steps.

Luke was cramming powder into the cannon muzzle.
Sweets ran back down the stairs. Other people carried cannonballs up the steps to the tower one at a time.

Leo came up. "What did you find, Sheriff, when you went
back?"

There was a cool breeze for a few seconds in the courthouse tower. Lindley breathed a few deep breaths, remembering. "Pretty rough. There was some of them still working
after that thing had gone. They were building another one just
like it." He pointed toward the machine, which was firing up
houses to the northeast side of town, swinging the ray back
and forth. They could hear its hum. Homes and chicken coops
burst into flames. A mooing cow was stilled.

"We threw in the dynamite and blew most of them up. One
was in a machine like a steam tractor. We shot up what was
left while they was hootin' and a-hollerin'. There was some

other things in there, live things maybe, but they was too
blowed up to put back together to be sure what they looked
like, all bleached out and pale. We fed everything there a diet
of buckshot till there wasn't nothin' left. Then we hightailed
it back here on horses, left the wagon sitting."

The machine came on toward the main street of town. Luke
finished with the powder. There were so many men with guns
on the building across the street it looked like a brick porcupine. It must have looked that way for the James Gang when
they were shot up in Northfield, Minnesota.

The courthouse was made of stone. Most of the wooden
buildings in town were scorched or already afire. When the
heat gun came this way, it blew bricks to dust, played flame
over everything. The air above the whole town heated up.

They had put out the lamps behind the clock faces. There
was nothing but moonlight glinting off the three-legged machine, flames of burning buildings, the faraway glows of prai-
rie fires. It looked like Pachuco City was on the outskirts of
Hell.

"Get ready, Luke," said the sheriff. The machine stepped
between two burning stores, its tentacles pulling out smolder-
ing horse tack, chains, kegs of nails, then heaving them this
way and that. Someone at the end of the street fired off a
round. There was a high, thin ricochet off the machine.

Sweets ran upstairs, something in his arms. It was a curtain
from one of the judge's windows. He'd ripped it down and
tied it to the end of one of the janitor's long window brushes.

On it he had lettered in tempera paint COME AND TAKE IT.

There was a ragged, nervous cheer from the men on the
building as they read it by the light of the flames.

"Cute, Sweets," said Lindley, "too cute."

The machine turned down Main Street. A line of fire
sprang up at the back side of town from the empty corrals.

"Oh, shit!" said Luke. "I forgot the wadding!"

Lindley took off his hat to hit him with. He looked at its
beautiful felt in the mixed moonlight and firelight.

The thing turned toward them. The sheriff thought he saw
eyes way up in the bell-thing atop the machine, eyes like a
big cat's eyes seen through a dirty windowpane on a dark
night.

"Gol Dang, Luke, it's my best hat, but I'll be damned if I let them cooters burn down my town!"

He stuffed the Stetson, crown first, into the cannon barrel. Luke shoved it in with the ramrod, threw in two thirty-five-pound cannon balls behind it, pushed them home, and swung the barrel out over Main Street.

The machine bent to tear up something.

"Okay, boys," yelled Lindley. "Attract its attention."

Rifle and shotgun fire winked on the rooftop. It glowed like a hot coal from the muzzle flashes. A great slather of ricochets flew off the giant machine.

It turned, pointing its heat gun at the building. It was fifty feet from the courthouse steps.

"Now," said the sheriff.

Luke touched off the powder with his cigarillo.

The whole north side of the courthouse bell tower flew off, and the roof collapsed. Two holes you could see the moon through appeared in the machine: one in the middle, one smashing through the dome atop it. Sheriff Lindley saw the lower cannonball come out and drop lazily toward the end of burning Main Street.

All six of the tentacles of the machine shot straight up into the air, and it took off like a man running with his arms above his head. It staggered, as fast as a freight train could go, through one side of a house and out the other, and ran part-way up Park Street. One of its three legs went higher than its top. It hopped around like a crazy man on crutches before its feet got tangled in a horse-pasture fence, and it went over backward with a shudder. A great cloud of steam came out of it and hung in the air.

No one in the courthouse tower heard the sound of the steam. They were all deaf as posts from the explosion. The barrel of the cannon was burst all along the end. The men on the other roof were jumping up and down and clapping each other on the back. The COME AND TAKE IT sign on the courthouse had two holes in it, neater than you could have made with a biscuit-cutter.

First a high whine, then a dull roar, then something like normal hearing came back to the sheriff's left ear. The right one still felt like a kid had its fist in there.

"Dang it, Sweets!" he yelled. "How much powder did Luke use!"

"Huh?"

Luke was banging on his head with both his hands.

"How much powder did he use?"

"Two, two and a half cans," said Sweets.

"It only takes half a can a ball!" yelled the sheriff. He reached for his hat to hit Luke with, touched his bare head. "I feel naked," he said. "Come on, we're not through yet. We got fires to put out and some hash to settle."

Luke was still standing, shaking his head. The whole town was cheering.

It looked like a pot lid slowly boiling open, moving just a little. Every time the end unscrewed a little more, ashes and cinders fell off into the second pit. There was a piled ridge of them. The back turned again, moved a few inches, quit. Then it wobbled, there was a sound like a stove being jerked up a chimney, and the whole back end rolled open like a mad bank vault and fell off.

There were 184 men and 11 women all standing behind the open end of the thing, their guns pointing toward the interior. At the exact center were Sweets and Luke with the other courthouse cannon. This time there was one can of powder, but the barrel was filled to the end with everything from the blacksmith-shop floor—busted window glass, nails, horse-shoes, bolts, stirrup buckles, and broken files and saws.

Eyes appeared in the dark interior.

"Remember the Alamo," said the sheriff.

Everybody, and the cannon, fired.

When the third meteor came in that evening, south of town at thirteen minutes past six, they knew something was wrong. It wobbled in flight, lost speed, and dropped like a long, heavy leaf.

They didn't have to wait for this one to cool and open. When the posse arrived, the thing was split in two and torn. Heat and steam came up from the inside.

One of the pale things was creeping forlornly across the ground with great difficulty. It looked like a thin gingerbread man made of glass with only a knob for a head.

"It's probably hurting from the gravity," said Leo.

"Fix it, Sweets," said Lindley.

"Sure thing, Sheriff."

There was a gunshot.

No fourth meteor fell, though they had scouts out for twenty miles in all directions, and the railroad tracks and telegraph wires were fixed again.

"I been doing some figuring," said Leo. "If there were ten explosions on Mars last month, and these things started landing in England last Thursday week, then we should have got the last three. There won't be any more."

"You been figurin', huh?"

"Sure have."

"Well, we'll see."

Sheriff Lindley stood on his porch. It was sundown on Sunday, three hours after another meteor should have fallen, had there been one.

Leo rode up. "I saw Sweets and Luke heading toward the Atkinson place with more dynamite. What are they doing?"

"They're blowing up every last remnant of them things—lock, stock and asshole."

"But," said Leo, "the professors from the University will be here tomorrow, to look at their ships and machines! You can't destroy them!"

"Shit on the University of Texas and the horse it rode in on," said the sheriff. "My jurisdiction runs from Deer Piss Creek to Buenos Frijoles, back to Olatunji, up the Little Clear Fork of the North Branch of Mud River, back to the Creek, and everything in between. If I say something gets blowed up, it's on its way to Kingdom Come."

He put his arms on Leo's shoulders. "Besides, what little grass grows in this county's supposed to be green, and what's growing around them things is red. I *really* don't like that."

"But, Sheriff! I've got to meet Professor Lowell in Waxahachie tomorrow morning . . ."

"Listen, Leo. I appreciate what you done. But I'm an old man. I been kept up by Martians for three nights, I lost my horse and my new hat, and they busted my favorite gargoyle off the courthouse. I'm going in and get some sleep, and I only want to be woke up for the Second Coming, by Jesus Christ Himself."

Leo jumped on his horse and rode for the Atkinson place.

Sheriff Lindley crawled into bed and went to sleep as soon as his head hit the pillow.

He had a dream. He was a king in Babylon, and he lay on a couch at the top of a ziggurat, just like the Tower of Babel in the Bible. He surveyed the city and the river. There were women all around him, and men with curly beards and golden headdresses. Occasionally someone would feed him a great big fig from a golden bowl.

His dreams were not interrupted by the sounds of dynamiting, first from one side of town, then another, and then another.

INTRODUCTION TO

FRENCH SCENES

LET me tell you about living in small town America where your contact with the real world, when you're a kid, is the library, *Uncle Scrooge Comics*, *Life Magazine* and television.

God knows things were happening in the late Fifties, but if it wasn't in one of those four places, or at an occasional movie, you wouldn't prove it by me.

Arlington, Texas, was a 7000 person burg surrounded by ten miles of open land in all directions when my family moved there in 1950. The city well was at the intersection of Center and Main. (It went dry in the drought of the Fifties—the town built a lake that was supposed to fill in seven years at the drought rate; the drought broke in '57, the lake filled up in 27 days, flooded and wiped out roads and homes all over the place. But that's another story.)

Movies. You better believe I saw movies. They changed three times a week at the Arlington Theater. (Hosey, the head usher, was reputed to pack heat; one of the rites of passage in town was to go to the show on Friday night and pick a fight with him; Hosey would, of course, put out your lights with one punch; then, of course, you and 49 of your closest friends would lay in wait for him after the last show.)

My father worked at an aircraft plant 60 miles away; when they were on overtime it was easier for him to rent a room there than try to drive the hour-and-a-half each way after working a twelve-hour day. My mother worked split shift (11–3, 6–9) as a waitress. The easiest place to keep me and my sister out of trouble was to park our butts three hours a night three nights a week at the theater. Besides, it only cost 50¢ a night for both of us.

I saw everything made between 1954 and 1962. I mean, ev-

erything. All the sci-fi, of course. Every muscleman epic that
came to Texas. Jeff Chandler-Doris Day-Barbara Rush-
Stephen Boyd. Disney. Made-in-Texas disasters. (I didn't
know who Larry Buchanan was then, but I knew what I *didn't*
like.) I could bore you to death. I hit puberty with *A Summer
Place.* I got my first kiss during *Pépé.* I took the first real date
I ever had to see *On the Beach.* (And Linda Rodden, wherever you are, I hope you've had an okay life, too.)

So I knew what movies were by the time I was fourteen.
Something was missing, though, and I knew what it was, because I'd read about it in *Life Magazine.* It was called the
nouvelle vague, or French New Wave.

As I understood it a bunch of Frenchmen had gone crazy
and made a lot of movies that made people's eyeballs jiggle.
Boy, did I want to see some of that!

And as soon as I got my driver's license, I did. There was
a theater near the SMU campus, the Fine Arts, in Dallas, and
another, way out on Maple, called the Festival, which was a
three-story house that had been gutted and turned into a
250-seater (the more things change, the more they stay the
same . . .) both of which showed *everything* foreign, to such
an extent that, like my '54-'62 orgy of American movies, I
realized that just because it was foreign didn't mean it was
good. (Nothing, nothing, *nothing* is worse than a bad Italian
movie, except a bad Italian SF movie . . .)

There were books I read, too, on New Wave films, directors, film history, Donald Keene, Robert Hughes, Pauline
Kael—the list goes ever on.

I knew a long time ago I was going to write a story about
new wave films—how to do it was what was holding me up.
Then one day I found myself in Denver at the World SF Convention, on a panel at which everyone knew what the panel
was supposed to be about except the moderator. We kept saying all this great stuff and he kept trying to get us back to
talking about whatever dull boring thing *he* wanted to.

Anyway, we got around to film, and new stuff, and I'll be
damned if Forrest J. Ackerman didn't say something that
made me know *immediately* how to do the story.

Forry has been around since Noe's Fludde; through him
and the magazines he edited he brought more people to SF
than any other single thing (so he has a lot to answer for, too).

He's given his whole life to a field which, when bad, is worse than *anything* (except a bad Italian SF movie), but when good, is something to be proud of. There's sort of a tribute to him in one of the other stories in this book—you won't have *any* trouble finding it.

As usual, I thought about the story for five or six more years before I got around to writing it for George Zebrowski's *Synergy 2*. So I had time to figure out how to put some more of my favorite character actors in it, and things like that, and make it so *even* an SF fan could understand it. . . .

Life goes on, 30 years late: the French New Wave comes to a small-town boy, the small-town boy grows up and writes the films he never saw.

Every man his own Godard, Lord help us all.

FRENCH SCENES

The fault, dear Brutus, is not in our stars,
But in ourselves . . .   Julius Cæsar *Act 1 Sc 2 1 1–2*

THERE was a time, you read, when making movies took so many people. Actors, cameramen, technicians, screenwriters, costumers, editors, producers and directors. I can believe it.

That was before computer animation, before the National Likeness Act, before the Noe's Fludde of marvels.

Back in that time they still used laboratories to make prints; sometimes there would be a year between the completion of a film and its release to theaters.

Back then they used *actual* pieces of film, with holes down the sides for the projector. I've even handled some of it; it is cold, heavy and shiny.

Now there's none of that. No doctors, lawyers, Indian chiefs between the idea and substance. There's only one person (with maybe a couple of hackers for the dogswork) who makes movies: the movie-maker.

There's only one piece of equipment, the GAX-600.

There's one true law: clean your mainframe and have a full set of specs.

I have to keep that in mind, all the time.

Lois was yelling from the next room where she was working on her movie *Monster Without a Meaning*.

"We've got it!" she said, storming in. "The bottoms of Morris Ankrum's feet!"

"Where?"

"Querytioup," she said. It was an image-research place across the city run by a seventeen-year-old who must have

seen every movie and tv show ever made. "It's from an un-
likely source," said Lois, reading from the hard copy. "*Tennessee Johnson*. Ankrum played Jefferson Davis. There's a
scene where he steps on a platform to give a secession
speech.

"Imagine, Morris Ankrum, alive and kicking, 360°, top and
bottom. Top was easy—there's an overhead shot in *Invaders
From Mars* when the guys in the fuzzy suits stick the ruby
hatpin-thing in his neck."

"Is that your last holdup? I wish *this* thing were that goddam easy," I said.

"No. Legal," she said.

Since the National Fair Likeness Act passed, you had to
pay the person (or the estate) of anyone even remotely famous, anyone recognizable from a movie, anywhere. (In the
early days after passage, some moviemakers tried to get
around it by using parts of people. Say you wanted a prissy
hotel clerk—you'd use Franklin Pangborn's hair, Grady
Sutton's chin, Eric Blore's eyes. Sounded great in theory but
what they got looked like a walking police composite sketch;
nobody liked them and they scared little kids. You might as
well pay and make Rondo Hatton the bellboy.)

"What's the problem now?" I asked.

"Ever tried to find the heirs of Olin Howlin's estate?" Lois
asked.

What I'm doing is called *This Guy Goes to Town* . . . It's a
nouvelle vague movie, it stars everybody in France in 1962.

You remember the French New Wave? A bunch of film
critics who wrote for a magazine, *Cahiers du Cinema*? They
burned to make films, lived, slept, ate films in the 1950s. Bad
American movies even their directors had forgotten, B Westerns, German silent Expressionistic bores, French cliffhangers
from 1916 starring the Kaiser as a gorilla, things like that.
Anything they could find to show at midnight when everybody else had gone home, in theaters where one of their cous-
ins worked as an usher.

Some of them got to make a few shorts in the mid-50s.
Suddenly studios and producers handed them cameras and
money. Go out and make movies, they said: talk is cheap.

Truffaut. Resnais. Godard. Rivette. Roehmer. Chris Marker.
Alain Robbe-Grillet.

*The Four Hundred Blows. Hiroshima, Mon Amour. Breath-
less. La Jetée. Trans-Europe Express.*

They blew moviemaking wide open.

And why I love them is that for the first time, underneath
the surface of them, even the comedies, was a sense of trag-
edy; that we were all frail human beings and not celluloid heroes and heroines.

It took the French to remind us of that.

The main thing guys like Godard and Truffaut had going
for them was that they didn't understand English very well.

Like in *Riot in Cell Block 11*, when Neville Brand gets shot
at by the prison guard with a Thompson, he yells:

"Look out, Monty! They got a chopper! Back inside!"

What the *Cahiers* people heard was:

"Steady, *mon frère*! Let us leave this place of wasted
dreams."

And they watched a *lot* of undubbed, unsubtitled films in
those dingy theaters. They learned from them, but not neces-
sarily what the films had to teach.

It's like seeing D. W. Griffith's 1916 *Intolerance* and listening to an old Leonard Cohen album at the same time. What
you're seeing doesn't get in the way of what you're thinking.
The words and images made for cultures half a century apart
mesh in a way that makes for sleepless nights and new ideas.

And, of course, every one of the New Wave filmmakers
was in love, one way or another, with Jeanne Moreau.

I'm playing Guy. Or my image is, anyway. For one thing,
composition, sequencing and specs on a real person take only
about fifteen minutes' easy work.

I stepped up on the sequencer platform. Johnny Rizzuli
pushed in a standard scan program. The matrix analyzer,
which is about the size of an old iron lung, flew around me
on its yokes and gimbals like the runaway merry-go-round in
Strangers on a Train. Then it flew over my head like the
cropduster in *North by Northwest*.

After it stopped the platform moved back and forth. I was
bathed in light like a sheet of paper on an old office copier.

Johnny gave me the thumbs-up.

I ran the imaging a day later. It's always ugly the first time you watch yourself tie your shoelaces, roll your eyes, scratch your head and belch. As close, as far away, from whatever angle in whatever lighting you want. And when you talk, you never sound like you think you do. I'm going to put a little more whine in my voice; just a quarter-turn on the old Nicholson knob.

The movie will be in English, of course, with subtitles. English subtitles.

(The screen starts to fade out.)

Director (voice off): Hold it. That's not right.

Cameraman (off): What?

Director (also me, with a mustache and jodhpurs, walking on-screen): I don't want a dissolve here. (He looks around) Well?

Cameraman (off): You'll have to call the Optical Effects man.

Director: Call him! (puts hands on hips)

Voices (off): Optical Effects! Optical Effects! Hey!

(Sounds of clanking and jangling. Man in coveralls ((Jean-Paul Belmondo)) walks on carrying a huge workbag marked Optical Effects. He has a hunk of bread in one hand.)

Belmondo: Yeah, Boss?

Director: I don't want a dissolve here.

Belmondo (shrugs): Okay. (He takes out a stovepipe, walks toward the camera p.o.v., jams the end of the stovepipe over the lens. Camera shudders. The circular image on the screen irises in. Camera swings wildly, trying to get away. Screen irises to black. Sound of labored breathing, then asphyxiation.)

Director's voice: No! It can't breathe! I don't want an iris, either!

Belmondo's voice: Suit yourself, Boss. (Sound of tearing. Camera p.o.v. Belmondo pulls off stovepipe. Camera quits moving. Breathing returns to normal.)

Director: What kind of effects you have in there?

Belmondo: All kinds. I can do anything.

Director: Like what?

Belmondo: Hey, cameraman. Pan down to his feet. (Camera pans down onto shoes.) Hold still, Monsieur Le Director! (Sound of jet taking off) There! Now pan up.

(Camera pans up. Director is standing where he was, back to us, but now his head is on backwards. He looks down his back.)

Director: Hey! Ow! Fix me!

Belmondo: Soon as I get this effect you want.

Director: Ow. Quick! Anything! Something from the old Fieullade serials!

Belmondo: How about this? (He reaches into the bag, brings out a Jacob's Ladder, crackling and humming.)

Director: Great. Anything! Just fix my head!

(Belmondo sticks the Jacob's Ladder into the camera's p.o.v. Jagged lightning bolt wipe to the next scene of a road-way down which Guy ((me)) is walking.)

Belmondo (v.o.): We aim to please, Boss.

Director (v.o.): Great. *Now* could you fix my head?

Belmondo (v.o.): Hold still. (Three Stooges' sound of nail being pried from a dry board.)

Director (v.o.): Thanks.

Belmondo (v.o.): Think nothing of it. (Sound of clanking bag being dragged away. Voice now in distance.) Anybody seen my wine?

(Guy ((me)) continues to walk down the road. Camera pans with him, stops as he continues offscreen left. Camera is focused on a road sign:)

Nevers 32 km
Alphaville 60 km
Marienbad 347 km
Hiroshima 14497km
Guyville 2 km

To get my mind off the work on the movie, I went to one of the usual parties, with the usual types there, and on the many screens in the house were the usual undergrounds.

On one, Erich von Stroheim was doing Carmen Miranda's dance from *The Gang's All Here* in full banana regalia, a three-minute loop that drew your eyes from anywhere in line of sight.

On another, John F. Kennedy and Marilyn Monroe tore up a bed in Room 12 of the Bates Motel.

In the living room, on the biggest screen, Laurel and Hardy were doing things with Wallace Beery and Clark Gable they had never thought of doing in real life. I watched for a moment. At one point a tired and puffy Hardy turned to a drunk and besmeared Laurel and said: "Why don't you do something to *help* me?"

Enough, enough. I moved to another room. There was a tv there, too. Something seemed wrong—the screen too fuzzy, sound bad, acting unnatural. It took me a few seconds to realize that they had the set tuned to a local low-power tv station and were watching an old movie, King Vidor's 1934 *Our Daily Bread*. It was the story of a bunch of Depression-era idealistic have-nots making a working, dynamic, corny and totally American commune out of a few acres of land by sheer dint of will.

I had seen it before. The *Cahiers du Cinema* people always wrote about it when they talked about what real Marxist movies should be like, back in those dim pre-*Four Hundred Blows* days when all they had were typewriters and theories.

The house smelled of butyl nitrate and uglier things. There were a dozen built-in aerosol dispensers placed strategically about the room. The air was a stale mix of vassopressins, pheromones and endorphins which floated in a blue mist a couple of meters off the floors. A drunk jerk stood at one of the dispensers and punched its button repeatedly, like a laboratory animal wired to stimulate its pleasure center.

I said my goodbyes to the hostess, the host having gone upstairs to show some new arrivals "some really interesting stuff."

I walked the ten blocks home to my place. My head slowly cleared on the way, the quiet buzzing left. After awhile, all the parties run together into one big Jello-wiggly image of people watching movies, people talking about them.

The grocer (Pierre Brasseur) turns to Marie (Jeanne Moreau) and Guy (me).

"I assure you the brussels sprouts are very fine," he says.

"They don't look it to me," says Marie.

"Look," says Guy (me) stepping between them. "Why not artichokes?"

"This time of year?" asks the grocer.

"Who asked you?" says Marie to Guy (me). She plants her feet. "I want brussels sprouts, but not these vile disgusting things."

"How dare you say that!" says the grocer. "Leave my shop. I won't have my vegetables insulted."

"Easy, mac," I (Guy) say.

"Who asked you?" he says and reached behind the counter for a baseball bat.

"Don't threaten him," says Marie.

"Nobody's threatening me," Guy (I) say to her.

"He is," says Marie. "He's going to hit you!"

"No, I'm not," says the grocer to Marie. "I'm going to hit *you*. Get out of my shop. I didn't fight in the *maquis* to have some chi-chi tramp disparage me."

"Easy, mac," Guy (I) say to him.

"And *now*, I *am* going to hit you!" says the grocer.

"I'll take these brussels sprouts after all," says Marie, running her hand through her hair.

"Very good. How much?"

"Half a kilo," she says. She turns to me (Guy). "Perhaps we can make it to the bakery before it closes."

"Is shopping here always like this?" I (Guy) ask.

"I wouldn't know," she says. "I just got off the bus."

It was the perfect ending for the scene. I liked it a lot. It was much better than what I had programmed.

Because from the time Marie decided to take the sprouts, none of the scene was as I had written it.

"You look tired," said Lois, leaning against my office doorjam, arms crossed like Bacall in *To Have and Have Not*.

"I am tired. I haven't been sleeping."

"I take a couple of dexadryl a day," she said. "I'm in this last push on the movie, so I'm making it a point to get at least two hours' sleep a night.

"Uh, Lois . . ." I said. "Have you ever programmed a scene one way and have it come out another?"

"That's what that little red reset button is for," she said. She looked at me with her grey-blue eyes.

"Then it's happened to you?"

"Sure."

"Did you let the scene play all the way through?"

"Of course not. As soon as anything deviated from the program, I'd kill it and start over."

"Wouldn't you be interested in letting them go and see what happens?"

"And have a mess on my hands? That was what was wrong with the old way of making movies. I treat it as a glitch, start again, and get it *right*." She tilted her head. "Why do you ask?"

"Lot of stuff's been . . . well, getting offtrack. I don't know how or why."

"And you're letting them run on?"

"Some," I said, not meeting her gaze.

"I'd hate to see your studio timeshare-bill. You must be *way* over budget."

"I try not to imagine it. But I'm sure I've got a better movie for it."

She took my hand for a second, but only a second. She was wearing a blue rib-knit sweater. Blue was definitely her color.

"That way lies madness," she said. "Call Maintenance and get them to blow out the low level format of your ramdisk a couple of times. Got to run," she said, her tone changing instantly. "Got a monster to kill."

"Thanks a lot. Really," I say. She stops at the door.

"They put a lot of stuff in the GAX," she said. "No telling what kind of garbage is floating around in there, unused, that can leak out. If you want to play around, you might as well put in a bunch of fractals and watch the pretty pictures.

"If you want to make a movie, *you've* got to tell it what to do and sit on its head while it's doing it."

She looked directly at me. "It's just points of light fixed on a plane, Scott."

She left.

Delphine Seyrig is giving Guy (me) trouble.

She was supposed to be the woman who asks Guy to help her get a new chest-of-drawers up the steps of her house.

We'd seen her pushing it down the street in the background of the scene before with Marie and Guy (me) in the bakery.

While Marie (Moreau) is in the vintner's, Seyrig asks Guy (me) for help.

Now she's arguing about her part.

"I suppose I'm here just to be a tumble in the hay for you?" she asks.

"I don't know what you're talking about, lady. Do you want help with the bureau, or what?"

"Bureau? Do you mean FBI?" asks a voice behind Guy (me). Guy (me) turns. Eddy Constantine, dressed as Lemmy Caution in a cheap trenchcoat and a bad hat stares at Guy (me) with his cue-ball eyes.

"No! Chest-of-drawers," says Seyrig.

"Chester Gould? *Dick Tracy*?" asks Constantine.

Guy (me) wanders away, leaving them to argue semantics on the steps. As he turns the corner the sound of three quick shots comes from the street he has just left. He heads toward the wine shop where Marie stands, smoking.

I almost forgot about the screening of *Monster Without A Meaning*. There was a note on my screen from Lois. I didn't know she was through or anywhere near it, but then, I didn't even know what day it was.

I took my cup of bad black coffee into the packed screening room. Lois wasn't there—she said she'd never attend a showing of one of her movies. There were the usual reps, a few critics, some of her friends, a couple of sequencer operators and a dense crowd of the usual bit-part unknowns.

Boris, Lois' boyfriend, got up to speak. (Boris had been working off and on for five years on his own movie, *The Beast With Two Backs*.) He said something redundant and sat down, and the movie started, with the obligatory GAX-600 logo.

Even the credits were right—they slimed down the screen and formed shaded hairy letters in deep perspective, like those from a flat print of an old 3-D movie.

John Agar was the scientist on vacation (he was catching a goddam *mackerel* out of what purported to be a high Sierra-Nevada lake; he used his fly rod with all the grace of a long-shoreman handling a pitchfork for the first time) when the decayed-orbit satellite hits the experimental laboratory of the twin hermit mad scientists (Les Tremayne and Leo G. Carroll).

An Air Force major (Kenneth Tobey) searching for the satellite meets up with both Agar and the women (Mara Corday, Julie Adams) who were on their way to take jobs with the mad doctors when the shock wave of the explosion blew their car into a ditch. Agar had stopped to help them, and the jeep with Tobey and the comic relief (Sgt. Joe Sawyer, Cpl. Sid Melton) drives up.

Cut to the Webb farmhouse—Gramps (Olin Howlin), Patricia (Florida Friebus), Aunt Sophonsiba (Kathleen Freeman) and Little Jimmy (George "Foghorn" Winslow) were listening to the radio when the wave of static swept over it. They hear the explosion, and Gramps and Little Jimmy jump into the woodie and drive over to the The Old Science Place.

It goes just like you imagine from there, except for the monster. It's all done subjective camera—the monster sneaks up (you've always seen something moving in the background of the long master shot before, in the direction from which the monster comes). It was originally a guy (Robert Clarke) coming in to get treated for a rare nerve disorder. He was on Les Tremayne's gurney when the satellite hit, dousing him with experimental chemicals and "space virus" from the newly discovered van Allen belt.

The monster gets closer and closer to the victims—they see something in a mirror, or hear a twig snap, and they turn around—they start to scream, their eyeballs go white like fried marbles, blood squirts out their ears and nose, their gums dissolve, their hair chars away, then the whole face; the clothes evaporate, wind rushes toward their radioactive burning—it's all over in a second but it's all there, every detail perfect.

The scene where Florida Friebus melts is a real shocker. From the way the camera lingers over it, you know the monster's enjoying it.

By the time General Morris Ankrum, Colonel R.G. Armstrong and Secretary of State Henry Hull wise up, things are bad.

At one point the monster turns and stares back over its shoulder. There's an actual charred trail of destruction stretching behind it; burning houses like Christmas tree lights in the far mountains, the small town a few miles back looking like the ones they built for the Project Ivy A-bomb tests in Nevada. Turning its head the monster looks down at the quiet night-time city before it. All the power and wonder of death are in that shot.

(Power and wonder are in me, too, in the form of a giant headache. One of my eyes isn't focusing anymore. A bad sign, and rubbing doesn't help.)

I get up to go—the movie's great but the light is hurting my eyes too much.

Suddenly here come three F-84 Thunderjets flown by Cpt. Clint Eastwood, 1st Lt. Leonard Nimoy and Colonel James Whitmore.

"The Reds didn't like the regular stuff in Korea. This thing shouldn't like this atomic napalm, either," says Whitmore. "Let's go in and spread a little honey around, boys."

The jets peel off.

Cut to the monster's p.o.v. The jets come in with a roar. Underwing tanks come off as they power back up into a climb. The bombs tumble lazily toward the screen. One whistles harmlessly by, two are dropping short, three keep getting bigger and bigger, then blam—woosh. You're the monster and you're being burned to death in a radioactive napalm firestorm.

Screaming doesn't help; one hand comes up just before the eyes melt away like lumps of lard on a floor furnace—the hand crisps to paper, curls, blood starts to shoot out and evaporates like verga over the Mojave. The last thing the monster hears are its auditory canals boiling away with a screeching hiss.

Cut to Agar, inventor of the atomic napalm, holding Mara Corday on a hill above the burning city and the charring monster. He's breathing hard, his hair is singed; her skirt is torn off one side, exposing her long legs.

Up above, Whitmore, oxygen mask off, smiles down and wags the jet's wings.

Pull back to a panorama of the countryside; Corday and Agar grow smaller; the scene lifts, takes in jets, county, then state; miles up now the curve of the earth appears, grows larger, continue to pull back, whole of U.S., North and Central America appears. Beeping on soundtrack. We are moving along with a white luminescence which is revealed to be a Sputnik-type satellite.

Beeping stops. Satellite begins to fall away from camera, lurching some as it hits the edges of the atmosphere. As it falls, letters slime down the screen: The End?

Credits: A movie by Lois B. Traven.

The lights come up. I begin to breathe again. I'm standing in the middle of the aisle, applauding as hard as I can.

Everybody else is applauding, too. Everybody.

Then my head *really* begins to hurt, and I go outside into the cool night and sit on the studio wall like Humpty-Dumpty.

Lois is headed for the Big Time. She deserves it.

The notes on my desk are now hand-deep. Pink ones, then orange ones from the executive offices. Then the bright red-striped ones from accounting.

Fuckem. I'm almost through.

I sat down and plugged on. Nothing happened.

I punched Maintenance.

"Sorry," says Bobo. "You gotta get authorization from Snell before you can get back online, says here."

"Snell in accounting, or Snell in the big building?"

"Lemme check." There's a lot of yelling around the office on the other end. "Snell in the big building."

"Yeah, yeah, okay."

So I have to eat dung in front of Snell, promise him anything, renegotiate my contract *right then and there* in his office without my business manager or agent. But I *have* to get this movie finished.

Then I have to go over to Accounting and sign a lot of stuff. I call Bernie and Chinua and tell them to come down to the studio and clean up the contractual shambles as best they can, and not to expect to hear from me for a week or so.

Then I call my friend Jukai, who helped install the first GAX-600 and talk to him for an hour and a half and learn a few things.

Then I go to Radio Shack and run up a bill of $6124, buy two weeks worth of survival food at Apocalypse Andy's, put everything in my car and drive over to the office deep under the bowels of the GAX-600.

I have locked everyone else out of the mainframe with words known only to myself and Alain Resnais. Let *them* wait.

I have put a note on the door.
Leave me alone. I am finishing the movie. Do not try to stop me. You are locked out of the 600 until I am through. Do not attempt to take me off-line. I have rewired the 600 to wipe out everything, every movie in it but mine if you do. Do not cut my power; I have a generator in here—if you turn me off, the GAX is history. (See attached receipt.) Leave me alone until I have finished; you will get everything back, and a great movie too.

They *were* knocking. Now they're pounding on the door. Screwem. I'm starting the scene where Guy (me) and Marie hitch a ride on the garbage wagon out of the communist pig farm.

The locksmith was quiet but he couldn't do any good, either. I've put on the kind of locks they use on the *outsides* of prisons.
They tried to put a note on the screen. BACK OFF, I wrote.
They began to ease them, pleading notes, one at a time through the razor-thin crack under the fireproof steel door.
Every few hours I would gather them up. They quit coming for a while.
Sometime later there was a polite knock.
A note slid under.
"May I come in for a few moments?" it asked. It was signed *A. Resnais.*
GO AWAY, I wrote back. YOU HAVEN'T MADE A GOOD MOVIE SINCE *LA GUERRE EST FINIE.*
I could imagine his turning to the cops and studio heads in his dignified humble way (he must be pushing ninety by now), shrugging his shoulders as if to say, well, I tried my best, and walking away.   • • •

"You must end this madness," says Marie. "We've been here a week. The room smells. I smell. You smell. I'm tired of dehydrated apple chips. I want to talk on the beach again, get some sunlight."

"What kind of ending would that be?" I (Guy) ask.

"I've seen worse. I've *been* in much worse. Why do you have this obsessive desire to recreate movies made fifty years ago?"

I (Guy) look out the window of the cheap hotel, past the edge of the taped roller shade. "I (Guy) don't know." I (Guy) rub my chin covered with a scratchy week's stubble. "Maybe those movies, those, those things were like a breath of fresh air. They led to everything we have today."

"Well, we could use a breath of fresh air."

"No. Really. They came in on a stultified, lumbering dinosaur of an industry, tore at its flanks, nibbled at it with soft rubbery beaks, something, I don't know what. Stung it into action, showed it there were *other* ways of doing things— made it question itself. Showed that movies could be free— not straight jackets."

"Recreating *them* won't make any new statements," said Marie (Moreau).

"I'm trying to breathe new life into *them*, then. Into what they were. What they meant to . . . to me, to others," I (Guy) say.

What I want to do more than anything is to take her from the motel, out on the sunny street to the car. Then I want to drive her up the winding roads to the cliffs overlooking the Mediterranean. Then I want her to lean over, her right arm around my neck, her hair blowing in the wind, and give me a kiss that will last forever, and say, "I love you, and I'm ready."

Then I will press down the accelerator, and we will go through the guard rail, hang in the air, and begin to fall faster and faster until the eternal blue sea comes up to meet us in a tender hand-shaped spray, and just before the impact she will smile and pat my arm, never taking her eyes off the windshield.

"Movies are freer than they ever were," she says from the bed. "I was there. I know. You're just going through the motions. The things that brought about those films are remem-

bered only by old people, bureaucrats, *film critics*," she says
with a sneer.

"What about you?" I (Guy) ask, turning to her. "You remember. You're not old. You're alive, vibrant."

My heart is breaking.

She gives me (Guy) a stare filled with sorrow. "No I'm not.
I'm a character in a movie. I'm points of light, fixed on a
plane."

A tear-gas canister crashes through the window. There is a
pounding against the door.

"The cops!" I (Guy) say, reaching for the .45 automatic.

"The pimps!" Marie says.

The room is filling with gas. Bullets fly. I fire at the door,
the window shades as I reach for Marie's hand. The door
bursts open.

Two quick closeups: her face, terrified; mine, determined,
with a snarl and a holy wreath of cordite rising from my pistol.

My head is numb. I see in the dim worklight from my
screen the last note they stuck under the door fluttering as the
invisible gas is pumped in.

I type *fin*.

I reach for the nonexistent button which will wipe everything but *This Guy Goes to Town* ... and mentally push it.

I (Guy) smile up at them as they come through the doors
and walls; pimps, Nazis, film critics, studio cops, deep-sea di-
vers, spacemen, clowns and lawyers.

Through the windows I can see the long geometric rows of
the shrubs forming quincuxes, the classical statuary, people
moving to and fro in a garden like a painting by Fragonard.

I must have been away a long time; someone was telling
me, as I was making my way toward these first calm
thoughts, that *This Guy* ... is the biggest hit of the season. I
have been told that while I was on my four-week vacation
from human cares and woes that I have become that old-time
curiosity: the rich man who is crazy as a piss ant.

Far less rich of course than I would have been had I not re-
negotiated my contract before my last, somewhat spectacular,
orgy of movie-and-lovemaking in my locked office.

I am now calm. I am not looking forward to my recovery, but suppose I will have to get some of my own money out of my manager's guardianship.

A nurse comes in, opens the taffeta curtains at another set of windows, revealing nice morning sunlight through the tiny, very tasteful, bars.

She turns to me and smiles.

It is Anouk Aimee.

INTRODUCTION TO

THE PASSING OF THE WESTERN

AS it happens to all genres, something is happening to the Western (it may be the Eighties, my personal opinion is that it's something in the water, but all the genres and forms of once-mass entertainment went through sea changes in the last decade—see the intro for "Thirty Minutes Over Broadway!" for what happened to comic books).

As always, a large part of this was three guys, and further on, a bunch of writers who were *ready*. Two of them are editors—Greg Tobin and Pat LoBrutto—the other's a writer, Joe Lansdale. For years, LoBrutto handled the Western (and SF and mystery) lines at Doubleday. Tobin came to Bantam some few yeas ago and revitalized its shootemups (Westerns-except-for-Louis-L'Amour-don't-sell was the publishing dictum everywhere else) by getting a bunch of recognized classics back into print, and, among other things, getting Chad Oliver to write "the Custer book" (*Broken Eagle*, Bantam, 1989) he'd been talking about for twenty-five years.

Lansdale, who's written horror, SF, mysteries, suspense, and for all I know, tortilla cookbooks, and who is, I'm afraid to say, younger than I am, was also a Western writer, with a love for the field that knows no bounds. He wrote the primo book *The Magic Wagon*, which, if you haven't read it, you ain't squat. (What the people who automatically picked up every Double-D western that hits the library shelf thought they were getting when they opened it, I don't know. My theory is that they're still sitting wherever it was when they read it, eyes bugged out, smoke coming out the holes where their ears used to be. I can't describe the book—it's got Wild Bill Hickok's mummy, a wrestling chimpanzee, a medicine show, a town you'd never want to find yourself in—it's just plain wonderful.)

Well, all this stuff was going on, and Ed Gorman was editing the Western Writers of America anthologies, with, like stream-of-consciousness rustler's tales, and descriptions of brandings from the calf's point of view, and Neal Barrett was writing about Emily Dickinson stealing all her poetry from Liver-Eater Johnson—you know, things were *happening*.

Three or four years ago, Joe asked me the question that *always* gets me in trouble, the one all my writer friends ask: "I may get to edit an original anthology someday. If I do, will you write a story for me?" and I always give the same answer, "Sure. You bet. Can't wait."

About 18 months ago I get a call: "We're doing the book. It's called *Razored Saddles*. Where's your story?"

Yow!

Well, one had been clanging around in the back of my mind for years—like most of the ones just sitting there, it's an alternate world story. Also, I wanted an homage to a guy who's given the SF field more than it will ever give back to him, mostly by his just *being* there (see the intro to "French Scenes," in case you're reading this book backwards). So it had to be about this guy's area of expertise. I wrote it in a day or so, once I got the initial image that tied everything together.

I sent it off to Joe and Pat LoBrutto, the co-editors. Then I took it up to Kansas City to read at an SF convention.

My friend George R. R. Martin heard me read it. Afterwards, we were all sitting around somebody's room party, and George started in about how he'd tried and tried to teach me how to write through the years, and that it hadn't taken.

"Look, Howard. Somebody else with that idea would have set it in the *time* it took place."

"Uh-huh."

"Somebody really out to end their career would have described the *movies* about the *time* the story's about."

"Uh-huh."

"Somebody who knew absolutely nothing about writing at all is the only one who would write the story about the *filming* of the *movies* about the *time* the story's about!"

"Uh-huh."

"But no-o-o-o-o!" said George. "You, you write *articles* about *filming* the *movies* about the *time* the story's about!"

"Uh-huh?"

"Nobody can write stories that way, Howard! It's like Homer never existed! Did you know you did all that, Howard? Did you know how tertiary your thinking is? Did you know all that? Didja? Didja, huh?"

Everybody was looking at me.

"Well, George," I said. "I went through all that convoluted thinking stuff you just did. But I did it in about ten seconds, and I knew it was the *only* way to write the story, so I did."

George threw his hands into the air and ran screaming from the room.

Sorry.

THE PASSING
OF THE WESTERN

FROM *Film Review World*, April 1972:

A few months ago, we sensed something in the national psyche, a time for reevaluation, and began to put together this special issue of *Film Review World* devoted to that interesting, almost forgotten art form, the American western movie.

The genre flourished between 1910 and the late 1930s, went into its decline in the 1940s (while the country was recovering from The Big Recession, and due perhaps more to actual physical problems such as the trouble of finding suitable locations, and to the sudden popularity of costume dramas, religious spectacles and operettas). There was some renewed interest in the late 1940s, then virtually nothing for the next twenty years.

Now that some Europeans (and some far less likely people) have discovered something vital in the form, and have made a few examples of the genre (along with their usual output of historical epics and heavy dramas), we felt it was time for a retrospective of what was for a while a uniquely American art form, dealing as they did with national westward expansion and the taming of a whole continent.

We were originally going to concentrate on the masters of the form, but no sooner had we assigned articles and begun the search for stills to illustrate them than we ran across (in the course of reviewing books in the field *and* because we occasionally house-sit with our twelve-year-old nephew) no less than *three* articles dealing in part with a little-known (but well-remembered by those who saw them) series of Westerns made between 1935 and 1938 by the Metropolitan-Goldfish-Mayer Studios. Admittedly, the last article appeared in a magazine aimed specifically at teenagers with no knowledge of

American film industry history (or anything *else* for that matter) edited by a man with an encyclopedic knowledge of film and an absolutely abominable writing style—who has nevertheless delved into movie arcana in his attempt to fill the voracious editorial maw of the six magazines he edits (from his still-and-poster-laden Boise garage) for a not-so-nice guy in Richmond.

That we could almost dismiss, but the other two we couldn't—two works by film scholars noted for their ability to find people, hunt up lost screenplays and production notes and to dig at the facts, both books to be published within a week of each other next month.

We've obtained permission to reprint the relevant portions of the two books, and the whole of that magazine article (including the stills) by way of introduction to this special issue dedicated to the Passing of the Western Movie from the American cinema—taken together, they seemed to strike exactly the right note about the film form we seem to have lost.

Join us, then, in a trip backwards in time—twice, as it were—to both the real events that inspired the films, and to the movies made about them fifty years later.

And, as they used to say on the Chisolm Road, "always keep to the high ground and have your slicker handy!"

—John Thomas Johns

From: *The Boise System: Interviews with 15 Directors Who Survived Life in the Studios*, by Frederick T. Yawts, Ungar (Film Book 3) 1972.

          (from the interview with James Selvors)

Selvors: ... the problems of doing Westerns of course in those days was finding suitable locations—that's why they set up operations in Boise in the first place. See, no matter what steps people had taken, they'd never really gotten any good constant rainfall in the Idaho part of the basin—oh, they could make it rain occasionally, but never like anywhere else—it was the mountains to the west. They call it orographic uplift, an orographic plain. There used to be one on the west coast of Peru, but they fixed that back in the Nineteen-teens by fooling with the ocean currents down there. They tried that up here, too, in

Washington State and Oregon, messed with the ocean currents; instead of raining in Idaho all they got was more rain on the Pacific slope, which they *did not need.*

Anyway, Griffith and Laemmle came out to Boise in '09, 1910, something like that, because they could be out in what was left of the Plains in a few hours and they could almost guarantee 150 good-weather days a year.

First thing the early filmmakers had to do was build a bunch of western towns, since there weren't any out there (nobody with any sense ever stopped and put down roots in the Idaho Plains when Oregon was just a few days away). What few towns there had been had all rotted away (there still wasn't much rain but it was a hell of a lot more than there had been 60 years before). The place actually used to be a desert—imagine that, with nothing growing but scrub; by the time the pioneer moviemakers got there it was looking like old pictures of Kansas and Nebraska from the 1850s—flat grasslands, a few small trees; really Western-looking. (God help anyone who wanted to make a movie set in one of the Old Deserts—you've got farms all up and down the Mojave River and Death Valley Reservoir and Great Utah Lake now that get 50 bales to the acre in cotton.) There was the story everybody's heard about making the Western in one of the new *nunatak* areas in Antarctica—the snow'd melted off some 3000 square miles—taking fake cactus and sagebrush down there in the late '40s. I mean, it *looked* like a desert, flat bare rock everywhere; everybody had to strip down to just shirt, pants and hats and put on fake sweat—we heard it froze; the snow's melted in Antarctica a whole lot, but don't let anyone tell you it's not still *cold* there—it has something with not getting as cold by a couple of degrees a year—like the mean temperature's only risen like four degrees since the 1880s. (Filming icebergs is another thing—you either have to do miniatures in a tank, which never worked, use old stock footage, ditto; or go to Antarctica and blast the tops off all jaggedy with explosives—the ones in Antarctica are flat, they're land ice; what everybody thinks of as northern icebergs were sea ice.) Somebody's gonna have to do an article sometime on how the weather's kept special effects people in business. . . .

Int: What was it about the *Cloudbusters* series that made them so popular?

Selvors: Lots of people saw them. (laughs)

Int: No, seriously. They were started as short subjects, then went to steady B-Westerns. Only Shadow Smith dying stopped production of them. . . .

Selvors: I've talked to lots of people over the years about that. Those things resonate. They're about exactly what they're about, if you know what I mean. Remember *Raining Cats and Dogs? The Second Johnstown Flood?* Those were A pictures, big budgets, big stars? Well, they all came later, after the last *Cloudbusters* movie was made. I mean, we set out to make a film about the real taming of the West—how it was done, in fact. All these small independent outfits, going from place to place, making it rain, fixing up things, turning the West into a garden and a lush pastureland. That was the real West, not a bunch of people killing off Indians and shooting each other over rights to a mudhole. That stuff happened early on, just after the Civil War. By 1880 all that was changing.

We wanted just to make a short, you know, a three-reeler, about thirty minutes—there was a hot documentary and a two-reel color cartoon going out with the A picture *Up and Down the Front*, about Canadians in the Big 1920 Push during the Great World War (that being the closest the U.S. got to it)—this was late '34, early '35 ((release date April 23, 1935—Int)). So that package was too much stuff for even a 55 minute B-picture. Goldfish and Thalberg came to me and George Mayhew and asked us if we had a three-reeler ready to go—we didn't but we told them we did, and sat up all night working. Mayhew'd wanted to do a movie about the rainmakers and pluvicultists for a long time. There'd been an early silent about it, but that had been a real stinker ((*Dam Burst at Sun Dog Gap*, Universal 1911—Int.)), so Mayhew thought up the plot, and the mood, and we knew Shadow Smith was available, and Mayhew'd written a couple of movies with "PDQ" Podmer in them so he thought up the "Doodad" character for him, and we went back to Thalberg next day and shook hands on it and took off for Boise the next morning.

Int: It was a beautiful little film—most people remember it being a feature.

Selvors: Mayhew kicked butt with that script—lots of stuff in it, background and things, lots of action, but nothing seemed jammed in sideways or hurried. You remember that one was self-contained; I mean, it ended with the rain and everybody jumping up and down in mud-puddles, and the Cloudbusters rolling out for the next place. I think if we'd never made another one, people would still remember *The Cloudbusters*.

Int: It was the first one to show the consequences, too—it ended with the Cloudbusters sitting in the Thunder Wagon bogged up to the wheelhubs and having to be pulled out by two teams of oxen.

Selvors: That's right. A beautiful touch. But it wasn't called the Thunder Wagon yet. Most people remember it that way but it wasn't, not in that one. That all came later.

Int: Really?

Selvors: Really. Wasn't until the second one their wagon was referred to as the Thunder Wagon. And it wasn't painted on the side until the third one.

Int: How did the features, and the rest of the series come about?

Selvors: Thalberg liked it. So did the preview audiences, better than anything but the cartoon. It even got bookings outside the package and the chains.

Int: I didn't know that. That was highly unusual.

Selvors: So much so they didn't know what to do. But by
             then we were into the second, maybe the third. All
             I know is they set up a points system for us.
Int: Even though you were on salary?
Selvors: Me and Mayhew were in pig heaven. Smith got
             part of it, but the brightest man of all was Podmer.
             He wasn't on contract—he was, like, a loose can-
             non; sometimes him and Andy Devine or Eric
             Blore would work on two or three movies on dif-
             ferent lots a day. Anyway, he sure cut some sweet
             deal with M.G.M. over the series. Podmer talked
             like a hick and walked like a hick—it was that we
             wanted in the character of "Doodad" and he was
             brilliant at it—but he could tear a pheasant with the
             best of them. . . .
Int: So if you and Mayhew set out to tell a realistic
             story, about the rainmakers and the real business of
             winning the West . . .
Selvors: I know what you're going to ask next. (laughs)
Int: What?
Selvors: You're going to ask about The Windmill Trust.
Int: What about The Windmill Trust?
Selvors: That part, we made up.

From: *The Sidekick: Doppelgangers of the Plains* by Marvin
Ermstien, UCLA Press, 1972.
             (This interview with Elmer "PDQ" Podmer took
             place in 1968, a few months before his death at the
             age of 94. It was recorded at the Boise Basin Yacht
             Club.)
             . . .
ME: Let's talk about the most popular series you did at
             M.G.M.
Podmer: You mean *The Cloudbusters*?
ME: You've been in, what, more than 300 movies . . . ?
Podmer: 374, and I got another one shooting next month,
             where I play Burt Mustin's father.
ME: I'm still surprised that people remember you best
             as "Doodad" Jones. Three of the films were shorts,
             five were B-movies, and I don't think any of them
             have been on television for a while. . . .

Podmer: Izzat a fact? Well, I know last time I saw one was mebbe ten year ago when I was over to my great grandniece's house. I remember when Bill Boyd was goin' on and on about television, way back in 1936 or so. He told all us it was the wave o' the future and to put all our money in Philco. He was buying up the rights to all his Roman Empire movies, that series he made, Hoplite Cassius. We all thought he was crazy as a bedbug at the time. He made quite a bundle, I know that.

ME: About *The Cloudbusters* ...

Podmer: Well, it was a good character part. It was just like me, and the director and writer had some pretty good ideas what to do with him. Also, you remember I was the star of the last one ...

ME: *The Thunder Wagon*. That was the one being made when Shadow Smith died.

Podmer: That was it. Well, originally of course it had pretty much another script—they'd filmed some of it—in fact they'd filmed the scene that was used in the movie where Shadow talks to me and then rides off to do some damn thing or other. Next day we got the news about Shadow drowning in the Snake River while he was hauling in a 14 pound rainbow trout. They found his rod and reel two mile downriver and the trout was still hooked....

ME: There were lots of ironic overtones in the death notices at the time.

Podmer: You mean about him being in *The Cloudbusters* and then dying that way? Yeah, I remember. He was a damn fine actor, a gentleman, just like his screen character. We was sure down for a while.

ME: So the script was rewritten?

Podmer: Yep. Mayhew wanted to make it a tribute to Smith, and also do some things he hadn't been able to do before, so he turned out a hum-dinger! I got top billing for the first and only time in my life. In the cutting on the new version, they had Smith say whatever it is, then as he turns to ride away they had this guy who could do Smith's voice tell me where to take the Thunder Wagon, which sets up

the plot. That puts me and Chancy Raines (that
was Bobby Hornmann, a real piss-ass momma's
boy, nothing like the character he played) smack
dab up against Dryden and the Windmill Trust on
our own. 'Course the real star of that last picture
was the wagon itself. Mayhew's screenplay really
put that thing through some paces. . . .

ME: Tell us about the Wagon.

Podmer: You seen the movies, ain't you?

ME: Three or four times each.

Podmer: Then why ask me?

ME: Well, it looked like *you* firing off the Lightning
           Rockets and the Nimbus Mortars. . . .

Podmer: It was me. I didn't use no stuntman! I wisht I had
           a nickel for every powder burn I got on that series.
           Some days I'd be workin' at M.G.M. mornings and
           hightailing it all the way across Boise to the First
           National lot, and runnin' on the set sayin' my
           lines, and the makeup men would be bitching be-
           cause I'd burnt half my real beard off, or had pow-
           der burns on my arms, or something. One of those
           other films I ain't got no eyebrows in a couple of
           scenes.

ME: What about the Sferics Box? I know some critics
           complained there was nothing like it in use among
           the rainmakers in the real Old West.

Podmer: Do I look like a goddamn engineer? I'm a thes-
           pian! Ask Mayhew or Selvors about that stuff. I do
           know I once got a letter from a guy what used to
           be a rainmaker back then—hell, he must have been
           older when he wrote that letter than I am *now*—
           who said he used something like that there Sferics
           Box—they'd listen for disturbances in the ether
           with them. Had something to do with sunspots, I
           think.

ME: That was twenty years before deForest sent the
           first messages. . . .

Podmer: They wasn't interested in talkin' to each other, they
           was interested in makin' a gullywasher! That's
           what the guy wrote, anyway.

ME: In all those films, Shadow Smith never used a gun, right?

Podmer: Well, just that once. People talked about that stuff for a long time. It was the next to last one ((*The Watershed Wars*, 1937—ME)) and they was that shootist for the Windmill Trust that called Shadow out to a street duel—Shadow'd just gone into the saloon to find him after all those people were killed when the Windmill Trust tried to make Utah Great Lake salty again, and Shadow's so mad he picks up a couple of guns from the bar and goes out, then you cut out onto the street, bad guy's standing in it, and Shadow comes out the saloon doors a quarter-mile away and starts shooting, just blasting away and walking up the boardwalk, bullets hitting all over the streets around the shootist, and he just takes off and runs, hightails it away. When Shadow realizes what he's done, that he's used gun-violence, he gets all upset and chagrined. People still talk about that. What few Westerns were made later, even the ones they started filming a few years ago in what was left of the Sahara Plains, they'd never done that—always romanticized it, one-to-one, always used violence. Never like in *The Cloudbusters*, where we used brains and science. . . .

ME: It wasn't just Shadow Smith's death that finished the series, then?

Podmer: It wuz everything. Smith died. Thalberg had been dead a year by then, and Goldfish wanted to move Selvors up to the A pictures; he never could leave well-enough alone. The next one we knew was gonna be directed by just someone with a ticket to punch. Selvors tried to stay, but they told him their way or the highway. That was the middle of '38, just when the European market fell apart, and people was nervous over here—they didn't have to wait but till August before our market started The Long Fall, and people started the Back-to-the-Land movement; they ate all right but there wasn't any *real* money around. Anyway, that's about the time

Mayhew had the garish-headline divorce and we'd be damned if we'd let other people write *and* direct *The Cloudbusters*. Also they took Bill Menzies away from us, too—he'd designed the Thunder Wagon, and most of the props and did the sets, and about half the effects on the movies—remember the credits, with that big thunderhead rolling in on you and suddenly spelling out *The Cloudbusters*?—that was Menzies' doing all along.

So we all got together, just after we wrapped *The Thunder Wagon* and we made a gentlemen's agreement that there wouldn't be any more Cloudbuster films—it was hard to do, we'd been a real family except for that shitty Hornmann kid, I hope he's burning in hell—((Robert Hornmann was killed in a fight in a West Boise nightclub in 1946—ME)) and for me it was walking away from a goldmine, and my only chance to get top billing again. But it was easiest for me, too, since I had a picture-to-picture deal and all I did was line up enough work to stay busy for the solid next year. I also put out the word to all the other comic relief types not to go signin' anything with the name Cloudbusters on it. . . .

ME: Have you seen Sergio Leone's *A Faceful of Rain-
           water*?
Podmer: Was that the wop western about the Two Forks
           War?
ME: Yes. It's supposedly an homage to the Cloud-
           busters, much grittier but not as good, I don't think.
Podmer: Nope. Ain't seen it.

From: *Blazing Screens! The Magazine of Celluloid Thrills*, June 1972.
SOUNDTRACK THUNDER AND NITRATE LIGHTNING!
            by Formalhaut J. Amkermackam

Imagine a time when most of the American continent was a vast dry desert from the Mississippi to the Pacific Coast!

Imagine when there were no lush farmlands from sea to sea, when coffee, rubber and tea had to be imported into this country!

Imagine that once men died crossing huge sandy wastes & when the only water for a hundred miles might turn out to be poison, when the Great Utah Lake was so salty it supported no aquatic life!

Imagine when the Midwest was only sparse grasslands, suitable for crops only like wheat & oats, or an economy based on the herding of cattle & sheep!

Imagine a time when rainfall was so scarce the only precipitation was snow on the high mountains in the winter & when that was melted there was no more till next year!

These things were neither a nightmare nor the fevered dreams of the fantasy writer—this was the American West— where our forefathers actually tried to make a living—*less than one hundred years ago!*

YOU CAN TAKE A PLUVICULTURE BUT YOU CAN'T MAKE IT DRINK

Then came the men & women who not only talked (as Mark Twain once said) about the weather but they did something about it! They called themselves storm wizards, rainmakers and even pluviculturists (which is the fancy word for rainmaker!) & their theories were many & varied but what they did & how they did it & how they changed our lives & the destiny of the world was the stuff of legend. But at first everybody just talked about them & nobody did anything about them.

Until 1935 that is!!!

TWO THUNDERHEADS ARE BETTER THAN ONE

That year George Mayhew (the screenwriter of *Little Lost Dinosaur* & *Wild Bill Barnacle*) teamed up with James Selvors (director of such great movies as *The Claw-Man Escapes*, *His Head Came C.O.D.* and the fantastic musical war movie *Blue Skies & Tailwinds*) to bring to the screen a series of films dealing with the life & times of the men who broke the weather & transformed the American West to a second Garden of Eatin'—*The Cloudbusters*!

THE GUN THAT DROWNED THE WEST

Aided by the marvellous & mysterious Thunder Wagon (in which they kept all their superscientific paraphernalia & their downpour-making equipment) they roamed the west through five feature films & three shorts that will never be forgotten by those who've seen them.

SHADOWS OF THINGS TO COME

For the lead in the films (except for the last one where he had only a brief appearance due to his untimely & tragic death) they chose Shadow Smith, the big (6′5-½″) actor who'd starred in such films as *Warden, Let Me Out!*, *My Friend Frankenstein* & lots more. Before the Cloudbusters films, his best-known role was as Biff Bamm in *Spooks in the Ring*, *Singing Gloves* and *Biff Bamm Meets Jawbreaker* all for Warner Bros. Shadow was born in 1908 in Flatonia, Texas & had worked in films from 1928 on, after a stint as an egg-handler & then college in Oklahoma City.

He fit the role perfectly (his character name was Shadow Smith also) & according to people who knew him was just like his screen character—softspoken, shy and a great lover of the outdoors. It is interesting that the Shadow Smith character in the Cloudbusters *never* used a firearm to settle a score—sometimes resorting to scientific wrestling holds & fisticuffs, but most usually depending on his quick wits, brain and powers of logic.

who dat who say "doodad"?

As comic relief & sidekick "Doodad" Jones was played by Elmer "PDQ" Podmer (the "PDQ" in the name of this old-time character actor stuck with him for the alacrity with which he learned & assayed his many roles, and the speed with which he went from one acting job to another, sometimes working on as many as three different films at three different studios in one day!). The character of "Doodad" was one of the most interesting he ever had. Many characteristics were the usual—he used malapropisms like other sidekicks ("aspersions to greatness", "some hick yokelramus" & he once used "matutinal absolution" for "morning bath") but was deferred to by Shadow Smith for his practical knowledge & mechanical abilities, especially when something went wrong with the "consarned idjit contraptions" in the Thunder Wagon.

Their young assistant, Chancy Raines (played by Bobby Hornmann, who died tragically young before he could fulfill his great talents as an actor) was added in the second film as an orphan picked up by Smith and "Doodad" after a drought & sudden flash flood killed his mother & father & little sister.

Together they roamed the West, in three short (3-reel or 28 minute) films and five full-length features made between

1935 and 1938. They went from small towns and settlements to the roaring hellcamps of Central City and Sherman Colorado to the Mojave Desert in California, and as far north as the Canadian border, bringing with them storms & lifegiving rains which made the prairies bloom—always in their magnificent Thunder Wagon!

SKYWARD HO!

The Thunder Wagon! A beautiful & sleek yellow and blue (we were told) wagon pulled by a team of three pure white horses (Cirrus, Stratus and Cumulus) and one pure black horse (Nimbus)!

Designed by director/cameraman/set designer/special effects man Bill C. Menzies (who had come from Germany via England to the M.G.M. studios in Boise in 1931) the Thunder Wagon seemed both swift & a solid platform from which Shadow, "Doodad" and Chancy made war on the elements with their powerful Lightning Rockets, Nimbus Mortars (& the black horse neighed every time that weapon was fired) and the Hailstone Cannons, which they fired into the earth's atmosphere & caused black clouds & thunderstorms (& in one case a blizzard) to form & dump their precipitation on the hopeful thirsty farmers and ranchers who'd hired them.

DON QUIXOTES OF THE PLAINS!

But the weather wasn't the only thing Cloudbusters fought in the course of their movies. For they also had to battle the deadly Windmill Trust!

The Windmill Trust! A group of desperate Eastern investors, led by the powerful Mr. Dryden, dedicated to keeping the status quo of low rainfall & limited water resources in the Western territories! Their tentacles were everywhere—they owned the majority of the railroads & all the well-drilling & windmill manufacturing firms in the United States & they kept in their employ many shootists & desperadoes whom they hired to thwart the efforts of all the rainmakers & pluviculturalists to bring moisture to the parched plains. These men resorted to sabotage, missending of equipment, wrongful processes of law, and in many cases outright murder and violence to retain their stranglehold on the American West and its thirsty inhabitants!

DESICCATED TO THE ONE I LOVE

Through these eight films, with their eye-popping special effects (even the credits were an effects matte shot of a giant cloud forming & coming toward you & suddenly spelling out the series' name!) their uncharacteristic themes & their vision of a changing America (brought on by the very rainmakers these films were about!) there were thrills & images people would never forget.

If you ever get to see these (& someone should really put the first three shorts together in one package & release it to TV) you'll see:

A race to the death between raging flood waters, the Thunder Wagon, & the formerly-unbelieving Doc Geezler & a wagonload of orphans!

"Doodad" Jones using the Nimbus Mortars to cause a huge electrical storm & demolish the Giant Windmill (30 stories high!) sucking the water from & drying up the South Platte River & threatening the town of Denver with drought!

The henchmen of the Windmill Trust (led by Joe Sawyer) dressed as ghosts in a *silent* (no sound of hoofbeats, only the snap of quirts and jingle of spurs heard in an eerie scene) raid on the town of Central City, Colorado!

The climactic fight on the salt-drilling platform above Utah Great Lake in the hailstorm between Shadow Smith and Dryden & three others seemingly plunging to their deaths far below!

The great blizzard forming over the heated floor of the (once) Great Mojave Desert, with its magical scenes of cacti in the snow & icicles on the sagebrush!

ACTION! THRILLS! WET SOCKS!

You can see all this and more, if you travel back via the silver screen & your TV set to a time not so long ago, when the Cloudbusters rode the Wild American West in their eight films:

The Cloudbusters (1935—a short, introducing Shadow Smith, "Doodad" & the Thunder Wagon!)

44 Inches or Bust! (1935—the second short—the title refers to the rainfall they promise a parched community—introducing Chancy Raines & the Windmill Trust!)

Storms Along the Mojave (1936—the last short)

The Desert Breakers (1936—the first feature, introducing Dryden as head of The Windmill Trust!)

The Dust Tamers (1936—with the magic blizzard scenes!)

Battling the Windmill Trust (1936—with the giant windmill that threatens Denver!)

The Watershed Wars (1937—Dryden and Shadow Smith in hand-to-hand combat above Utah Great Lake!)

The Thunder Wagon (1938—the best film tho not most representative due to the death of Shadow Smith ((who appears only in an early scene & to whom the picture is dedicated)) but the Thunder Wagon is the star along with "Doodad" & Chancy—they have to cause rain in three widely-separated places & use the Hailstone Cannons to freeze an underground stream!)

So through these films you can ride (or saddle up again if you were lucky enough to see them the first time) with Shadow Smith, "Doodad" Jones & Chancy Raines, fighting the Windmill Trust & bringing the West the rain it so sorely needs & experience a true part of American history & thrill to the science & adventures of *The Cloudbusters*!

INTRODUCTION TO

THE ADVENTURE OF
THE GRINDER'S WHISTLE

LIKE with most things from the Seventies, this is Philip José Farmer's fault. (As, in the Fifties in the field, everything was Boucher's, Gold's or Campbell's fault, and in the Sixties, it was Harlan Ellison's fault—I'm talking bad and good here, folks.)

You remember Kurt Vonnegut's Kilgore Trout? The scuffling, mangy SF writer, who wrote brilliant books, but sent them off invariably to a porno publisher ("2BR02B was published as *Mouth Crazy*.")? His life was based on an amalgam of the lives of all the writers this field has ignored, shuffled aside, not understood, or in general pissed on (for real examples, see Malzberg and Greenberg's *Forgotten Visions* anthology). In my opinion, the guys Trout most resembled were Phil Dick (for most of his career) and the early P.J. Farmer.

Well, through the various machinations of the publishing world, Kilgore Trout's *Venus on the Half-Shell* was published. (Evidently this was all very straightforward, with Vonnegut in on the deal. But Vonnegut did not write the book, and the photo on the book jacket of Trout looked suspiciously like Farmer, wearing Boss Mule work gloves, beagle puss and mustache, sunglasses, mufflers, etc.)

Anyway, at the same time word went round that "Kilgore Trout" was going to edit an anthology of "Fictional Author" stories—people were going to write stories "as" fictional authors—all those characters in fiction who were authors, newspapermen, or to whom a book had been ascribed, preferably in the style of the author who wrote about the character.

I immediately wrote "Kilgore Trout," explaining I was the agent for the narrator of this story, that I thought "Trout" would be interested, etc. (I also told him he should write Steve Utley, agent for Gideon Spillett, the journalist in Verne's *Mysterious Island*, for the battle he witnessed between the *Albatross* and the *Nautilus*—not for nothing did Joanna Russ, in a review, once refer to me and Steve as "The Malaprop Kids, Adrift in the Classics.")

"Kilgore Trout" thought this was the bee's knees.

Then people started coming up to Kurt Vonnegut and insisting to his face what a shitty book *Venus on the Half-Shell* was. He took it for about three months, then the word came down: No more Kilgore Trout, unless it was in a book he, K.V., personally wrote with his name on it. (I thought that was extremely fair at the time, although it put a meteor *into* my career.)

I wasn't discouraged, no sir. (Not just me, either. Gene Wolfe wrote a great David Copperfield story that was published somewhere else; Farmer published a bunch himself; we're still reaping the rewards, in a different way, in "O. Niemand's" series *written like* great American authors—they're dead right on—I told "O. Niemand" (who is not, for a change, P.J. Farmer) that I thought the stories were great, and so did every other writer I knew, but that he was beating his head against a brick wall, as most SF fans had not only never *read* any Faulkner, Hemingway or Sherwood Anderson, they'd never *heard* of them (unless, like Melvin Belli, they'd done a guest shot on *Star Trek*).

Anyway, I sent this a few places. (Its story had a hold on me I can't explain rationally—mainly, like when I wrote "God's Hooks!" I couldn't understand why no one had done it before, and how come I was the only one who put 2 and 2 together?)

It ended up, like so many of my things of the time, at *Chacal* (later to be *Shayol*, a late-lamented, glossy, wonderfully edited and illustrated semi-prozine edited by Pat Cadigan and one of the guys who are now the publishers of *this* sterling collection).

This is the oldest story in the book (it's the oldest story, in terms of when it was written, that I've put in a collection ex-

cept for "All About Strange Monsters of the Recent Past"
which was in the last Ursus book). What that means, I don't
know.

If you don't like it, don't write me. Write Philip José
Farmer.

THE ADVENTURE OF THE GRINDER'S WHISTLE

by Edward Malone

AUTHOR'S Foreword: *Retelling events which happened when one was seven years of age, from a vantage point eighty-six years removed, is a dangerous undertaking. Events blur and change in the mind, and one summer or fall, one neighborhood and another, this vista and that bit of scenery become confused.*

I confess this is normally so. There is one singular event in my life which has never, and will never, lose its sharp edges. Of that, I am sure. Those which came later; the adventure with Professor Challenger in Maple White Land, the aftermath of the comet, and with the earth needle were surely excitement enough for any man's life. That I was privileged, during the last war, to write the history of His Majesty's part in the development of the fission bomb was an additional boon which time gave me.

My part in the affair of which I write was small, and will not detain the reader for very long. My agent has insisted that I commit this memory to print. I am, I believe, giving an account which has not been told before.

A few words of explanation. I came to London with my mother soon after the death of my father in the late summer of 1888. We were living with my aunt's family, and I was very happy at the time since I was held out of school for that fall term. How I fell in with the rough gang to be described is not important. It involved several fistfights, most of which I won, and an initiation which, if my widowed mother had ever known about it, would have assured

that I had been returned to the halls of academe forth-
with.

Let us go back, then, to the era of fog and gaslights. . . .

It was a foggy night, and we were following around behind
the lamplighter and turning off the gas.

Jenkins, our leader, was a gangly lad of fifteen. He towered
far over me, as he did the others, all except for Neddie, who
was a big lug, if ever there were one.

We'd sneak behind the lampman, old Mr. Soakes. Very
quiet-like, Jenkins would lift one of the younger of us (sometimes myself or Aubrey) up and we'd twist off the supply and
all be gone giggling and laughing down the alleyways.

(I sometimes came home those days with traces of soot behind my ears I'd failed to clean off, and would suffer my
mother's reproofs.)

We were having to be very careful for constables. What
with the Ripper murders and all, they'd doubled the force in
our district.

My mother and I had a discussion about that, too. One
which I'd won by shocking her Calvinistic upbringing. She
said I wasn't to go out at night because the Ripper was about.
I told her that no one who wasn't a lady of easy virtue had
anything to worry about from the fiend.

Us fellows had had talks about the Ripper. He was the topic
of conversation in London, even in our circles, which were
none too high. Some of us thought he was a fine-dressed gentleman who came down to Whitechapel to work his way with
the ladies. Some thought him a butcher gone mad, or to be
like old Sweeny Todd, the Demon Barber of Fleet Street some
years ago. Jack Leatherapron, people were calling him, and
we could envision him all covered in blood from head to foot,
carrying off the heart of his victim. Others supposed he was
one of the mad Russian socialists who lived all together in the
big house over in Seldon Row West, out killing capitalists. He
was sure starting at the bottom of the money ladder if he
were, we agreed.

"Well," said Jenkins that night, after we'd put out the
twelfth light and had to cut through fences because old
Soakes had seen us and given the alarm. We'd heard some
bobby-whistles and club-thumping a few minutes later, but by

then we were holed up in the basement where we held our meetings.

"Well what, then?" asked Neddie, all out of breath. "The coppers have put the kibosh on the fun tonight. They'll be looking for us, sure."

"Let's go filch from the pruneseller in the Square," said Aubrey, who was older than me, but even shorter.

"Aw, who wants prunes?" asked Neddie.

Toldo Wigmore, who read a lot but didn't say much, grunted.

"What is it, Toldo?" asked Jenkins, all attention.

"I's just thinkin' 'pon what we kin do tomorrer," said Toldo. He hitched up the leg of his knicker and scratched. "We could all go out to Maxon Heath and see the new steam combine-tractor. It's just in from Americker."

"Capital idea!" I said, and they all looked at me, expectant. "But you can't. I re—" and you must remember I wanted to be one of the gang, so I couldn't let on that I read, yet. My mother'd taught me to read before I was five, she was being somewhat of a progressive. So I caught my slip in time. "I mean, my mom told me it was stolen early this morning."

"Was not!" yelled Toldo. "Leastwise, I ain't seen that in no newspapers. Yer mother's lying!"

Before the fight could start, there was somewhat of a noise upstairs, and Jenkins went to see what it was. He came bounding downstairs with a whoop in a few seconds. "Line up, men!" he hollers, all official like a sergeant major.

We hopped to and stood before him in the basement.

"We've been hired by a gentleman," he said. We gave a ragged cheer. I joined in, though I'd only heard about working from one of the boys who'd been in the gang longer.

"Alright, you newer members," said Jenkins, pacing back and forth before us, looking especially hard at Aubrey and myself. "You're to remember that we do anything within reason for the gentleman, and when we're paid off, half the money is to go to the club funds."

I didn't like that very well. I knew that meant Jenkins would end up with most of the money before this was over. And they'd told me about looking for tarbarrels all one night once, down at the quays and such. I didn't look to have a very pleasant night ahead of me.

"All right," says Jenkins. "Let's go!"

We ran, whooping and hollering and raising a commotion through the streets and alleys, and got two more boys on the way. Our yelling caught in our throats, though, when we saw the bobbies and their lanterns ahead of us in the fog.

We got very respectable. A sergeant of police stopped us. He was wearing his slicker and his hardpot hat with the shield on it. It was the first bobby I'd really seen up close. He had a great thick mustache. I was very impressed.

"Here, boys," he said, spreading his arms like a railcrossing signal. "You can't come through here. There's been a foul deed perpetrated."

"I'll bet it's the Ripper!" said Toldo, out of the corner of his mouth.

Jenkins became very respectful-looking, and took off his cap. "We've been sent for by that gentleman over there, sergeant," he said, pointing into the fog.

"He sent for you, did he?" asked the policeman. "Just a mo'." He walked to a plainclothes-dressed man and spoke to him. The fellow looked us over from under his bowler hat and said something to the sergeant. There were others moving around in the fog like ghosts. I couldn't see what had happened, but there was a great knot of police standing toward one of the building corners.

"All right, you boys," said the sergeant, returning. "Stand about out of the way. And don't you touch nothing."

"Fine, sir," said Jenkins. "We sha'n't."

We moved to the building wall opposite the gathering of policemen. Jenkins kept us all quiet and in line.

There was a bluff-looking man with a mustache standing with the bobbies. He didn't look like any policeman to me. He held one of his shoulders just a little higher than the other, and was talking with two of the plainclothes detectives.

"Would you look at thart," said Toldo, to me, and pointed.

There was a man crawling around on the paving of the street.

"Is he hurt?" I asked Jenkins. "Maybe he's the one that's hurt?"

"Naw. That's the man who hired us," said the leader. "That's . . ."

"Step over here a moment, Watson, and have a look at

this," said the man on the ground, peering toward the knot of policemen.

"Of course, Holmes," said the man with the off-shoulder. We were quite near them, so I heard all this.

The man on all fours moved around until he got the gaslight shining before him.

"This Ripper business is ghastly, what?" said the bluff man.

"What do you make of these?" asked Holmes, getting to one knee above the cobbles.

Watson peered at the uneven pavings. I couldn't see what they were looking at.

"Faint scratches of some sort," he said.

"Quite right, Watson, quite right." Holmes dropped to the ground again and looked left and right.

"Whatever are you doing, Holmes?" asked the other.

"Be a good fellow and see if Lestrade needs any help. I should imagine your bedside manner could calm the woman," said Mr. Holmes.

For the first time I noticed there was a woman among the police. She seemed to be talking, and I heard some whimpers from the crowd. It may have been her, but the fog muffled voices so I couldn't tell.

Two of the plainclothesmen came toward Watson as he got up. As they left the group of constables, I saw a lumpy greatcoat lying on the street. Someone had thrown it over a body, for a great pool of blood was drying around it. I nudged Aubrey and he poked Toldo and Toldo jabbed Jenkins, but Jenkins just nodded his head wisely.

That's why he's the leader.

"Dr. Daniels agrees with you, Dr. Watson. However, it remains to be seen what will come out at the inquest. I'm not entirely convinced at all. Not at all," said the plainclothesman in the bowler hat.

"What do you propose is happening, Lestrade?" asked Holmes, getting up from the street and wiping his hands.

"Certainly no mad Jack Ripper is committing these deeds. I refuse to believe a man to be capable of such violence."

"You may be right, there, Lestrade," said Holmes, but I don't think the policeman was paying any attention. He seemed to be waiting to be asked something.

"Well," asked Dr. Watson. "What's your explanation, Inspector?"

"Suicide," said Lestrade, with a note of triumph.

"Suicide?" asked Watson.

Toldo started to giggle, but Jenkins silenced him with a foot in the ankle.

"Certainly," said the plainclothesman. "These unfortunate women of the streets, in remorse for having sunk to such a low level, drink themselves senseless, stumble to some doorway here in Whitechapel, and do themselves in with repeated jabs of large knives. It's all very simple."

"So is the inspector," whispered Toldo.

"But, Lestrade, what becomes of the murder weapon?" asked Watson.

"With their last ounce of strength, they fling the knives away from themselves. I'm sure my men's search of the rooftops and curbs will reveal the instrument of suicide." The inspector put his hands in his vest pockets and rocked back and forth on his heels.

"Very interesting, Inspector," said Holmes. "Might I now interview the woman you have there? I have certain questions of my own."

"Certainly, Mr. Holmes. Though she claims to have heard this non-existent Leather Apron. She's frightened, like the rest of the inhabitants of the district, by the newspaper headlines and the penny-dreadfuls. She'll not be of any use to you if it's the truth you're after."

And, to this day, I'll swear I heard Mr. Holmes say this to Inspector Lestrade. He said: "Often, in the search for truth, the frightened have more to offer than the brave."

A P.C. had finished taking down notes from the woman, and brought her towards us. She looked shabby-respectable, like someone's great-auntie fallen on bad times.

"She manages the doss house across the way," said Lestrade to Mr. Holmes, under his breath.

The woman was holding her head in her hands and moaning.

"Oh, it was 'orrible, 'orrible!" she said.

"Madame," said Holmes. "Though I quite realize you are in distress, there are certain things I must ask you."

"Oh, it was 'orrible!" she said, as if Holmes were not there.

Someone brought her some brandy from a house down the way. She drank at it and seemed to calm down. Holmes stood patiently, watching until she had finished. He was a tall man, with a nose like a beak. He reminded me of a heron, except that he had bright eyes, like a cat's. They caught glints from the gaslamps and police lanterns as I watched. My knicker leg was working free of the sock and I bent to rebutton it. I didn't hear the woman when she first started talking again.

". . . way she was screaming. Like the devil himself was after her. And he was, too. Him with his satanic whistle. He . . ."

"Whistle? Whistle, did you say?" asked Mr. Holmes, all rushing. "What type of whistle? Any melody?"

"No, no tune to it, at all. That's what made it so eerie. That, an' 'im sharpenin' 'is knives again and again, over and over . . ."

"A sound like, say, someone using a large whetstone? Like a scissors-grinder?" asked Holmes, all nervous-like.

"That's it! That's it exactly!" said the old woman.

"Just as I thought!" yelled Mr. Holmes. "Watson, you have your revolver?"

"Yes, Holmes, of course. What is it?"

"No time, Watson. The game's afoot."

Jenkins snapped to, with a call of "Attention!" This made the police and some of the bystanders jump.

"Ah," said Holmes. "Jenkins."

"Baker Street Irregulars reporting for duty, Mr. Holmes."

"Good," said Holmes. "Then I shan't worry about needing reinforcements from the Yard.

"Inspector," said Holmes, turning to Lestrade. "If I remember correctly, the lowest road to be reached from here, by . . . say, a coach and four . . . is Bremick Road. Do . . ."

I spoke before the Inspector. "The lowest place is near the drain into the river, Mr. Holmes." I stumbled, then continued. "In the alleyways across from the pier. Though a coach-and-four would have to take several short streets between here and there."

"Good!" said Holmes. "Bright lad." He turned again to Lestrade. "Meet me, then, at Bremick Road with five armed men as soon as you're done here. Come, Watson! Irregulars, ho!"

"But where?" asked Lestrade, as we hurried away.

"The Irregulars will lead you," yelled Mr. Holmes, as we ran into the thickening fog.

It made me proud.

We all ran so fast I was winded quickly. But it was Doctor Watson who began to slow after we had run twenty blocks. "Dammit, Holmes," he yelled. "I'm afraid I can't keep this up much longer. The jezail bullet in my shoulder, you know?"

"Quite alright," said Mr. Holmes, bending low to the cobbles as he had every hundred feet or so since we left the police. "The fog is thickening. I propose the Ripper will come with it. We're quite close enough already. I've lost the trail some time back. I must station the Irregulars and flush out our Cheeky Jack."

We rushed onto the Road. Holmes surveyed about him through the fog. "Station yourself there, Watson, with your revolver handy. You—" he pointed to me.

"Malone," said I.

"Malone, keep watch with Dr. Watson. Be his ears and eyes if he needs them."

He turned, motioned to Jenkins and the others, then faced back to Watson.

"When the Ripper comes, Watson, and he surely shall, you must aim for the glasses."

"His glasses? Whatever do you mean, Holmes? What? How will I know the Ripper when he comes?"

"You'll know him well enough, Watson. He'll be whistling and sharpening his knives."

"But Holmes!" said Watson, frustrated.

"He shall come from that alley, and you'll know him, Watson. Be a steady fellow." And then he was gone with the other members of the gang into the roiling fog.

"But, Holmes . . ." said Dr. Watson, into the mist.

I was shivering with excitement and the cold.

Dr. Watson turned to me. "What the devil did Holmes mean, I must aim for his glasses? And how does he know where the Ripper will come from? And why with the fog?"

"I—I'm sure I don't know," I said to him.

"Oh . . . oh. Pardon me, lad," he said. "I'm quite sure you don't." He had the air of someone distracted. He was a large man himself, and his greatcoat made him seem all the larger. He had a reddish mustache, blockish features and reminded me of an uncle of mine on my father's side.

"There's danger here, er . . . Malone," he said. "We must wait quietly and make no noise. You're up to danger, aren't you?"

"Yes, sir," I said, very resolutely, though my heart was in my throat.

Though there was a light cold breeze off the River, the fog grew thicker than it had been all evening. I stood in place and trembled.

We had been waiting about ten minutes, I guess, when we both thought we heard something. Was that a whistle? My skin went all gooseflesh. Coming face to face with Jack the Ripper would not be as much fun as I had once imagined. Doctor Watson cocked his head and gripped his Webley revolver more tightly. Little beads of moisture were collecting on his hand and dripping down his coatfront. I was becoming soaked through, and my teeth began to chatter.

Then the sound came to us again. It was like the old lady said: a high, keening tuneless whistle. I looked toward the fog in the alleyway across from us, the place Mr. Holmes said the Ripper would come from. I could barely see the buildings to each side.

Doctor Watson regripped his pistol. The tuneless whistle came, now soft, now loud, as if the Ripper were moving to and fro across the alley, perhaps checking doorways for victims. I could see him in my mind: a huge formless man, all covered with gore from head to heel, eating the liver . . .

I jumped as Doctor Watson brushed my arm.

The sound was coming toward us.

It was then I heard the sound with it, as must have the doctor. A sharp clicking sound. I had heard sounds like it, but much smaller, when on vacation at Blackpool with my mother and father.

I could only liken it to the opening and closing of the claws of a giant crab.

I saw Doctor Watson take aim along his revolver barrel where the alleyway entered the thoroughfare. Then the mists thickened, and all across the street was lost to view. He lowered his pistol and stepped into the roadway from our hiding place. I went out with him. My heart wasn't in it.

The noises came louder. The eerie whistle sent shivers along my damp spine. The tenor of the clicking grew and changed; they now sounded exactly as if someone were sharpening a large knife again and again. What a sound . . .

I started to wet my pants but held back.

I could see now why those poor women the Ripper killed must have frozen in their tracks when they heard him coming, while he bore down on them and perpetrated his outrages.

The fog roiled. The whistling grew louder. A shape moved at the edge of the alleyway, and the whistling and whetting fairly screamed toward us.

Doctor Watson braced his legs, swung his barrel in line with the shape. He fired twice, the discharges lighting his face and arm pure white. He couldn't have missed, that close.

Like a juggernaut of doom, the Ripper came down at us. He was immense. I couldn't see anything distinct, but sensed something *big*, like in a nightmare, coming for me. He was whistling louder, sharpening his knife like a demon as he charged across the alley for me and the doctor.

A voice on the rooftop behind us yelled, "The glasses, Watson! *The glasses!*"

At the same time, I saw a glint of light above the ground, reflected from the gaslight down the way, as the Ripper came for me.

So did Doctor Watson. He emptied his Webley at it.

There was a loud shrill whistle and a scream, and the Ripper slowed his movement. A few seconds later, the sound of whetting died away in the fog.

"Good show, Watson," said Mr. Holmes, climbing down from the rooftop. "Well done, old man."

Through the fog, I heard police whistles, pounding of feet and nightsticks, and the yells of the Irregulars coming toward us.

I *had* wet my pants.

"You mean to tell me, Holmes," Watson said loudly as the detective examined the silent machinery with Lestrade and the constables, "that you were watching all the time! Why, we might have been killed!"

"Things were well in hand, Watson. If you failed to shoot out the pressure glasses on the combine machine, I was prepared to jump from the rooftop and engage the hand brake, there." He pointed to the operating levers of the steam behemoth.

"What a ghastly machine," remarked Lestrade. "Five murders, by this?"

"Wrong, Lestrade," said Holmes, examining the tractor. "The Ripper still stalks Whitechapel. This steam combine is responsible only for the death of the streetwalker tonight."

"Whatever put you on to it, Mr. Holmes?" asked Lestrade.

"The marks in the street, and the mutilations of the body," said the detective, lighting a pipe with a match struck against the boiler of the tractor. "That, and the comment of the witness to the whistle and continuous sharpening of the knives. Whistles suggest steam, continuous motion suggests machinery. Steam-driven machinery, simply.

"Deduction tells us," he continued after a puff, "that the farmers who thought the machine stolen had not properly extinguished the boiler fires. They only banked them. Something in the valves failed, probably due to humidity in the fogs. The steam combine trundled itself away. It followed the lowest courses into London. The valve must have closed in the evening, banking the fires once more. At nightfall, the return of the fog opened the valve once more. The unfortunate woman happened in its way. She was either too drunk or too frightened to move, and was caught up in the rakes."

"How dreadful," said Lestrade.

"Eventually," said Mr. Sherlock Holmes, "the steam machine would have run into the Thames. And this Jack Leatherapron, at least, would disappear from the face of London."

"But what of the real Ripper?" asked Lestrade.

"Your superintendent has already engaged the services of Doctor Doyle, Lestrade," said Holmes. "I sha'n't be needed."

"Jenkins," said Holmes, turning to us. "Your Irregulars behaved admirably, especially young Malone, there." He winked at me with his bright eyes like glass. "I wouldn't mind having to depend upon him in a tight." Holmes handed Jenkins coins. "Your usual pay, plus a bonus. Now, perhaps you'd better get out of Lestrade's way."

We took off then, back to Baker Street, hollering. There Jenkins divided up the money. Then I had to tell them how it was a dozen times or more. By morning, we were laughing. Near dawn, the whole thing seemed miles away, and comical, and already we were calling it Jack the Reaper.

They never did notice my pants.

INTRODUCTION TO

THIRTY MINUTES
OVER BROADWAY!

SOMETHING was happening in all the genres in the 1980s, as I've said elsewhere.

Comic books led the way. There was the *Dark Knight* stuff. Marvel and DC sloughed off their various universes, supposedly to simplify and codify them. The high point of comic book narrative so far, *The Watchmen*, used every convention of the genre to tell a story which could have been told in no other way, and did it brilliantly. (And if Terry Gilliam does the movie, I want to see it.)

There was something in the air, because I didn't know about *any* of this when I started thinking about Jetboy.

And it's time to set the record straight.

"Thirty Minutes Over Broadway!" was the first story in the first volume of George R. R. Martin's *Wild Cards*, which has now reached seven or eight books and is still going strong. The machiavellian dealings of George in wheedling writers, making stories segue, doing overall plotting, fixing things up, are legendary. More than one writer has run screaming away from the series; others are beating down the door to get in. Go figure.

There's just something about a real, virus-caused, plausible, alternate-world-comic-book-universe-original-anthology-series that appeals to the 12- and 43-year-old in all of us.

See, longbout 1982, I wanted to write a story as an homage to my favorite comic book, *Airboy*, the 1942–1954 Hillman ones. (I still remember the day we moved, in 1954, to 716 Drummond Drive, and I went out to the garage, and there, in the back, with the rusted gasoline can and the busted garden hose, was a pile of thirty or forty comic books, including nine or ten *Airboys* and some prize *Frankensteins*. Mine, all mine . . .)

Anyway, I thought about the story, and thought about it. It would involve an A-Bomb, and President Truman, and Washington DC and be set in 1945 or so . . .

Jessica Amanda Salmonson sent a letter around about writing *different* stuff for one of her *Heroic Visions* books. I thought this might be a nice home for the Jetboy (as I'd begun to call him) story. I mentioned this to someone.

"Oh? WWII, huh? Maybe you should get ahold of George R. R. Martin. He and that Albuquerque bunch have spent the last couple of years pulling their puds and wasting all their time playing some damn superhero role-playing game, and now I think they're talking about doing some kinda funnybook world anthology."

Well, there was a time when I would have known this, since George and I had been best friends for going on thirty years now, and used to have two letters a week going back and forth since we were both pimply-butted kids. But that was a long time ago.

So I wrote George and said, see, I got this story . . .

Faster than you can say Ticonderoga (if you can say Ticonderoga . . .), not only was there a shared world anthology, but a three-book deal for big bucks, etc etc and something called The Master Agreement, on which reading I said, "George, this is a rip-off," and George said, "Yes, Howard, but we're ripping *ourselves* off, and giving it right back to *us*!" which, I supposed, was the way to do it, with points for character creation and use, for stories, with the pie getting bigger and bigger, and, if you're a team player, your *share* of the pie gets bigger and . . .

Well, you know what a team player *I* am.

So I saw, with the clarity of a man's last few seconds when he knows how green the grass is, and why the sky is blue, what all this would eventually lead to.

"George," I said. "I'll write the Jetboy story, but that's all. That's it. Nada. No more. All I need to know from you is the size of the canister and what Tachyon looks like." Meanwhile, these newsletters called *Cut and Shuffle* are piling up, telling me all this stuff I need to know. I ignore them.

(In fact, and ironically, they still come in. One came this

very day as I'm typing this, telling me how very very small my share of the very very large pie is . . .)

"But, your share of the pie . . ." said George.

"The pie gets bigger, my five big shares are worth more."

"But, but . . ."

"Later."

About a month later the phone rings.

"Yo!"

"Roger Zelazny."

"*¿En que puedo servile?*"

"What day *was* September 15, 1946?"

"Tuesday."

"Sure?"

"*Certainement!*"

"Okay." *Click bzzzzzz*

I was *certain* September 15, 1946 was Tuesday, because that was my birthdate. I *like* the idea that the world changed forever the day I was born. I was always told I'd been born on a Tuesday. Roger needed to know this because his story takes place just as mine is ending, and he wanted to make sure it was a weekday, because his kid-character Croyd is walking home from school, and Tuesday is *perfect* for that. (After the book came out, someone came up to Roger at a convention and told him for real and true September 15, 1946 was a Sunday and showed him a calendar. Roger said a naughty word, took his ever-present pipe from his mouth, and threw it down, breaking it. I owe Roger a pipe.)

Anyway, grouchy old George kept wanting the story, I kept saying buzz off, then I did a nifty great first draft with all this neat stuff in it (including six pages of stream-of-consciousness from inside Harry S Truman's head) and sent it in, and went off to a convention, expecting a check from George and a letter telling me it was the best thing I'd ever written on my return.

My first hint of trouble was when Melinda Snodgrass, creator of Dr. Tachyon, (known affectionately as "the wimp" in some circles) came running up to me when I entered the convention hotel and asked, "Why did you make Tachyon a Nazi?!"

I said "Huh?"

As usual, George had explained what I'd done in my first draft, and he'd explained it all wrong to her.

Anyway, when I get home, there's this letter from George telling me what an asshole I am, and the virus doesn't work like that, and if only I read the *Cut and Shuffles* like a good team player I'd know that, and that I've got the position so messed up nobody will ever be able to play it again, and the easiest way out of the hole I've dug for the book is to cut from the bottom of page 34 to the top of page 40.

Which is of course the Harry S Truman part.

Now *I'm* getting cranky. I read the *Cut and Shuffles*, do the revisions I think necessary, and send it back.

Right in the middle of all this, there's *Watchmen* and *Dark Knight*, and, *avec*! Eclipse revives *Airboy*.

I say, hmmmm, this might lead to friction. I go to a convention and meet Tim Truman, world's nicest guy. He even does an illo of Jetboy for *Amazing Heroes*. No friction at all.

All these strange things happen in the field, not the least of which is the appearance of *Wild Cards*, a comic-book-universe anthology by people who really can write.

I still love this story.

Following it is "The Annotated Jetboy" which is pretty much self-explanatory, and shows to what lengths I will go to write a story for people who don't appreciate me enough, anyway.

Just kidding, George.

(And a footnote: Several people have pointed out to me that the first New York Dolls album, from 1970 for chrissakes!; an album I have never, ever heard, has two songs on it. One's called "Jet Boy" and the other's "Something Happened Over Manhattan." I'm not making this up.)

THIRTY MINUTES
OVER BROADWAY!

Jetboy's Last Adventure!

BONHAM'S Flying Service of Shantak, New Jersey was socked in. The small searchlight on the tower barely pushed away the darkness of the swirling fog.

There was the sound of car tires on the wet pavement in front of Hangar 23. A car door opened, a moment later it closed. Footsteps came to the Employees Only door. It opened. Scoop Swanson came in, carrying his Kodak Autograph Mark II and a bag of flashbulbs and film.

Lincoln Traynor raised up from the engine of the surplus P-40 he was overhauling for an airline pilot who had got it at a voice-bid auction for $293. Judging from the shape of the engine, it must have been flown by the Flying Tigers in 1940. A ball game was on the workbench radio. Linc turned it down.

" 'Lo, Linc," said Scoop.

" 'Lo."

"No word yet?"

"Don't expect any. The telegram he sent yesterday said he'd be in tonight. Good enough for me."

Scoop lit a Camel with a Three Torches box match from the workbench. He blew smoke toward the Absolutely No Smoking sign at the back of the hangar. "Hey, what's this?" He walked to the rear. Still in their packing cases were two long red wing extensions and two 300 gallon teardrop underwing tanks. "When these get here?"

"Air Corps shipped them yesterday from San Francisco. Another telegram came for him today. You might as well read it, you're doing the story." Linc handed him the War Department orders.

> TO: Jetboy (Tomlin, Robert NMI)
>   HOR: Bonham's Flying Service
>   Hangar 23
>   Shantak, New Jersey
>
> 1. Effective this date 1200Z hours 12 Aug '46, you are no longer on active duty, United States Army Air Force.
> 2. Your aircraft (model—experimental) (ser. no. JB-1) is hereby decommissioned from active status, United States Army Air Force and reassigned you as private aircraft. No further materiel support from USAAF or War Department will be forthcoming.
> 3. Records, commendations and awards forwarded under separate cover.
> 4. Our records show Tomlin, Robert NMI, has not obtained pilot's license. Please contact CAA for courses and certification.
> 5. Clear skies and tailwinds,
>
>   For
>   Arnold, H.H.
>   CofS, USAAF
> ref: Executive Order #2, 08 Dec '41

"What's this about him having no pilot's license?" asked the newspaperman. "I went through the morgue on him—his file's a foot thick. Hell, he must have flown faster and further, shot down more planes than anyone—five hundred planes, fifty ships! He did it without a pilot's license?"

Linc wiped grease from his mustache. "Yep. That was the most plane-crazy kid you ever saw. Back in '39, he couldn't have been more than twelve, he heard there was a job out here. He showed up at 4 A.M.—lammed out of the orphanage to do it. They came out to get him. But of course Professor Silverberg had hired him, squared it with them."

"Silverberg's the one the Nazis bumped off? The guy who made the jet?"

"Yep. Years ahead of everybody, but weird. I put together the plane for him, Bobby and I built it by hand. But

Silverberg made the jets—damnedest engines you ever saw. The Nazis and Italians, and Whittle over in England had started theirs. But the Germans found out something was happening here."

"How'd the kid learn to fly?"

"He always knew, I think," said Lincoln. "One day he's in here helping me bend metal. The next, him and the Professor are flying around at 400 miles per. In the dark, with those early engines."

"How'd they keep it a secret?"

"They didn't, very well. The spies came for Silverberg— wanted him *and* the plane. Bobby was out with it. I think he and the Prof knew something was up. Silverberg put up such a fight the Nazis killed him. Then, there was the diplomatic stink. In those days the JB-1 only had six .30 cals on it— where the Professor got them I don't know. But the kid took care of the car full of spies with it, and that speedboat on the Hudson full of embassy people. All on diplomatic visas."

"Just a sec," Linc stopped himself. "End of a doubleheader in Cleveland. On the Blue Network." He turned up the metal Philco radio that sat above the toolrack.

". . . Sanders to Papenfuss to Volstad, a double-play. That does it. So the Sox drop two to Cleveland. We'll be right . . ." Linc turned it off. "There goes five bucks," he said. "Where was I?"

"The Krauts killed Silverberg, and Jetboy got even. He went to Canada, right?"

"Joined the RCAF, unofficially. Fought in the Battle of Britain, went to China against the Japs with the Tigers, was back in Britain for Pearl Harbor."

"And Roosevelt commissioned him?"

"Sort of. You know, funny thing about his whole career. He fights the *whole* war, longer than any other American—late '39 to '45, then right at the end, he gets lost in the Pacific, missing. We all think he's dead for a year. Then they find him on that desert island last month, and now he's coming home."

There was a high thin whine like a prop plane in a dive. It came from the foggy skies outside. Scoop put out his third Camel. "How can he land in this soup?"

"He's got an all-weather radar set—got it off a German

nightfighter back in '43. He could land that plane in a circus tent at midnight."

They went to the door. Two landing lights pierced the rolling mist. They lowered to the far end of the runway, turned and came back on the taxi strip.

The red fuselage glowed in the grey shrouded lights of the airstrip. The twin-engine high-wing plane turned toward them and rolled to a stop.

Linc Traynor put a set of double chocks under each of the two rear tricycle landing gears. Half the glass nose of the plane levered up and pulled back. The plane had four 20mm cannon snouts in the wing roots between the engines, and a 75mm gun port below and to the left of the cockpit rim.

It had a high thin rudder, and the rear elevators were shaped like the tail of a brook trout. Under each of the elevators was the muzzle of a rear-firing machine gun. The only markings on the plane were four non-standard USAAF stars in a black roundel, and the serial number JB-1 on the top right and bottom left wings and beneath the rudder.

The radar antennae on the nose looked like something to roast weenies on.

A boy dressed in red pants, white shirt and a blue helmet and goggles stepped out of the cockpit and onto the dropladder on the left side.

He was nineteen, maybe twenty. He took off his helmet and goggles. He had curly, mousy brown hair, hazel eyes and was short and chunky.

"Linc," he said. He hugged the pudgy man to him, patted his back for a full minute. Scoop snapped off a shot.

"Great to have you back, Bobby," said Linc.

"Nobody's called me that in years," he said. "It sounds real good to hear it again."

"This is Scoop Swanson," said Linc. "He's gonna make you famous all over again."

"I'd rather be asleep," he shook the reporter's hand. "Any place around here we can get some ham and eggs?"

The launch pulled up to the dock in the fog. Out in the harbor a ship finished cleaning its bilges and was turning to steam back southward.

There were three men in the mooring, Fred and Ed and

Filmore. One man stepped out of the launch with a suitcase in his hands. Filmore leaned down and gave the guy at the wheel of the motorboat a Lincoln and two Jacksons. Then he helped the guy with the suitcase.

"Welcome home, Dr. Tod."

"It's good to be back, Filmore." Tod was dressed in a baggy suit, and had on an overcoat even though it was August. He wore his hat pulled low over his face, and from it a glint of metal was reflected in the pale lights from a warehouse.

"This is Fred and this is Ed," said Filmore. "They're here just for the night."

"'Lo," said Fred.

"'Lo," said Ed.

They walked back to the car, a '46 Merc that looked like a submarine. They climbed in, Fred and Ed watching the foggy alleys to each side. Then Fred got behind the wheel, and Ed rode shotgun. With a sawed-off 10-gauge.

"Nobody's expecting me. Nobody cares," said Dr. Tod. "Everybody who had something against me is either dead or went respectable during the war and made a mint. I'm an old man and tired. I'm going out in the country and raise bees and play the horses and the market."

"Not planning anything, boss?"

"Not a thing."

He turned his head as they passed a streetlight. Half his face was gone, a smooth metal plate reaching from jaw to hatline, nostril to left ear.

"I can't shoot anymore, for one thing. My depth perception isn't what it used to be.

"I shouldn't wonder," said Filmore. "We heard something happened to you in '43."

"Was in a somewhat profitable operation out of Egypt while the Afrika Korps was falling apart. Taking people in and out for a fee in a nominally neutral air fleet. Just a sideline. Then ran into that hotshot flier."

"Who?"

"Kid with the jet plane, before the Germans had them."

"Tell you the truth, boss, I didn't keep up with the war much. I take a long view on merely territorial conflicts."

"As I should have," said Dr. Tod. "We were flying out of

Tunisia. Some important people were with us that trip. The pilot screamed. There was a tremendous explosion. Next thing, I came to, it was the next morning, and me and one other person are in a life raft in the middle of the Mediterranean. My face hurt. I lifted up. Something fell into the bottom of the raft. It was my left eyeball. It was looking up at me. I knew I was in trouble."

"You said it was a kid with a jet plane?" asked Ed.

"Yes. We found out later they'd broken our code, and he'd flown 600 miles to intercept us."

"You want to get even?" asked Filmore.

"No. That was so long ago I hardly remember that side of my face. It just taught me to be a little more cautious. I wrote it off as character-building."

"So no plans, huh?"

"Not a single one," said Dr. Tod.

"That'll be nice for a change," said Filmore.

They watched the lights of the city go by.

He knocked on the door, uncomfortable in his new brown suit and vest.

"Come in, it's open," said a woman's voice. Then it was muffled. "I'll be ready in just a minute."

Jetboy opened the oak hall door and stepped into the room, past the glass-brick room divider.

A beautiful woman stood in the middle of the room, a dress halfway over her arms and head. She wore a camisole, garter belt and silk hose. She was pulling the dress down with one of her hands.

Jetboy turned his head away, blushing and taken aback.

"Oh," said the woman. "Oh! I, who?"

"It's me, Belinda," he said. "Robert."

"Robert?"

"Bobby, Bobby Tomlin."

She stared at him a moment, her hands clasped over her front, though she was fully dressed.

"Oh, Bobby," she said, and came to him and hugged him and gave him a big kiss right on the mouth.

It was what he had waited six years for.

"Bobby. It's great to see you. I—I was expecting someone else. Some—girlfriends. How did you find me?"

"Well, it wasn't easy."

She stepped back from him. "Let me look at you."

He looked at her. The last time he had seen her she was fourteen, a tomboy, still at the orphanage. She had been a thin kid with mousy blonde hair. Once, when she was eleven, she'd almost punched his lights out. She was a year older than he.

Then he had gone away, to work at the airfield, then to fight with the Brits against Hitler. He had written her when he could all during the war, after America entered it. She had left the orphanage and been put in a foster home. In '44 one of his letters had come back from there marked "Moved—No Forwarding Address." Then he had been lost all during the last year.

"You've changed, too," he said.

"So have you."

"Uh."

"I followed the newspapers all during the war. I tried to write you but I don't guess the letters ever caught up with you. Then they said you were missing at sea, and I sort of gave up."

"Well, I was, but they found me. Now I'm back. How have you been?"

"Real good, once I ran away from the foster home," she said. A look of pain came across her face. "You don't know how glad I was to get away from there. Oh, Bobby," she said. "Oh, I wish things were different!" She started to cry a little.

"Hey," he said, holding her by the shoulders. "Sit down. I've got something for you."

"A present?"

"Yep." He handed her a grimy, oil-stained paper parcel. "I carried these with me the last two years of the war. They were in the plane with me on the island. Sorry I didn't have time to rewrap them."

She tore the English butcher paper. Inside were a copy of *The House at Pooh Corner* and *The Tale of the Fierce Bad Rabbit*.

"Oh," said Belinda. "Thank you."

He remembered her dressed in the orphanage coveralls, just in, dusty and tired from a baseball game, lying on the reading-room floor with a Pooh book open before her.

"The Pooh book's signed by the real Christopher Robin,"

he said. "I found out he was an RAF officer at one of the bases in England. He said he usually didn't do this sort of thing, that he was just another airman. I told him I wouldn't tell anyone. I'd searched high and low to find a copy, and he knew that, though.

"This other one's got more of a story behind it. I was coming back near dusk, escorting some crippled B-17s. I looked up and saw two German nightfighters coming in, probably setting up patrol, trying to catch some Lancasters before they went out over the Channel.

"To make a long story short, I shot down both of them; they packed in near a small village. But I had run out of fuel and had to set down. Saw a pretty flat sheep pasture with a lake at the far end of it, and went in.

"When I climbed out of the cockpit, I saw a lady and a sheepdog standing at the edge of the field. She had a shotgun. When she got close enough to see the engines and decals, she said, 'Good shooting! Won't you come in for a bite of supper and to use the telephone to call Fighter Command?'

"We could see the two ME-110s burning in the distance.

" 'You're the very famous Jetboy,' she said. 'We have followed your exploits in the Sawrey paper. I'm Mrs. Heelis.' She held out her hand.

"I shook it. 'Mrs. William Heelis? And this is Sawrey?'

" 'Yes,' she said.

" 'You're Beatrix Potter!' I said.

" 'I suppose I am,' she said.

"Belinda, she was this stout old lady in a raggedy sweater and a plain old dress. But when she smiled, I swear all of England lit up!"

Belinda opened the book. On the fly leaf was written:

To Jetboy's American Friend,
Belinda,
from
Mrs. William Heelis
("Beatrix Potter")
April 12, 1943

Jetboy drank the coffee Belinda made for him.

"Where are your friends?" he asked.

"Well, he—they should have been here by now. I was thinking of going down the hall to the phone and trying to call them. I can change, and we can sit around and talk about old times. I really can call."

"No," said Jetboy. "Tell you what. I'll call you later on in the week; we can get together some night when you're not busy. That would be fun."

"Sure would." .

Jetboy got up to go.

"Thank you for the books, Bobby. They mean a lot to me, they really do."

"It's real good to see you again, Bee."

"Nobody's called me that since the orphanage. Call me real soon, will you?"

"Sure will," he leaned down and kissed her again.

He walked to the stairs. As he was going down, a guy in a modified zoot suit—pegged pants, long coat, watch chain, bow tie the size of a coathanger, hair slicked back, reeking of Brylcreem and Old Spice—went up the stairs two at a time, whistling "It Ain't the Meat, It's the Motion."

Jetboy heard him knocking at Belinda's door.

Outside, it had begun to rain.

"Great. Just like in a movie," said Jetboy.

The next night was quiet as a graveyard.

Then dogs all over the Pine Barrens started to bark. Cats screamed. Birds flew in panic from thousands of trees, circled, swooping this way and that in the dark night.

Static washed over every radio in the Northeastern U.S. New television sets flared out, volume doubling. People gathered around nine-inch Dumonts jumped back at the sudden noise and light, dazzled in their own living rooms and bars and sidewalks outside appliance stores all over the east coast.

To those out in that hot August night it was even more spectacular. A thin line of light, high up, moved, brightened, still falling. Then it expanded, upping in brilliance, changed into a blue-green bolide, seemed to stop, then flew to a hundred falling sparks which slowly faded on the dark starlit sky.

Some people said they saw another, smaller light a few minutes later. It seemed to hover, then sped off to the west, growing dimmer as it flew. The newspapers had been full of stories of the "ghost rockets" in Sweden all that summer. It was the silly season.

A few calls to the Weather Bureau or Army Air Force bases got the answer that it was probably a stray from the Aquariad meteor shower.

Out in the Pine Barrens, somebody knew differently, though he wasn't in the mood to communicate it to anyone.

Jetboy, dressed in a loose pair of pants, a shirt and a brown aviator's jacket, walked in through the doors of the Blackwell Printing Company. There was a bright red and blue sign above the door: "Home of the Cosh Comics Company."

He stopped at the receptionist's desk.

"Robert Tomlin to see Mr. Farrell."

The secretary, a thin blonde job with glasses with swept-up rims that made it look like a bat was camping on her face, stared at him. "Mr. Farrell passed on in the winter of 1945. Were you in the service or something?"

"Something."

"Would you like to speak to Mr. Lowboy? He has Mr. Farrell's job now."

"Whoever's in charge of *Jetboy Comics*."

The whole place began shaking as printing presses cranked up in the back of the building. On the walls of the office were garish comic book covers, promising things only *they* could deliver.

"Robert Tomlin," said the secretary to the intercom.

"Scratch* squawk never heard of him *squich."

"What was this about?" asked the secretary.

"Tell him Jetboy wants to see him."

"Oh," she said, looking at him. "I'm sorry. I didn't recognize you."

"Nobody ever does."

Lowboy looked like a gnome with all the blood sucked out. He was as pale as Harry Langdon must have been, like a weed grown under a burlap bag.

"Jetboy!" he held out a hand like a bunch of grub worms. "We all thought you'd died until we saw the papers last week. You're a real national hero, you know?"

"I don't feel like one."

"What can I do for you? Not that I'm not pleased to finally meet you. But you must be a busy man."

"Well, first, I found out none of the licensing and royalty checks have been deposited in my account since I was reported Missing and Presumed Dead last summer."

"What, really? The legal department must have put it in escrow or something until somebody came forward with a claim. I'll get them right on it."

"Well, I'd like the check now, before I leave," said Jetboy.

"Huh? I don't know if they can do that. That sounds awfully abrupt."

Jetboy stared at him.

"Okay, okay, let me call accounting." He yelled into the telephone.

"Oh," said Jetboy. "A friend's been collecting my copies. I checked the statement of ownership and circulation for the last two years. I know *Jetboy Comics* have been selling 500,000 copies an issue lately."

Lowboy yelled into the phone some more. He put it down. "It'll take 'em a little while. Anything else?"

"I don't like what's happening to the funny book," said Jetboy.

"What's not to like? It's selling a half million copies a month!"

"For one thing, the plane's getting to look more and more like a bullet. And the artists have swept back the wings, for Christ's sakes!"

"This is the Atomic Age, kid. Boys nowadays don't like a plane that looks like a red leg of lamb with coathangers sticking out the front!"

"Well, it's always looked like that. And another thing. Why's the damned plane blue in the last three issues?"

"Not me! I think red's fine. But Mr. Blackwell sent down a memo, said no more red except for blood. He's a big Legionnaire."

"Tell him the plane has to look right, and be the right color. Also, the combat reports were forwarded. When Farrell was sitting at your desk, the comic was about flying and combat, and cleaning up spy rings—real stuff. And there were never more than two ten-page Jetboy stories an issue."

"When Farrell was at this desk, the book was only selling a quarter-million copies a month," said Lowboy.

Robert stared at him again.

"I know the war's over, and everybody wants a new house and eye-bulging excitement," said Jetboy. "But look what I find in the last eighteen months . . .

"I never fought anyone like the Undertaker, any place called The Mountain of Doom. And come on! The Red Skeleton? Mr. Maggot? Professor Blooteaux? What is this with all the skulls and tentacles? I mean, evil twins named Sturm and Drang Hohenzollern? The Arthropoid Ape, a gorilla with six sets of elbows? Where do you get all this stuff?"

"It's not me, it's the writers. They're a crazy bunch, always taking benzedrine and stuff. Besides, it's what the kids want!"

"What about the flying features, and the articles on real aviation heroes? I thought my contract called for at least two features an issue on real events and people."

"We'll have to look at it again. But I can tell you, kids don't want that kind of stuff anymore. They want monsters, spaceships, stuff that'll make 'em wet the bed. You remember? You were a kid once yourself!"

Jetboy picked up a pencil from the desk. "I was thirteen when the war started, fifteen when they bombed Pearl Harbor. I've been in combat for six years. Sometimes I don't think I was ever a kid."

Lowboy was quiet a moment.

"Tell you what you need to do," he said. "You need to write up all the stuff you don't like about the book and send it to us. I'll have the legal department go over it, and we'll try to do something, work things out. Of course, we print three issues ahead, so it'll be Thanksgiving before the new stuff shows up. Or later."

Jetboy sighed. "I understand."

"I sure do want you happy, 'cause *Jetboy*'s my favorite comic. No, I really mean that. The others are just a job. My god, what a job, deadlines, working with drunks and worse, riding herd over printers, you can just imagine! But I like the work on *Jetboy*. It's special."

"Well, I'm glad."

"Sure, sure." Lowboy drummed his fingers on the desk. "Wonder what's taking them so long?"

"Probably getting out the other set of ledgers," said Jetboy.

"Hey, now! We're square here!" Lowboy came to his feet. "Just kidding."

"Oh. Say, the paper said you were, what, marooned on a desert island or something? Pretty tough?"

"Well, lonely. I got tired of catching and eating fish. Mostly it was boring, and I missed everything. I don't mean missed, I mean missed out. I was there from April 29 of '45, until last month.

"There were times when I thought I'd go nuts. I couldn't believe it one morning when I looked up, and there was the U.S.S. *Reluctant* anchored less than a mile offshore. I fired off a flare, and they picked me up. It's taken a month to get someplace to repair the plane, rest up, get home. I'm glad to be back."

"I can imagine. Hey, lots of dangerous animals on the island? I mean, lions and tigers and stuff?"

Jetboy laughed. "It was less than a mile wide, and a mile and a quarter long. There were birds and rats and some lizards."

"Lizards? Big lizards? Poisonous?"

"No. Small. I must have eaten half of them before I left. Got pretty good with a wrist-rocket made out of an oxygen hose."

"Huh! I bet you did!"

The door opened, and a tall guy with an ink-smudged shirt came in.

"That him?" asked Lowboy.

"I only seen him once, but it looks like him," said the man.

"Good enough for me!" said Lowboy.

"Not for me," said the accountant. "Show me some ID and sign this release."

Jetboy sighed and did. He looked at the amount on the check. It had far too few digits in front of the decimal. He folded it up and put it in his pocket.

"I'll leave my address for the next check with your secretary. And I'll send a letter with the objections this week."

"Do that. It's been a real pleasure meeting you. Let's hope we have a long and prosperous business together."

"Thanks, I guess," said Jetboy. He and the accountant left. Lowboy sat back down in his swivel chair. He put his hands behind his head and stared at the bookcase across the room.

Then he rocketed forward, jerked up the phone, and dialed nine to get out. He called up the chief writer for *Jetboy Comics*.

A muzzy hungover voice answered on the twelfth ring.

"Clean the shit out of your head, this is Lowboy. Picture this: 52-page special, single story issue. Ready? *Jetboy on Dinosaur Island!* Got that? I see lots of cave men, a broad, a what-you-call-it—king rex. What? Yeah, yeah, a tyrannosaur. Maybe a buncha holdout Jap soldiers. You know. Yeah, maybe even samurai. When? Blown off course in 1100 A.D.? Christ. Whatever. You know exactly what we need.

"What's this? Tuesday. You got till 5 P.M. Thursday, okay? Quit bitchin'. It's a hundred and a half fast bucks! See you then."

He hung up. Then he called up an artist and told him what he wanted for the cover.

Ed and Fred were coming back from a delivery in the Pine Barrens.

They were driving an eight-yard dump truck. In the back until a few minutes ago had been six cubic yards of new-set concrete. Eight hours before, it had been five and a half yards of water, sand, gravel, cement and a secret ingredient.

The secret ingredient had broken three of the Five Unbreakable Rules for carrying on a tax-free, unincorporated business in the state.

He had been taken by other businessmen to a wholesale construction equipment center, and been shown how a cement mixer works, up close and personal.

Not that Ed and Fred had anything to do with that. They'd been called an hour ago and been asked if they could drive a dump truck through the woods for a couple of grand.

It was dark out in the woods, not too many miles from the city. It didn't look like they were within a hundred miles of a town over 500 population.

The headlights picked out ditches where everything from old airplanes to sulfuric acid bottles lay in clogged heaps. Some of the dumpings were fresh. Smoke and fire played about a few. Others glowed without combustion. A pool of metal bubbled and popped as they ground by.

Then they were back into the deep pines again, jouncing from rut to rut.

"Hey!" yelled Ed. "Stop!"

Fred threw on the brakes, killing the engine. "Goddamn!" he said. "What the hell's the matter with you?"

"Back there! I swear I saw a guy pushing a neon cat's-eye marble the size of Cleveland!"

"I'm sure as hell not going back," said Fred.

"Nah! Come on! You don't see stuff like that every day."

"Shit, Ed! Some day you're gonna get us both killed!"

It wasn't a marble. They didn't need their flashlights to tell it wasn't a magnetic mine. It was a rounded canister that glowed on its own, with swirling colors on it. It hid the man pushing it.

"It looks like a rolled-up neon armadillo," said Fred, who'd been out west.

The man behind the thing blinked at them, unable to see past their flashlights. He was tattered and dirty, with a tobacco-stained beard and wild steel wool hair.

They stepped closer.

"It's mine!" he said to them, stepping in front of the thing, holding his arms out across it.

"Easy, old-timer," said Ed. "What you got?"

"My ticket to Easy Street. You from the Air Corps?"

"Hell no. Let's look at this."

The man picked up a rock. "Stay back! I found it where I found the plane crash. The Air Corps'll pay plenty to get this atomic bomb back!"

"That doesn't look like any atomic bomb I've ever seen," said Fred. "Look at the writing on the side. It ain't even English."

"Course it's not! It must be a secret weapon. That's why they dressed up so weird."

"Who?"

"I told you more'n I meant to. Get outta my way."

Fred looked at the old geezer. "You've piqued my interest," he said. "Tell me more."

"Outta my way, boy! I killed a man over a can of lye hominy once!"

Fred reached in his jacket. He came out with a pistol with a muzzle that looked like a drainpipe.

"It crashed last night," said the old man, eyes wild. "Woke me up. Lit up the whole sky. I looked for it all day today, figured the woods would be crawlin' with Air Corps people and State Troopers, but nobody came.

"Found it just before dark tonight. Tore all hell up, it did. Knocked the wings completely off the thing when it crashed. All these weird-dressed people all scattered around. Women too." He lowered his head a minute, shame on his face. "Anyway, they was dead. Must have been a jet plane, didn't find no propellors or nothing. And this here atomic bomb was just lying there in the wreck. I figured the Air Corps would pay real good to get it back. Friend of mine found a weather balloon once and they gave him a dollar and a quarter. I figure this is about a million times as important as that!"

Fred laughed. "A buck twenty-five, huh? I'll give you ten dollars for it."

"I can get a million!"

Fred pulled back the hammer on the revolver.

"Fifty," said the old man.

"Twenty."

"It ain't fair. But I'll take it."

"What are you going do to with that?" asked Ed.

"Take it to Dr. Tod," said Fred. "He'll know what to do with it. He's the scientific type."

"What if it is an A-bomb?"

"Well, I don't think A-bombs have spray nozzles on them. And the old man was right. The woods would have been crawling with Air Force people if they'd lost an atomic bomb. Hell, only five of them have ever been exploded. They can't have more than a dozen, and you better believe they know where every one of them is, all the time."

"Well, it ain't a mine," said Ed. "What do you think it is?"

"I don't care. If it's worth money, Doctor Tod'll split with us. He's a square guy."

"For a crook," said Ed.

They laughed and laughed, and the thing rattled around in the back of the dumptruck.

The MPs brought the red-haired man into his office and introduced them.

"Please have a seat, Doctor," said A.E. He lit his pipe.

The man seemed ill at ease, as he should have been after two days of questioning by Army Intelligence.

"They have told me what happened at White Sands, and that you won't talk to anyone but me," said A.E.

"I understand they used sodium pentathol on you, and that it had no effect?"

"It made me drunk," said the man, whose hair in this light seemed orange and yellow.

"But you didn't talk?"

"I said things, but not what they wanted to hear."

"Very unusual."

"Blood chemistry."

A.E. sighed. He looked out the window of the Princeton office. "Very well, then. I will listen to your story. I am not saying I will believe it, but I *will* listen."

"All right," said the man, taking a deep breath. "Here goes."

He began to talk, slowly at first, forming his words carefully, gaining confidence as he spoke. As he began to talk faster, his accent crept back in, one A.E. could not place, something like a Fiji Islander who had learned English from a Swede. A.E. refilled his pipe twice, then left it unlit after filling it the third time. He sat slightly forward, occasionally nodding, his gray hair an aureole in the afternoon light.

The man finished.

A.E. remembered his pipe, found a match, lit it. He put his hands behind his head. There was a small hole in his sweater near the left elbow.

"They'll never believe any of that," he said.

"I don't care, as long as they do something!" said the man. "As long as I get it back."

A.E. looked at him. "If they did believe you, the implications of all this would overshadow the reason you're here. The fact that *you* are *here*, if you follow my meaning."

"Well, what can we do? If my ship were still operable, I'd

be looking myself. I did the next best thing, landed somewhere that would be sure to attract attention, asked to speak
to you. Perhaps other scientists, research institutes . . ."

A.E. laughed. "Forgive me. You don't realize how things
are done here. We will need the military. We will *have* the
military and the government whether we want them or not, so
we might as well have them on the best possible terms, ours,
from the first. The problem is that we have to think of something that is *plausible* to them, yet will still mobilize them in
the search.

"I'll talk to the Army people about you, then make some
calls to friends of mine. We have just finished a large global
war, and many things had a way of escaping notice, or being
lost in the shuffle. Perhaps we can work something from
there.

"The only thing is, we had better do all this from a phone
booth. The MPs will be along, so I will have to talk quietly.
Tell me," he said, picking up his hat from the corner of a cluttered bookcase, "do you like ice cream?"

"Lactose and sugar solids congealed in a mixture kept just
below the freezing point?" asked the man.

"I assure you," said A.E., "it is better than it sounds, and
quite refreshing." Arm in arm, they went out the office door.

Jetboy patted the scarred side of his plane. He stood in
Hangar 23. Linc came out of his office, wiping his hands on
a greasy rag.

"Hey, how'd it go?" he asked.

"Great. They want the book of memoirs. Going to be their
big spring book, if I get it in on time, or so they say."

"You still bound and determined to sell the plane?" asked
the mechanic. "Sure hate to see her go."

"Well, that part of my life's over. I feel like if I never fly
again, even as an airline passenger, it'll be too soon."

"What do you want me to do?"

Jetboy looked at the plane.

"Tell you what. Put on the high altitude wing extensions,
and the drop tanks. It looks bigger and shinier that way.
Somebody from a museum will probably buy it, is what I
figure—I'm offering it to museums first. If that doesn't work,
I'll take out ads in the papers. We'll take the guns out later,

if some private citizen buys it. Check everything to see it's tight. Shouldn't have shaken much on the hop from San Fran, and they did a pretty good overhaul at Hickham Field. Whatever you think it needs."

"Sure thing."

"I'll call you tomorrow, unless something can't wait."

HISTORICAL AIRCRAFT FOR SALE: Jetboy's twin-engine jet. 2×1200 lb. thrust engines, speed 600 mph at 25000 ft, range 650 miles, 1000 w/drop tanks (tanks and wing exts. inc.) length 31 ft, w/s 33 ft (49 w exts.). Reasonable offers accepted. Must see to appreciate. On view at Hangar 23, Bonham's Flying Service, Shantak, New Jersey.

Jetboy stood in front of the bookstore window, looking at the pyramids of new titles there. You could tell paper rationing was off. Next year, his book would be one of them. Not just a comic book but the story of his part in the war. He hoped it would be good enough so that it wouldn't be lost in the clutter.

Seems like, in the words of someone, every goddam barber and shoeshine boy who was drafted had written a book about how he won the war.

There were six books of war memoirs in one window, by everyone from a lieutenant colonel to a major general (maybe those PFC barbers didn't write that many books?).

Maybe they wrote some of the two dozen war novels that covered another window of the display.

There were two books near the door, piles of them in a window by themselves, runaway bestsellers, that weren't war novels or memoirs. One was called *The Grasshopper Lies Heavy* by someone named Abendsen (Hawthorne Abendsen, obviously a pen name). The other was a thick book called *Growing Flowers by Candlelight in Hotel Rooms* by someone so self-effacing she called herself "Mrs. Charles Fine Adams." It must be a book of unreadable poems that the public, in its craziness, had taken up. There was no accounting for taste.

Jetboy put his hands in the pockets of his leather jacket and walked to the nearest movie show.

● ● ●

Tod watched the smoke rising from the lab and waited for the phone to ring. People ran back and forth to the building a half-mile away.

There had been nothing for two weeks. Thorkeld, the scientist he'd hired to run the tests had reported each day. The stuff didn't work on monkeys, dogs, rats, lizards, snakes, frogs, insects, or even on fish in suspension in water. Doctor Thorkeld was beginning to think Tod's men had paid twenty dollars for an inert gas in a fancy container.

A few moments ago there had been an explosion. Now he waited.

The phone rang.

"Tod—oh, god, this is Jones at the lab, it's—" static washed over the line. "Oh, sweet Jesus! Thorkeld's—they're all—" there was a thumping near the phone receiver on the other end. "Oh, my—"

"Calm down," said Tod. "Is everyone outside the lab safe?"

"Yeah, yeah. The . . . oooh." The sound of vomiting came over the phone.

Tod waited.

"Sorry, Doctor Tod. The lab's still sealed off. The fire's— it's a small one on the grass outside. Somebody dropped a butt."

"Tell me what happened."

"I was outside for a smoke. Somebody in there must have messed up, dropped something. I . . . I don't know. It's— They're most of them dead, I think. I hope. I don't know. Something's—wait, wait. There's someone still moving in the office, I can see from here, there's—"

There was a click of someone picking up a receiver. The volume on the line dropped.

"Tog, Tog," said a voice, an approximation of a voice.

"Who's there?"

"Torgk—"

"Thorkeld?"

"Guh. Hep. Hep. Guh."

There was a sound like a sack full of squids being dumped on a corrugated roof. "Hep." Then came the sound of jelly being emptied into a cluttered desk drawer.

There was a gunshot, and the receiver bounced off the desk.

"He—he shot—it—himself," said Jones.

"I'll be right out," said Tod.

After the cleanup, Tod stood in his office again. It had not been pretty. The canister was still intact. Whatever the accident had been had been with a sample. The other animals were okay. It was only the people. Three were dead outright. One, Thorkeld, had killed himself. Two others he and Jones had *had* to kill. A seventh person was missing, but had not come out any of the doors or windows.

Tod sat down in his chair and thought a long, long time. Then he reached over and pushed the button on his desk.

"Yeah, Doctor," asked Filmore, stepping into the room with a batch of telegrams and brokerage orders under his arm.

Dr. Tod opened the desk safe and began counting out bills. "Filmore. I'd like you to get down to Port Elizabeth, North Carolina, and buy me up five type B blimp balloons. Tell them I'm a car salesman. Arrange for one million cubic feet of helium to be delivered to the south Pennsy warehouse. Break out the hardware and give me a complete list of what we have—anything we need we can get surplus. Get ahold of Captain Mack, see if he still has that cargo ship. We'll need new passports. Get me Cholley Sacks, I'll need a contact in Switzerland. I'll need a pilot with a lighter-than-air license. Some diving suits and oxygen. Shot ballast, couple of tons. A bombsight. Nautical charts. And bring me a cup of coffee."

"Fred has a lighter-than-air license," said Filmore.

"Those two never cease to amaze me," said Dr. Tod.

"I thought we'd pulled our last caper, boss?"

"Filmore," he said, and looked at the man he'd been friends with for twenty years, "Filmore, some capers you *have* to pull, whether you want to or not."

"Dewey was an Admiral at Manila Bay,
    Dewey was a candidate just the other day.
    Dewey were her eyes when she said I do;
    Do we love each other? I should say we do!"

The kids in the courtyard of the apartment jumped rope. They'd started the second they got home from school.

At first it bothered Jetboy. He got up from the typewriter and went to the window. Instead of yelling, he watched.

The writing wasn't going well, anyway. What had seemed like just the facts when he'd told them to the G-2 boys during the war looked like bragging on paper, once the words were down:

"Three planes, two ME-109s and a TA-152 came out of the clouds at the crippled B-24. It had suffered heavy flak damage. Two props were feathered and the top turret was missing.

"One of the 109s went into a shallow dive, probably going into a snap roll to fire up at the underside of the bomber.

"I eased my plane in a long turn and fired a deflection shot while about 700 yards away and closing. I saw three hits, then the 109 disintegrated.

"The TA-152 had seen me and dived to intercept. As the 109 blew up, I throttled back and hit my airbrakes. The 152 flashed by less than 50 yards away. I saw the surprised look on the pilot's face. I fired one burst with my 20mms as he flashed by. Everything from his canopy back flew apart in a shower.

"I pulled up. The last 109 was behind the Liberator. He was firing with his machine guns and cannon. He'd taken out the tail gunner and the belly turret couldn't get enough elevation. The bomber pilot was wig-wagging the tail so the waist gunners could get a shot, but only the left waist gun was working.

"I was more than a mile away, but had turned above and to the right. I put the nose down and fired one round with the 75mm just before the gunsight flashed across the 109.

"The whole middle of the fighter disappeared—I could see France through it. The only image I have is that I was looking down on top of an open umbrella and somebody folded it suddenly. The fighter looked like Christmas tree tinsel as it fell.

"Then the few gunners left on the B-24 opened up on me, not recognizing my plane. I flashed my IFF code, but their receiver must have been out.

"There were two German parachutes far below. The pilots of the first two fighters must have gotten out. I went back to my base.

"When they ran maintenance, they found one of my 75mm rounds missing, and only twelve 20mm shells. I'd shot down three enemy planes.

"I later learned the B-24 had crashed in the Channel and there were no survivors."

Who needs this stuff? Jetboy thought. The war's over. Does anybody really want to read *The Jet-Propelled Boy* when it's published? Does anybody except morons even want to read *Jetboy Comics* anymore?

I don't even think *I'm* needed. What can I do now? Fight crime? I can see strafing getaway cars full of bank robbers. That would be a *real* fair fight. Barnstorming? That went out with Hoover, and besides, I don't want to fly again. This year more people will fly on airliners on vacation than have been in the air all together in the last 43 years, mail pilots, crop-dusters and wars included.

What can I do? Break up a trust? Prosecute wartime prof-iteers? *There*'s a real dead-end job for you. Punish mean old men who are robbing the state blind running orphanages and starving and beating the kids? You don't need me for that, you need Spanky and Alfalfa and Buckwheat.

> "A-tisket A-tasket
> Hitler's in a casket.
> Eeenie-meenie-Mussolini
> Six feet underground!"

said the kids outside, now doing double-dutch, two ropes go-ing opposite directions. Kids have too much energy, he thought. They hot-peppered a while, then slowed again.

> "Down in the dungeon, twelve feet deep,
> Where old Hitler lies asleep,
> German boys, they tickle his feet,
> Down in the dungeon, twelve feet deep!"

Jetboy turned away from the window. Maybe what I need is to go to the movies again.

Since his meeting with Belinda, he'd done nothing much but read, write and go see movies. Before coming home, the last two movies he'd seen, in a crowded post auditorium in France in late '44, had been a cheesy double bill. *That Nazty Nuisance*, a United Artists film made in '43, with Bobby Watson as Hitler, and one of Jetboy's favorite character actors,

Frank Faylen, had been the better of the two. The other was a PRC hunk of junk, *Jive Junction*, starring Dickie Moore, about a bunch of hepcats jitterbugging at the malt shop.

The first thing he'd done after getting his money and finding an apartment, was to find the nearest movie theater, where he'd seen *Murder, He Says* about a house full of hillbilly weird people, with Fred McMurray and Marjorie Main, and an actor named Porter Hall playing identical twin brother murderers named Bert and Mert. "Which one's which?" asked McMurray, and Marjorie Main picked up an axe handle and hit one of them in the middle of the back, where he collapsed from the waist up in a distorted caricature of humanity, but stayed on his feet. "That there's Mert," said Main, throwing the axehandle on the woodpile. "He's got a trick back." There was radium and homicide galore, and Jetboy thought it was the funniest move he had ever seen.

Since then he'd gone to the movies every day, sometimes going to three theaters and seeing from six to eight movies a day. He was adjusting to civilian life like most soldiers and sailors had, by seeing films.

He had seen *Lost Weekend* with Ray Milland, and Frank Faylen again, this time as a male nurse in a psycho ward; *A Tree Grows in Brooklyn, The Thin Man Goes Home*, with William Powell at his alcoholic best, *Bring on the Girls, It's in the Bag* with Fred Allen, *Incendiary Blonde, The Story of G.I. Joe* (Jetboy had been the subject of one of Pyle's columns back in '43), a horror film called *Isle of the Dead* with Boris Karloff, a new kind of Italian movie called *Open City* at an art house, and *The Postman Always Rings Twice*.

And there were other films, Monogram and PRC and Republic westerns and crime movies, pictures he'd seen in 24-hour nabes, but had forgotten about ten minutes after leaving the theaters. By the lack of star names and the 4-F look of the leading men, they'd been the bottom halves of double bills made during the war, all clocking in at exactly 59 minutes running time.

Jetboy sighed. So many movies, so much everything he'd missed during the war. He'd even missed V-E and V-J days, stuck on that island, before he and his plane had been found by the crew of the *U.S.S. Reluctant*. The way the guys on the

Reluctant talked, you'd have thought they missed most of the war and the movies, too.

He was looking forward to a lot of films this fall, and to seeing them when they came out, the way everybody else did, the way he'd used to do at the orphanage.

Jetboy sat back down at the typewriter. If I don't work, I'll never get this book done. I'll go to the movies tonight.

He began to type up all the exciting things he'd done on July 12, 1944.

In the courtyard, women were calling kids in for supper as their fathers came home from work. A couple of kids were still jumping rope out there, their voices thin in the afternoon air:

> "Hitler, Hitler looks like this,
> Mussolini bows like this,
> Sonja Henie skates like this,
> And Betty Grable misses like *this*!"

The Haberdasher in the White House was having a piss-ass of a day.

It had started with a phone call a little after six A.M.—the Nervous Nellies over at the State Department had some new hot rumors from Turkey. The Soviets were moving all their men around on that nation's edges.

"Well," the Plain Speaking Man from Missouri said, "call me when they cross the damn border and not until."

Now this.

Independence's First Citizen watched the door close. The last thing he saw was Einstein's heel disappearing. It needed half-soleing.

He sat back in his chair, lifted his thick glasses off his nose, rubbed vigorously. Then the President put his fingers together in a steeple, his elbows resting on his desk. He looked at the small model plow on the front of his desk (it had replaced the model of the M-1 Garand that had sat there from the day he took office until V-J Day). There were three books on the right corner of the desk—a Bible, a thumbed thesaurus and a pictorial history of the United States. There were three buttons on his desk for calling various secretaries, but he never used them.

Now that peace has come, I'm fighting to keep ten wars from breaking out in twenty places, there's strikes looming in

every industry and that's a damn shame, people are hollering
for more cars and refrigerators, and they're as tired as I am of
war and war's alarm.

And I have to kick the hornet's nest again, get everybody
out looking for a damn germ bomb that might go off and in-
fect the whole U.S. and kill half the people or more.

We'd have been better off still fighting with sticks and
rocks.

The sooner I get my ass back to 219 N. Delaware in Independence, the better off me and this whole damn country will
be.

Unless that sonofabitch Dewey wants to run for President
again. Like Lincoln said, I'd rather swallow a deer-antler
rocking chair than let that bastard be President.

That's the only thing that'll keep me here when Mr. Roosevelt's term is over.

Sooner I get this snipe hunt underway, the faster we can put
World War Number Two behind us.

He picked up the phone.

"Get me the Chiefs of Staff," he said.

"Major Truman speaking."

"Major, this is the other Truman, your boss. Put General
Ostrander on the horn, will you?"

While he was waiting he looked out past the window fan
(he hated air-conditioning) into the trees. The sky was the
kind of blue that quickly turns to brass in the summer.

He looked at the clock on the wall. 10:23 A.M. Eastern
Daylight Time. What a day. What a year. What a century.

"General Ostrander here, sir."

"General, we just had another bale of hay dropped on
us . . ."

A couple of weeks later, the note came: Deposit 20 Million
Dollars account #43Z21, Credite Suisse, Berne, by 2300Z 14
Sept or lose a major city. You know of this weapon; your people have been searching for it. I have it; I will use half of it
on the first city. The price goes to 30 Million Dollars to keep
me from using it a second time. You have my word it will not
be used if the first payment is made and instructions will be
sent on where the weapon can be recovered.

The Plain-Speaking Man from Missouri picked up the
phone.

"Kick everything up to the top notch," he said. "Call the Cabinet, get the Joint Chiefs together. And, Ostrander . . ."

"Yessir?"

"Better get ahold of that kid flier, what's his name. . .?"

"You mean Jetboy, sir? He's not on active duty anymore."

"The hell he's not. He is now!"

"Yessir."

It was 2:24 P.M. on the Tuesday afternoon of September 15, 1946 when the thing first showed up on the radar screens.

At 2:31 it was still moving slowly toward the city at an altitude of nearly 60,000 feet.

At 2:41 they blew the first of the air raid sirens, which had not been used in New York City since April of 1945 in a blackout drill.

By 2:48 there was panic.

Someone in the CD office hit the wrong set of switches. The power went off everywhere except hospitals and police and fire stations. Subways stopped. Things shut down, and traffic lights quit working. Half the emergency equipment, which hadn't been checked since the end of the war, failed to come up.

The streets were jammed with people. Cops rushed out to try to direct traffic. Some of the policemen panicked when they were issued gas masks. Telephones jammed. Fistfights broke out at intersections, people were trampled at subway exits and on the stairs of skyscrapers.

The bridges clogged up.

Conflicting orders came down. Get the people into bomb shelters. No, no, evacuate the island. Two cops on the same corner yelled conflicting orders at the crowds. Mostly people just stood around and looked.

Their attention was soon drawn to something in the southeastern sky. It was small and shiny.

Flak began to bloom ineffectually two miles below it.

On and on it came.

When the guns over in Jersey began to fire, the panic really started.

It was 3 P.M.

• • •

"It's really quite simple," said Dr. Tod. He looked down toward Manhattan which lay before him like a treasure trove.
He turned to Filmore and held up a long cylindrical device
which looked like the offspring of a pipe bomb and a combi-
nation lock. "Should anything happen to me, simply insert
this fuse in the holder in the explosives," he indicated the
taped-over portion with the opening in the canister covered
with the Sanskrit-like lettering. "Twist it to the number 500,
then pull this lever." He indicated the bomb-bay door latch.
"It'll fall of its own weight, and I was wrong about the bomb-
sights. Pinpoint accuracy is not our goal."

He looked at Filmore through the grill of his diving helmet.
They all wore diving suits with hoses leading back to a central oxygen supply.

"Make sure, of course, everyone's suited with their helmet
on. Your blood would boil in this thin air. And these suits
only have to hold pressure for the few seconds the bomb
door's open."

"I don't expect no trouble, boss."

"Neither do I. After we bomb New York City, we get out
to our rendezvous with the ship, rip the ballast, set down and
head for Europe. They'll be only too glad to pay us the
money then. They have no way of knowing we'll be using the
whole germ weapon. Seven million or so dead should quite
convince them we mean business."

"Look at that," said Ed, from the co-pilot's seat. "Way
down there. Flak!"

"What's our altitude?" asked Dr. Tod.

"Right on 58,000 feet," said Fred.

"Target?"

Ed sighted, checked a map. "Sixteen miles straight ahead.
You sure called those wind currents just right, Dr. Tod."

They had sent him to an airfield outside Washington DC to
wait. That way he would be within range of most of the major
east coast cities.

He had spent part of the day reading, part asleep, and the
rest of it talking over the war with some of the other pilots.
Most of them, though, were too new to have fought in all but
the closing days of the war.

Most of them were jet pilots, like him, who had done their

training in P-59 Airacomets or P-80 Shooting Stars. A few of
those in the ready-room belonged to a P-51 prop-job squadron. There was a bit of tension between the blowtorch jockeys
and the piston-eaters.

All of them were a new breed, though. Already there was
talk Truman was going to make the Army Air Force into a
separate branch, just the Air Force, within the next year.
Jetboy felt, at 19, that time had passed him by.

"They're working on something," said one of the pilots,
"that'll go through the sonic wall. Bell's behind it."

"A friend of mine out at Murdoc says wait till they get the
Flying Wing in operation. They're already working on an all-
jet version of it. A bomber that can go 13,000 miles at 500
per, carries a crew of 13, bunk beds for seven, can stay up for
a day and a half!" said another.

"Anybody know anything about this alert?" asked a very
young nervous guy with 2nd Looie bars. "The Russians up to
something?"

"I heard we were going to Greece," said someone. "Ouzo
for me, gallons of it."

"More like Czech potato-peel vodka. We'll be lucky if we
see Christmas."

Jetboy realized he missed ready-room banter more than he
had thought.

The intercom hissed on and a klaxon began to wail. Jetboy
looked at his watch. It was 2:25 P.M.

He realized he missed something more than Air Corps ba-
dinage. That was flying. Now, it all came back to him. When
he had flown down to Washington the night before it was just
a routine hop.

Now was different. It was like wartime again. He had a
vector. He had a target. He had a mission.

He also had on an experimental Navy T-2 pressure suit. It
was a girdle manufacturer's dream, all rubber and laces, pressure bottles and a real space helmet, like out of *Planet Comics*, over his head. They had fitted him for it the night before,
when they saw his high-altitude wings and drop tanks on the
plane.

"We'd better tailor this down for you," said the flight sergeant.

"I've got a pressurized cabin," said Jetboy.

"Well, in case they need you, and in case something goes wrong, then."

The suit was still too tight, and it wasn't pressurized yet. The arms were built for a gorilla, and the chest for a chimpanzee. "You'll appreciate the extra room if that thing ever inflates in an emergency," said the sergeant.

"You're the boss," said Jetboy.

They'd even painted the torso white and the legs red to match his outfit. His blue helmet and goggles showed through the clear plastic bubble.

As he climbed with the rest of the squadron, he was glad now that he had the thing. His mission was to accompany the flight of P-80s in, and to engage only if needed. He had never been exactly a team player.

The sky ahead was blue as the background curtain in Bronzino's *Venus, Cupid, Folly and Time*, with a two-fifths cloud to the north. The sun stood over his left shoulder. The squadron angled up. He wig-wagged the wings. They spread out in a staggered box and cleared their guns.

Chunder chunder chunder chunder went his 20mm cannons.

Tracers arced out ahead from the six .50 cals on each P-80. They left the prop planes far behind and pointed their noses toward Manhattan.

They looked like a bunch of angry bees circling under a hawk.

The sky was filled with jets and prop fighters climbing like the wall clouds of a hurricane.

Above was a lumpy object that hung and moved slowly on toward the city. Where the eye of the hurricane would be was a torrent of flak, thicker than Jetboy had ever seen over Europe or Japan.

It was bursting far too low, only at the level of the highest fighters.

Fighter control called them. "Clark Gable Command to all squadrons. Target at 550, repeat 550 angels. Moving ENE at 25 knots. Flak unable to reach."

"Call it off," said the squadron leader. "We'll try to fly high enough for deflection shooting. Squadron Hodiak, follow me."

Jetboy looked up into the high blue **above**. The object continued its slow track.

"What's it got?" he asked Clark Gable Command.

"Command to Jetboy. Some type of bomb is what we've been told. It has to be a lighter-than-air craft of at least 500,000 cubic feet to reach that altitude. Over."

"I'm beginning a climb. If the other planes can't reach it, call them off, too."

There was silence on the radio, then, "Roger."

As the P-80s glinted like silver crucifixes above him, he eased the nose up.

"Come on, baby," he said. "Let's do some flying."

The Shooting Stars began to fall away, sideslipping in the thin air. Jetboy could only hear the sound of his own pressure-breathing in his ears, and the high thin whine of his engines.

"Come on, girl," he said. "You can make it!"

The thing above him had resolved itself in a bastard aircraft made of half a dozen blimps, with a gondola below it. The gondola looked as if it had once been a PT boat shell. That was all he could see. Beyond it, the air was purple and cold. Next stop, outer space.

The last of the P-80s slid sideways on the blue stairs of the sky. A few had made desultory firing runs, some snap-rolling as fighters used to do underneath bombers in the war. They fired as they nosed up. All their tracers fell away under the balloons.

One of the P-80s fought for control, dropping two miles before levelling out.

Jetboy's plane protested, whining. It was hard to control. He eased the nose up again, had to fight it.

"Get everybody out of the way," he said to Clark Gable Command.

"Here's where we give you some fighting room," he said to his plane. He blew the drop tanks. They fell away like bombs behind him. He pushed his cannon button. *Chunder chunder chunder chunder* they went. Then again and again.

His tracers arced toward the target, then they too fell away. He fired four more bursts until his cannon ran dry. Then he cleaned out the twin fifties in the tail, but it didn't take long for all 100 rounds to be spent.

He nosed over and went in a shallow dive, like a salmon sounding to throw a hook, gaining speed. A minute into the run he nosed up, putting the JB-1 into a long circling climb.

"Feels better, huh?" he asked.

The engines bit into the air. The plane, relieved of the weight, lurched up and ahead.

Below him was Manhattan with its seven million people. They must be watching down there, knowing these might be the last things they ever saw. Maybe this is what living in the atomic age would be like, always be looking up and thinking *is this it*?

Jetboy reached down with one of his boots and slammed a lever over. A 75 mm cannon shell slid into the breech. He put his hand on the auto-load bar, and pulled back a little more on the control wheel.

The red jet cut the air like a razor.

He was closer now, closer than the others had gotten, and still not close enough. He had only five rounds to do the job.

The jet climbed, beginning to stagger in the thin air, as if it were some red animal clawing its way up a long blue tapestry that slipped a little each time the animal lurched.

He pointed the nose up.

Everything seemed frozen, waiting.

A long thin line of machine-gun tracers reached out from the gondola for him like a lover.

He began to fire his cannon.

FROM: The statement of Patrolman Francis V. ("Francis the Talking Cop") O'Hooey, Sept. 15, 1946, 6:45 P.M.:

"We was watching from the street over at Sixth Avenue, trying to get people from shoving each other in a panic. Then they calmed down as they was watching the dogfights and stuff up above.

"Some birdwatcher had this pair of binocs, so I confiscated 'em. I watched pretty much the whole thing. Them jets wasn't having no luck, and the anti-aircraft from over in the Bowery wasn't doing no good either. I still say the Army oughta be sued 'cause them Air Defense guys got so panicky they forgot to set the timers on them shells and I heard that some of them came down in the Bronx and blew up a whole block of flats.

"Anyway, this red plane, that is Jetboy's plane, was climbing up and he fired all his bullets, I thought, without doing any damage to the balloon thing.

"I was out on the street, and this fire truck pulls up with its sirens on, and the whole precinct and auxiliaries were on it, and the Lieutenant was yelling for me to climb on, we'd been assigned to the west side to take care of a traffic smash-up and a riot.

"So I jump on the truck, and I try to keep my eyes on what's happening up in the skies.

"The riot was pretty much over. The air-raid sirens was still wailing, but everybody was just standing around gawking at what was happening up there.

"The lieutenant yells to at least get the people in the buildings. I pushed a few in some doors, then I took another gander in the field glasses.

"I'll be damned if Jetboy hasn't shot up some of the balloons (I hear he used his howitzer on 'em) and the thing looks bigger—it's dropping some. But he's out of ammo and not as high as the thing is and starts circlin'.

"I forgot to say all the time this blimp thing has got so many machine guns going it looks like a Fourth of July sparkler, and Jetboy's plane's taking these hits all the time.

"Then he just takes his plane around and comes right back and crashes right into the what-you-call-it—the gondola, that's it—on the blimps. They just sort of merged together. He must have been going awful slow by then, like stalling, and the plane just sort of mashed into the side of the thing.

"And the blimp deal looked like it was coming down a little, not a lot, just some. Then the lieutenant took the glasses away from me, and I shaded my eyes and watched as best I could.

"There was this flare of light. I thought the whole thing had blown up at first, and I ducked up under a car. But when I looked up the blimps was still there.

" 'Look out! Get inside!' yelled the lieutenant. Everybody had another panic then, and was jumping under cars and around stuff and through windows. It looked like a regular Three Stooges for a minute or two.

"A few minutes later, it rained red airplane parts all over the streets, and a bunch on the Hudson Terminal."

(continued)

• • •

There was steam and fire all around. The cockpit cracked
like an egg, and the wings folded up like a fan. Jetboy jerked
as the capstans in the pressure suit inflated. He was curved
into a circle, and must have looked like a frightened tomcat.

The gondola walls had parted like a curtain where the
fighter's wings crumpled into it. A wave of frost formed over
the shattered cockpit as oxygen blew out of the gondola.

Jetboy tore his hoses loose. His bailout bottle had five minutes of air in it. He grappled with the nose of the plane, like
fighting against iron bands on his arms and legs. All you were
supposed to be able to do in these suits was eject and pull the
D-ring on your parachute.

The plane lurched like a freight elevator with a broken cable. Jetboy grabbed a radar antenna with one gloved hand, felt
it snap away from the broken nose of the plane. He grabbed
another.

The city was twelve miles below him, the buildings making
the island look like a faraway porcupine. The left engine of
his plane, crumpled and spewing fuel, tore loose and flew
under the gondola. He watched it grow smaller.

The air was purple as a plum—the skin of the blimps bright
as fire in the sunlight, and the sides of the gondola were bent
and torn like cheap cardboard.

The whole thing shuddered like a whale.

Somebody flew by over Jetboy's head through the hole in
the metal, trailing hoses like the arms of an octopus. Debris
followed through the air in the explosive decompression.

The jet sagged.

Jetboy thrust his hand into the torn side of the gondola,
found a strut.

He felt his parachute harness catch on the radar array. The
plane twisted. He felt its weight.

He jerked his harness snap. His parachute packs were
ripped away from him, tearing at his back and crotch.

His plane bent in the middle like a snake with a broken
back, then dropped away, the wings coming up and touching
above the shattered cockpit as if it were a dove trying to beat
its pinions. Then it twisted sideways, falling to pieces.

Below it was the dot of the man who had fallen out of the

gondola, spinning like a yard sprinkler toward the bright city far below.

Jetboy saw the plane fall away beneath his feet. He hung in space twelve miles up by one hand.

He gripped his right wrist with his left hand, chinned himself up until he got a foot through the side, then punched his way in.

There were two people left inside. One was at the controls, the other stood in the center behind a large round thing. He was pushing a cylinder into a slot in it. There was a shattered machine gun turret on one side of the gondola.

Jetboy reached for the service .38 strapped across his chest. It was agony reaching for it, agony trying to run toward the guy with the fuse.

They wore diving suits. The suits were inflated. They looked like ten or twelve beach balls stuffed into suits of long underwear. They were moving as slowly as he was.

Jetboy's hand closed in a claw over the handle of the .38. He jerked it from its holster.

It flew out of his hand, bounced off the ceiling and went out through the hole he had come in.

The guy at the controls got off one shot at him. He dived toward the other man, the one with the fuse.

His hand clamped on the diving-suited wrist of the other just as the man pushed the cylindrical fuse into the side of the round cannister. Jetboy saw that the whole device sat on a hinged doorplate.

The man had only half a face—Jetboy saw smooth metal on one side through the grid-plated diving helmet.

The man twisted the fuse with both hands.

Through the torn ceiling of the pilot-house, Jetboy saw another blimp begin to deflate. There was a falling sensation. They were dropping toward the city.

Jetboy gripped the fuse with both hands. Their helmets clanged together as the ship lurched.

The guy at the controls was putting on a parachute harness and heading toward the rent in the wall.

Another shudder threw Jetboy and the man with the fuse together. The guy reached for the door lever behind him as best he could in the bulky suit.

Jetboy grabbed his hands and pulled him back.

They slammed together, draped over the canister, their hands entangled on each other's suits and the fuse to the bomb.

The man tried again to reach the lever. Jetboy pulled him away. The canister rolled like a giant beach ball as the gondola listed.

He looked directly into the eye of the man in the diving suit. The man used his feet to push the canister back over the bomb door. His hand went for the lever again.

Jetboy gave the fuse a half-twist the other way.

The man in the diving suit reached behind him. He came up with a .45 automatic. He jerked a heavy gloved hand away from the fuse, worked the slide. Jetboy saw the muzzle swing at him.

"Die, Jetboy! Die!" said the man.

He pulled the trigger four times.

STATEMENT: of Patrolman Francis V. O'Hooey, Sept. 15, 1946, 6:45 P.M. (continued):

"So when the pieces of metal quit falling, we all ran out and looked up.

"I saw the white dot below the blimp thing. I grabbed the binocs away from the lieutenant.

"Sure enough it was a parachute. I hoped it was Jetboy had bailed out when his plane crashed into the thing.

"I don't know much about such stuff, but I do know that you don't open a parachute that high up or you get in serious trouble.

"Then while I was watching, the blimps and stuff all blew up, all at once. Like they was there, then there was this explosion, and there was only smoke and stuff way up in the air.

"The people all around started cheering. The kid had done it—he'd blown the thing up before it could drop the A-bomb on Manhattan Island.

"Then the lieutenant said to get in the truck, we'd try to get the kid.

"We jumped in and tried to figure out where he was gonna land. Everywhere we passed, people was standing in the middle of the car wrecks and fires and stuff, looking up and cheering the parachute.

"I noticed the big smudge in the air after the explosion,

when we'd been driving around for ten minutes. Them other jets that had been with Jetboy was back, flying all around through the air, and some Mustangs and Thunderjugs, too. It was like a regular air show up there.

"Somehow we got out near the Bridge before anybody else did. Good thing, because when we got to the water, we saw this guy pile right in about twenty feet from shore. Went down like a rock. He was wearing this diving suit thing, and we swam out and I grabbed part of the parachute and a fireman grabbed some of the hoses and we hauled him out onto shore.

"Well, it wasn't Jetboy, it was the one we got the make on as Edward 'Smooth Eddy' Shiloh, a real small-time operator.

"And he was in bad shape, too. We got a wrench off the firetruck and popped his helmet, and he was purple as a turnip in there. It had taken him 27 minutes to get to the ground. He'd passed out of course with not enough air up there, and he was so frostbit I heard they had to take off one of his feet and all but the thumb on the left hand.

"But he'd jumped out of the thing before it blew. We looked back up, hoping to see Jetboy's chute or something, but there wasn't one, just that misty big smudge up there, and all those planes zoomin' round.

"We took Shiloh to the hospital.

"That's my report."

(Excerpt) Statement of Edward "Smooth Eddy" Shiloh, Sept. 16, 1946:

". . . all five shells into a couple of the gasbags. Then he crashed the plane right into us. The walls blew. Fred and Filmore were thrown out without their parachutes.

"When the pressure dropped, I felt like I couldn't move, the suit got so tight. I tried to get my parachute. I see that Dr. Tod has the fuse and is making it to the bomb thing.

"I felt the airplane fall off the side of the gondola. Next thing I know, Jetboy's standing right in front of the hole his plane made.

"I pull out my roscoe when I see he's packing heat. But he dropped his gat and he heads toward Tod.

" 'Stop him, stop him!' Tod's yelling over the suit radio. I get one clean shot, but I miss, then he's on top of Tod and the bomb, and right then I decide my job's been over about five minutes and I'm not getting paid any overtime.

"So I head out, and all this gnashing and screaming's coming across the radio, and they're grappling around. Then Tod yells and pulls out his .45 and I swear he put four shots in Jetboy from closer than I am to you. Then they fall back together, and I jumped out the hole in the side.

"Only I was stupid, and I pulled my ripcord too soon, and my chute don't open right and got all twisted, and I started passing out. Just before I did, the whole thing blew up above me.

"Next thing I know, I wake up here, and I got one shoe too many, know what I mean?

". . . what did they say? Well, most of it was garbled. Let's see. Tod says, 'Stop him, stop him,' and I shot. Then I lammed for the hole. They were yelling. I could only hear Jetboy when their helmets slammed together, through Tod's suit radio. They must have crashed together a lot, 'cause I heard both of them breathing hard.

"Then Tod got to the gun and shot Jetboy four times and said, 'Die, Jetboy! Die!' and I jumped and they must have fought a second, and I heard Jetboy say: 'I can't die yet. I haven't seen *The Jolson Story*.' "

It was eight years to the day after Thomas Wolfe died, but it was his kind of day. Across the whole of America and the northern hemisphere, it was one of those days when summer gives up its hold, when the weather comes from the poles and Canada again, rather than the Gulf and the Pacific.

They eventually built a monument to Jetboy—"the kid that couldn't die yet." A battle-scarred veteran of 19 had stopped a madman from blowing up Manhattan. After calmer heads prevailed, they realized that.

But it took a while to remember that. And to get around to going back to college, or buying that new refrigerator. It took a long time for anybody to remember what anything was like before September 15, 1946.

When people in New York City looked up and saw Jetboy blowing up the attacking aircraft, they thought their troubles were over.

They were as wrong as snakes on an eight-lane high-way.

—Daniel Deck,
GODOT IS MY CO-PILOT: A Life of Jetboy
Lippincott, 1963

From high up in the sky the fine mist began to curve down-ward.

Part of it stretched itself out in the winds, as it went through the jet stream, toward the east.

Beneath those currents, the mist reformed and hung like verga, settling slowly to the city below, streamers forming and reforming, breaking like scud near a storm.

Wherever it came down, it made a sound like gentle autumn rain.

THE ANNOTATED JETBOY

WRITING is a funny business, but sometimes not nearly so funny as you'd like to think.

The following annotations are for my opening story, "Thirty Minutes Over Broadway!" in the George R.R. Martin-edited shared-world anthology, *Wild Cards!*, Bantam Books, 1987.

People have always accused me of researching too much. It was three years between initial conception and the writing of this one—part of the time was working stuff out in the shared world with George and the other writers, but not that much. (With the result that my first draft had a couple of hundred stupidities which—along with four brilliant pages of stream-of-consciousness from inside Harry S Truman's head—I later took out.) The research was to lend what we in the riproaring days of Postmodernist Fiction used to call *verisimilitude*, but what is now referred to in the Reagan '80s as "making it seem real-like."

Some of these were notes to myself, some were things I already knew; most I found in research while writing the story.

I figure if I'm going to work this damn hard I might as well get some use out of it and some credit for it. Whether this adds to your enjoyment of the story, or only clutters up your mind as much as mine, I don't care. Here it (they) are:

page 87   Shantak, N.J. H.P. Lovecraft, *Dream Quest of Unknown Kadath*, others. Also, Bill Wallace and Joe Pumilia, "Some Notes on M.M. Moamrath," *Nickelodeon #1, 1976.*

page 87   Hangar 23. See Shea and Wilson, *The Illuminatus Trilogy.*

page   87   Kodak Autograph Mark II. Press camera of the
             '30s and '40s.

page   87   Surplus P-40. Israel built its air force of surplus
             P-51s, bought for $500 each, put in crates marked
             "tractor parts," sent to the docks at Jaffa, where a
             runway was built. The planes were assembled
             there and flown to airfields from shipside, a few
             weeks before Independence. The British looked
             the other way.

page   87   Lincoln Traynor. Link trainers were ground
             school dummy airplanes in which pilots trained
             for their instrument ratings. They maneuvered on
             three axes in response to the controls. Named for
             their developer.

page   88   Tomlin, Robert NMI. If you don't have a middle
             name, the Army puts NMN where it goes. No
             middle initial, they put NMI.

page   88   1200Z. Zulu Time. GMT, Greenwich Mean Time.

page   88   USAAF. At the start of the War it was USAAC,
             the Army Air Corps. In '44 or '45 it was changed
             to USAAF. On October 2, 1947, it became the US
             Air Force. (On that day in both the Army and the
             Air Force, all enlisted men were temporarily
             given the rank E-1, buck private: all officers 0-1,
             2nd looie, until both services decided how many
             of each rank they needed.)

page   88   . . . our records show . . . Orville Wright got his
             pilot's license in *1940*.

page   88   Clear Skies and Tailwinds. The way Robert O.
             Erisman, editor of *G-8 and His Battle Aces*, used
             to sign all his letters to Chad Oliver.

page   88   Arnold, H.H. Chief of Staff, Army Air Corps,
             WWII.

page   88   500 planes, 50 ships. The German *Stuka* pilot,
             Hans Rudel, had 367 planes and about 100 tanks
             to his credit when the war ended, mostly on the
             Eastern Front. And he only had one leg. (And he
             did most of his flying in a *Stuka*—by the end of
             the war, this was like going up against a P-47 in
             a Singer Sewing Machine.) Richard Bong, Amer-
             ica's Ace of Aces, had 40 planes to his credit,

mostly in the Pacific. He went through the war
without a scratch. He was killed in 1946 when the
jet he was testing had a flameout 20 feet above
the runway on takeoff.

page 88   Professor Silverbeg. Unless my brain was more
burned-out than I think before I stopped using
Nutrasweet, the names of some of the monks in
the monastery where the characters in *The Book
of Skulls* go in search of immortality are the same
as the monks who raised Airboy, in *Air Fighters
Comics*, during WWII.

page 89   Nazis and Italians and Whittle. The Germans had
an operational jet by 1939 and would have had the
ME-262 twin-engine jet fighter in *combat* by 1943
if Hitler wouldn't have been so *stupid*. He made
them strap a 500 kg bomb on them, slowing them
down by 100 mph. In the last days of the war the
Luftwaffe had three operational jets (ME-262, Arado
234, and HE-162—they were going to give 12-year-
old kids two weeks of glider training and then give
them the 600 mph jet to go after B-17s with), and
a rocket-powered interceptor, the ME-163. The Italians had the Caproni jet by 1939, the world's first
operational jet; like most things Italian, it burned
kerosene and flew about *half* as fast as a prop-
driven fighter. Whittle made almost all the British
jet engines. The Gloster Meteor was the only Allied
jet used in combat—but only over England against
V-1 buzz bombs. We had the P-59 Airacomet and
the P-80 Shooting Star but neither saw combat. The
Japanese had two jets, both copies of German designs, the most promising of which made its test
flight August 8, 1945. No more *arigato*.

page 89   Six .30 cals. Standard armament for fighters in
1939. By 1945, most fighters had from six to
twelve .50 caliber machine guns plus one or more
20mm or 37mm cannons. The fun was *over*.

page 89   The Blue Network. NBC had to divide itself into
two radio networks due to an antitrust suit. They
were the Blue and the Red Networks. One later
became ABC.

page 89   Sanders to Pappenfuss to Volstad. Larry, Darryl
           and Darryl on the *Newhart Show*. Actually San-
           de*rson*, but never stop to check when things are
           going good.

page 89   Sox drop two to Cleveland. See Jean Shepherd, *In
           God We Trust—All Others Pay Cash*, Doubleday,
           1966.

page 89   RCAF . . . China against the Japs. The war started
           in '39, America got in on Dec. 8, 1941. Many
           people went over into Canada and joined the
           Canadian Air Force, or went to Britain. See *A
           Yank in the RAF, Captains of the Clouds*. The
           AVG, American Volunteer Group, better known
           as "The Flying Tigers" under General Claire
           Chennault, 1939—41. Like Jetboy, when the war
           started for the U.S., they were made members of
           the Air Corps. See *Flying Tigers, God Is My Co-
           Pilot*.

page 89   All-weather radar set. The Germans were the first
           to equip their nightfighters with radar, though the
           British had better ground-based ones, and some
           Neanderthal stuff in their Beauforts and Beau-
           fighters by 1940. Most common German night-
           fighters were converted ME-110s and Heinkel
           177s. By the end of the war, they had built a
           plane especially for nightfighting—the HE-219
           "Owl." So had we—the P-61 Black Widow.

page 90   Tricycle landing gear. The most advanced type.
           You'd be surprised how many WWII planes had
           two main gear under the wings, and a little bitty
           wheel, like off a red Radio Flyer wagon, under
           the tail.

page 90   Four 20mm cannon and a 75mm gun port. Heavy
           but not unknown armament. B-25 Mitchell bomb-
           ers were powered-up and converted to shipping
           attack planes, the A-25, in the Pacific. They car-
           ried eight .50-cals in the nose, four more on the
           fuselage, four in the wing roots, four in the top
           turret which could be fired forward, plus a 75mm
           cannon. That's twenty .50-cals and a howitzer
           pointing at you, as the Japanese Navy soon found

out. One stripped-down Japanese nightfighter, the Gekko, used against B-29s at the end of the war, carried a 90mm cannon. It only carried two shells. One was *quant suff.*

page 90   ... something to roast weenies on. The British referred to them as "toasting fork antennae."

page 91   A Lincoln and two Jacksons. $45.

page 91   Dr. Tod. German for death.

page 91   '46 Merc. If you had a '46 anything, you had money or a brother in the car business.

page 91   ... raise bees. Like Sherlock Holmes, in Sussex. See *The Art of Bee-Keeping, with some notes on the segregation of the queen.*

page 92   600 miles to intercept us. The American P-38s which shot down Admiral Yamamoto in '43 flew more than 1000 miles and came around the end of an island to find his plane flying less than 600 yards away.

page 92   ... glass-brick room divider. Once common, they went out of style, and now cost $20 each brick. In the '40s you couldn't give them away; they were considered Art Deco and old-fashioned for the Atomic Age.

page 93   Christopher Robin. Milne, in the RAF in the war, now runs a bookstore in England.

page 94   ... trying to catch some Lancasters ... Both sides played this game. We made daylight raids, the Brits and Germans night raids. Our nightfighters got in the formations as their bombers took off; they did the same for us.

page 94   Mrs. Heelis. Sawrey. Just like it says. Beatrix Potter died in the winter of '43.

page 95   ... modified zoot suit ... The zoot suit came in in '41, was the cause of riots in California in '41–'42. In March '42 the War Production Board declared them to be "counter-productive to the war effort" as they used too much material, especially the coats. They had been worn mostly by alienated youths, blacks and Chicanos. In '46 they had a short renaissance during the be-bop days. See the book *The Zoot-Suit Murders*, and the movies *Zoot Suit* and *1941.*

page 95   "It Ain't the Meat, It's the Motion." Any guy
            whistling this in 1946 had the wrong kind of
            friends. Listen to *Copulatin' Blues*, Yazoo Rec-
            ords.

page 95   Pine Barrens. See Wallace and Pumilia, *op cit*.
            The place looks just like I say it does.

page 95   ... nine-inch Dumonts ... Anyone looking at a
            nine-inch Dumont in 1946 is either a) rich, b) in
            a bar, c) in front of an appliance store, or knows
            someone who is.

page 96   "ghost rockets". A 1946 summer phenomenon in
            Sweden. Between the "foo fighters" seen in
            '44–'45 by Allied and Axis pilots, and Kenneth
            Arnold's 1947 "flying saucer" sighting, this was
            the big story. Attributed to Russians testing cap-
            tured V-2s. They weren't. Not over Sweden, any-
            way.

page 96   *Cosh Comics*. A comic book company of the
            Golden Age, invented for a fanzine hoax, *Jeddak*
            #6, 1965. Paul Moslander, Clint Bigglestone and
            Steve Perrin made most of it up. I drew the
            covers they "reprinted." A sleazy publisher, ac-
            cording to Moslander's article. We put ads in
            other fanzines for a year before the article ran—
            "Wanted! Cosh Comics, any, but especially
            Captain Cosh 1–6, 8, 10, 12–14! Will pay top
            dollar!" In 1965, you could get any comic book
            ever published, including *Action #1*, for less than
            $10.

page 96   Lowboy. I never realized there might be confu-
            sion caused by Jetboy talking to Lowboy. I
            thought the difference in the first three letters of
            their names would alert most readers.

page 96   Harry Langdon. Silent comedian. Big as Chaplin
            or Keaton. Sound and total artistic control ruined
            him. (Sound and lack of total artistic control did
            Keaton in.)

page 97   ... statement of ownership and circulation ...
            Once a year, in every comic book and magazine
            since 1876. These figures, like all, can be doc-
            tored, but you Go Up The River for that.

page 97   ... no more red except for blood. Things like this
            actually happened among the most gung-ho
            American businessmen, once they saw the Rus-
            sians were the Enemy. This is the year before the
            Hollywood Ten trial, and the year Richard
            Milhous Nixon was elected to Congress.

page 98   ... taking benzedrine and stuff. Read the inter-
            view with Harry Harrison, *Graphic Story Maga-
            zine #16*. Harrison was a comic book art director
            in the late '40s. He and his friends once did a
            52-page comic book—writing, art, covers, separa-
            tions, etc.—in 37 straight hours.

page 99   U.S.S. *Reluctant*. Cargo tub aboard which Ensign
            Pulver and Mr. Roberts served. Thomas Heggen,
            Mr. Roberts, 1948.

page 100   *Jetboy on Dinosaur Island*. See both George R.R.
            Martin's and Lew Shiner's stories and epilogue in
            Wild Cards!.

page 100   ... samurai ... 1100 A.D. A novel-within-a novel
            I was going to write once. British kid, Japanese
            POW, goes with Japanese soldiers to island cov-
            ered with dinosaur skeletons and rusty samurai
            armor. Find scroll, which they spend half the
            book translating. About soldiers, circa 1100 A.D.,
            assigned to take a princess out of danger, be-
            ing blown off course in the same Divine Wind
            that destroys the Chinese-Mongol fleet. Ended
            up on lost island fighting dinosaurs. I was youn-
            ger then. Then J.G. Ballard wrote *Empire of the
            Sun*.

page 100   ... up close and personal. Or as we would say
            today, he's an off-ramp on I-95.

page 101   Armadillo. Forty years ago their range was con-
            fined to the Southwest. Now that wolves and coy-
            otes have been killed, they are as far east as
            Florida, as far north as Tennessee and Missouri.
            They cross the Mississippi River by holding their
            breaths and walking on the bottom.

page 102   ... a dollar and a quarter. In the days before
            microchips, weather balloon radiosondes carried
            half a hardware store worth of electronics with

them, and the Weather Bureau used to pay this for
their recovery.

page 102   ... only five of them have ever been exploded.
Trinity Site, Alamagordo July 16, 1945. Hiroshima and Nagasaki, August '45. Able and Baker
tests, Operation Crossroads, South Pacific, summer 1946. Large scale open air tests didn't start
till the '50s.

page 104   ... something that is *plausible* to them ... If you
told Harry Truman and the Air Corps you were an
alien and were looking for a galactic Doomsday
weapon that could wipe out 90% of the people on
the planet, they wouldn't believe you. If you told
them you were a holdover Nazi in a new kind of
plane looking for one of Hitler's Secret Weapons,
you'd get their attention.

page 104   Ice cream. Einstein snuck off every day with two
FBI agents to have an ice cream cone in the sum-
mertime during the War.

page 104   ... book of memoirs. *The Jet-Propelled Boy*.
Never published in full. Excerpts in *Harper's
Magazine*, April 1947.

page 105   Historical Aircraft For Sale. The JB-1, with these
specs, should have those speeds, endurances, etc.
Underpowered by 1946 standards.

page 105   ... paper rationing was off. July 1945. If you
could find it, you could print on it.

page 105   *The Grasshopper Lies Heavy*. Philip K. Dick, *The
Man in the High Castle*, 1962.

page 105   *Growing Flowers by Candlelight in Hotel Rooms*,
Richard Brautigan, *The Abortion: A Romance*,
1966.

page 106   Thorkeld. *Dr. Cyclops*, by Will Garth (Henry
Kuttner), also movie, 1940. Actually, Thork*e*l, but
never stop to check when things are going good.

page 107   Port Elizabeth, North Carolina. The Navy anti-
submarine blimp patrol base for the East Coast in
WWII.

page 107   "Dewey was an admiral ..." and the others. See
Jump-Rope Rhymes, Aldridge, 1966.

page 108   G-2. Army or Air Force Intelligence.

page 108   TA-152. The Kurt TAnk-modified Folk-Wulf 190,
             with a longer fuselage, different prop and better
             engine. A booger.

page 108   Snap-roll. A tactic used on bombers by fighters
             on both sides. The Sperry ball belly turret was de-
             signed to discourage such rude behavior.

page 108   Wig-wagging. A last ditch tactic—it exposes the
             whole bomber rather than the back-end silhouette.
             You do it when you're down to just waist-
             gunners, the tail, top and belly turret gunners be-
             ing dead or out of ammo.

page 108   The whole middle of the fighter ... Stranger
             things happen. Two second looies I knew in 1971
             left for Vietnam. They were back a month later.
             "What happened?" "Well, we were out in a Huey
             gunship helicopter with rockets on it. We looked
             up and here came a MiG-19 in on us. I pushed
             all the buttons to lighten my load, rockets, ma-
             chine guns, and headed for the trees. We looked
             back and there was this parachute coming down.
             The MiG-19 pilot had run right into our rock-
             ets and shot himself down." They got Silver
             Stars.

page 108   ... not recognizing my plane. *Even* recognizing
             it. Gunners popped off at everything. Better safe
             than sorry. Spitfires and ME-109s looked a lot
             alike from the snout, or business, end. And the
             only jets in the air over Europe, except Jetboy's,
             were German.

page 108   My IFF code. *I*dentification *F*riend or *F*oe. These
             flashed a signal which changed every day. If you
             didn't flash the right one back, they fired at you.
             Better safe than sorry.

page 109   This year more people will fly on airliners ... a
             true statistic for 1946.

page 109   Spanky, Alfalfa, Buckwheat. The last *Our Gang*
             comedy was made in 1944.

page 109   *That Nazty Nuisance, Jive Junction.* Real.

page 110   *Murder, He Says.* Real, and great.

page 110   *It's in the Bag.* Remade as *The Twelve Chairs* by
             Mel Brooks, 1969.

page 110   PRC. Producers Releasing Company. A studio you rented in Gower Gulch.

page 110   The way the guys on the *Reluctant* talked . . . *Mister Rogers, op. cit.*

page 111   . . . rumors from Turkey. Truman concern during '46.

page 111   . . . plow . . . M-1 Garand. True.

page 112   Major Truman. One half a comic book writing/art team.

page 112   General Ostrander. The other half.

page 112   . . . he hated air-conditioning. True.

page 113   Tuesday afternoon, September 15, 1946. Actually, it was a Sunday, but I told Roger Zelazny two months before I began this story to make it a Tuesday. It's also my birthdate.

page 113   . . . nearly 60,000. Above the operational levels of most aircraft, and nearly all anti-aircraft artillery in 1946.

page 114   . . . the number 500. Five hundred feet above sea level.

page 115   P-51. The North American Mustang, the fastest prop-driven fighter of WWII, maybe ever. A *real* booger.

page 115   They're working on something. The Bell XS-1, the "Glamourous Glennis" in which Chuck Yeager broke the sound barrier in October of 1947. I once wrote a story in which Chuck Yeager was the first man on the Moon.

page 115   The Flying Wing. The XB-35 was a four-engine prop-job version, the world's first all wing bomber. The B-35 was modified by having four jet engines attached outboard on the wings. Then the all-jet version, the YB-49 was tested. Through Congressional and Defense Department graft and corruption, we adopted the B-36 instead. That's why when I looked up in the '50s I saw ugly half-jet, half-prop B-36s taking off from Carswell AFB, rather than the beautiful B-49s. George Pal, no slouch, had a B-49 drop the A-bomb on the Martians in *War of the Worlds*, 1953. See my "Love Comes for the YB-49," *Crawdaddy #7*, 1970.

page 115   Navy T-2 pressure suit. *The* space suit. It covered
            the body with all these Bozo rings made of latex
            and old tires. It had a real space helmet—you
            wore your oxygen mask and flying helmet inside.
            It probably weighed a zillion pounds, but it was
            on the cover of *every* sf magazine, at one time or
            another, in the 1950s.

page 116   Bronzino's *Venus, Cupid, Folly and Time*. Real
            hubba-hubba stuff in the late 1600s.

page 116   *chunder*. Listen to Men At Work, *Business As
            Usual*, "Down Under." Aussie for Return Lunch
            Ticket. Technicolor Yawn. Blowing Beets.

page 116   Clark Gable Command. After Carole Lombard
            died, Gable tried to get in combat. The Air Corps
            had him flying a desk. He raised so much com-
            motion they had to let him go on bombing mis-
            sions. Also see *Command Decision*, 1948.

page 116   Squadron Hodiak. John Hodiak, bad American
            actor. *Dragonfly Squadron*, 1953. *On the Thresh-
            old of Space*, 1956. The name of my first bicycle.
            See "Hodiak, Son of Battle," *Prism #1*, 1973.

page 117   . . . at least 500,000 cubic feet. Big for 1946.
            Small for 1986.

page 118   "Francis the Talking Cop." Dolph Sweet, in
            Francis Ford Coppola's *You're A Big Boy Now*,
            1967.

page 118   Sixth Avenue. Avenue of the Americas.

page 118   Army oughta be sued. This happened in the "Bat-
            tle for Los Angeles," late December 1941, when a
            fake air raid panicked the West Coast, and the air
            defense artillerymen got so jumpy they forgot to
            set the timers on their shells. Spielberg's *1941* is
            based on this real incident.

page 120   . . . bailout bottle . . . Not enough air, thoughtful-
            ly provided with early pressure suits. Usually
            strapped to the leg or back. It was to keep the
            suit inflated and you breathing long enough to
            get down to thicker air, or bail out before you
            passed out or underwent a decompression explo-
            sion (your blood boils up there from your body
            heat).

page 122   ... that high up ... serious trouble. At 50,000 feet your chute won't open right, but it will slow you down long enough for you to pass out before you hit air you can *breathe*. Also, it's cold up there—about −50°F.

page 123   Roscoe. A heater.

page 123   Packing heat. Carrying a roscoe.

page 123   Gat. A roscoe.

page 124   Lammed. Opting for the path of least Jetboy.

page 124   "I can't die yet ..." Larry Fine of the Three Stooges, in one of their 1946 shorts.

page 124   ... eight years to the day ... Wolfe died September 15, 1938, in Johns Hopkins in Baltimore.

page 125   Daniel Deck. Usually called Danny. See *All My Friends Are Going To Be Strangers*, Larry McMurtry, Simon and Schuster, 1972.

page 125   Verga. The rain that hangs down from clouds over deserts but evaporates before it hits the ground.

INTRODUCTION TO

HOOVER'S MEN

ONE of my favorite cultural icons is a fuzzy, blurry picture of a Felix the Cat statuette.

Great, Howard.

No. Really. And it has a lot to do with this story.

See. Ellen Datlow of *Omni* called me up one day. She was running another of those, what I refer to, as six-authors-for-a-buck deals.

Normally, *Omni* prints one or two nifty items of fiction per issue. Once a year, though, Ellen goes *meshuggeneh* and asks five or six writers for short-shorts on a common theme or topic. They write them, she buys them, they all come out in the issue of *Omni*, then the stories squeal like pigs as they disappear, because, generally, nobody pays attention. But Ellen keeps doing it, and damned if she wasn't asking *me* for one. The theme was urban fantasy.

Hot diggety damn.

Because I'd been wanting to write this story (well, you know, a story *like* this) for a long time. Now I had to do it. Oh, the research! Oh, the pains I went to! Some asshole university professor had checked out every copy of Erik Barnouw's *A Tower in Babel*, the definitive work on the subject up to the time, in this one-reactor burg. So I had to piece together stuff from everywhere: old magazines, books that had been out of print 40 years, like that. (The kind of stuff I really love.)

Anyway, I did it. Anybody who thinks writing any but the jokiest, or one-punch kind of short-short is easy is loco. The less you write, the more it should do.

I was living without a phone (or tv!) at the time, sending

139

stuff Express Mail. I did three revisions of this 1800 word story. It took a month and a half. I was broke. I was kiping pears off a neighbor's tree as one of my two meals of the day. (This was not some dim starving in a garret past, this was two years ago, folks.) Anyway, some pages got lost, and I had to borrow the $8.75 to mail two pages to *Omni*.

Finally everything was hunky-dory and I got paid. When the issue came out, I was in there with Daniel Pinkwater, Joyce Carol Oates, T. Coraghessan Boyle, Barry Malzberg and K.W. Jeter (what I refer to as hot-shit company).

In the meantime: you remember all the work I'd done researching this? Well, PBS did its tribute to TV, and a book was published called *The Race for Television*, which had exactly everything I'd needed to know, in one place. This has happened before. It will no doubt happen again.

Back to the Felix the Cat statue—it was an image sent out over what became NBC, in the mid-Twenties.

And did you know we had transatlantic television broadcasts two months before Lindbergh made his flight? I didn't think so.

What really went on in those days was weirder than anything I could ever come up with. I just changed it around to the way I would have liked it to have happened.

So here's a story for all those mad Russians, and guys in basements in Cleveland, and visionary Scots who knew what they wanted, but didn't *quite* know how to get it. . . .

HOOVER'S MEN

ON March 30, 1929, three weeks after Al Smith's Presidential inauguration, four gunmetal grey Fords were parked on a New Jersey road. On the tonneau top of each was a large silver loop antenna.

There were fifteen men in all—some inside the cars in their shirt-sleeves, earphones on their heads, the others sitting on the running boards or standing in stylish poses. All those outside wore dark blue or grey suits, hats and dark ties with small checks on them. Each had a bulge under one of his armpits.

It was dusk. On the horizon, two giant aerials stood two hundred feet high, with a long wire connecting them. They were in silhouette and here and there they blotted out one of the early stars. Back to the east lay the airglow of Greater Manhattan.

Men in the cars switched on their worklights. Outside the first car Carmody uncrossed his arms, opened his pocket watch, noted the time on his clipboard. "Six fifty-two. Start your logs," he said. Word passed down the line.

He reached in through the window, picked up the extra set of headphones next to Dalmas and listened in:

"This is station MAPA coming to you from Greater New Jersey with fifty thousand mighty watts of power. Now, to continue with *The Darkies' Hour* for all our listeners over in Harlem, is Oran 'Hot Lips' Page with his rendition of 'Blooey!' featuring Floyd 'Horsecollar' Williams on the alto saxophone . . ."

"Jesus," said Dalmas, looking at his dials. "The station's all over the band, blocking out everything from 750 to 1245. Nothin' else is getting through nowhere this side of Virginia!"

Carmody made a note on his clipboard pages.

• • •

"The engineer—that's Ma—said sorry we were off the air this afternoon for a few minutes but we blew out one of our heptodes, and you know how danged particular they can be. She says we'll get the kinks out of our new transmitter real soon.

"Don't forget—at 7:05 tonight, Madame Sosostris will be in to give the horoscopes and read the cards for all you listeners who've written her, enclosing your 25¢ handling fee, in the past week. . . ."

"Start the wire recorders," said Carmody.

"Remember to turn off your radio sets for five minutes just before 7 P.M. That's four minutes from now. First, we're going up to what, Ma?—two hundred and ninety thousand watts—in our continuin' effort to contact the planet Mars, then we'll be down to about three quarters of a watt with our antenna as a receiver in our brand new effort to make friends with the souls of the departed.

"Here, to end our Negro music broadcast for this evening are Louis 'Satchmo' Armstrong and Dwight 'Ike' Eisenhower with their instrumental 'Do You Know What It Means to Miss New Orleans?' Hang on, this one will really heat up your ballast tubes . . ."

Some of the sweetest horn and clarinet music Dalmas had ever heard came out of the earphones. He swayed in time to the music. Carmody looked at him. "Geez. You don't have to enjoy this stuff so much. We have a job to do." He checked his pocket watch again.

He turned to Mallory. "I want precise readings on everything. I want recordings from all four machines. Mr. Hoover doesn't want a judge throwing anything out on a technicality like with the KXR2Y thing. Understood?"

"Yeah, boss," said Mallory from the third car.

"Let's go, then," said Carmody.

Just then the sky lit up blue and green in a crackling halo that flickered back and forth between the aerials on the horizon.

"Yikes!" yelled Dalmas, throwing the earphones off. The sound coming out of them could be heard fifty feet away.

"EARTH CALLING MARS! EARTH CALLING MARS! THIS IS STATION MAPA, MA AND PA, CALLING MARS. HOWDY TO ALL OUR MARTIAN LISTENERS. COME SEE US!

"EARTH CALLING MARS . . ."

They burst through the locked station door. Small reception room, desk piled high with torn envelopes and stacks of quarters, a glass wall for viewing into the studio, locked power room to one side. A clock on the wall that said 7:07. There was a small speaker box and intercom on the viewer window.

An old woman was sitting at a table at a big star-webbed carbon mike with a shawl wrapped around her shoulders and a crystal ball in front of her. An old man stood nearby holding a sheaf of papers in his hand.

". . . and a listener writes Dear Madame Sosostris—"

Carmody went to the intercom and pushed down the button. He held up his badge. "United States Government, Federal Radio Agency, Radio Police!" he said.

They both looked up.

"Cheese it, Pa! The Feds!" said the woman, throwing off her shawl. She ran to the racks of glowing and humming pentodes on the far wall, throwing her arms wide as if to hide them from sight.

"Go arrest some bootleggers, G-Man!" yelled Pa.

"Not my jurisdiction. And Prohibition ends May 1st. You'd know that if you were fulfilling your responsibilities to keep the public informed . . ." said Carmody.

"See, ladies and gentlemen in radioland," yelled Pa into the microphone, "this is what happens to private enterprise in a totalitarian state! The airwaves belong to *anybody*! My great uncle invented radio—he did!—Marconi stole it from him in a swindle. Government interference! Orville Wright doesn't have a pilot's license! He invented flying. My family invented radio . . ."

". . . you are further charged with violation of nineteen sections of the Radio Act of 1929," said Carmody, continuing to read from the warrant. "First charge, operating an unlicensed station broadcasting on the AM band, a public resource. Second, interfering with the broadcast of licensed operations—"

"See, Mr. and Mrs. Radio Listener, what putting one man in charge of broadcasting does! Ma! Crank it up all the way!" Ma twisted some knobs. The sky outside the radio station turned blue and green again. Carmody's hair stood up, pushing his hat off his head. His arms tingled.

"SOS!" yelled Pa. "SOS! Help! Help! This is station MAPA. Get your guns! Meet us at the station! Show these Fascists we won't put up with—"

"We'll add sending a false distress call over the airwaves, incitement to riot and breach of the peace," said Carmody, pencilling on his notes, "having astrologers, clairvoyants and mediums in contravention of the Radio Act of 1929 . . ."

The first of the axes went through the studio door.

". . . use of the airwaves for a lottery." Carmody looked up. "Give yourselves up," he said. He watched while Ma and Pa ran around inside the control room, piling the meager furniture against the battered door. "Very well. Resisting arrest by duly authorized Federal agents. Unlawful variation in broadcast power—"

"Squeak! Squeak! Help!" said Pa. Dalmas had bludgeoned his way into the shrieking power room and threw all the breaker switches. Ma and Pa turned into frantic blurs as all the needles dropped to zero. The sky outside went New Jersey dark and Carmody's hair lay back down.

"Good," he said, still reading into the intercom. "Advertising prohibited articles and products over the public airwaves. Broadcast of obscene and suggestive material. Use of . . ."

The door gave up.

"Book 'em, Dalmas," he said.

"Two minutes, Mr. Hoover," said the floor manager. He waved his arms. In a soundproof room an engineer put his foot on a generator motor and yanked on the starter cord. Then he adjusted some knobs and gave an okay signal with a circle thumb and finger.

Hoover sat down at the bank of microphones in front of him. A four-by-eight-foot panel of photosensitive cells lowered into place in front of him. In a cutout portion in its center was a disk punched with holes. As the panel came down the disk began to spin faster and faster. The studio lights came up to blinding intensity. Hoover blinked, shielded his eyes.

Carmody and Mallory stood in the control room behind the engineers, the director and the station manager. Before them on the bank of knobs and lights was a two by three inch flickering screen filled with lines in which Mallory could barely make out Mr. Hoover. Carmody and the other chiefs had turned in their reports to Hoover an hour before.

"I never thought he'd take this job," said an engineer.

"Aw, Hoover's a public servant," said the director.

The STAND BY sign went off. Hoover arranged his papers.

ON THE AIR blazed in big red letters over the control booth. The announcer at his mikes at the side table said:

"Good evening, ladies and gentlemen. This is Station WRNY and it's 11 P.M. in New York City. Tonight, live via coast-to-coast hookup on all radio networks, the Canadian Broadcasting System, and through the television facilities of WIXA2 New York and W2JA4 Washington DC, we present a broadcast from the head of the new Federal Radio Agency concerning the future of the airwaves. Ladies and gentlemen of the United States and Canada, Mr. Hoover."

The greying, curly-haired gentleman looked into the whirling Nipkow disk with the new Sanabria interlaced pattern and pushed one of the microphones a little further from him.

"I come to you tonight as the new head of the Federal Radio Agency. After the recent elections, in which I lost the Presidency to Mr. Alfred Smith, I assumed that after eight years as your Secretary of Commerce under the last two administrations I would be asked to leave government service.

"Imagine my delight and surprise when Mr. Smith asked me to stay on, but in the new position of head of the Federal Radio Agency. If I may quote the President: 'Who knows more about *raddio* than you, Herbert? It's all in a *turrible* mess and I'd like you to straighten it out, once and for all.'

"Well, tonight, I'm taking your President's words to heart. As chief enforcement officer under the new and valuable Radio Act of 1929, I'm announcing the following:

"Today my agents closed down fourteen radio stations. Nine were violating the total letter of the law; five were, after repeated warnings, still violating its spirit. Tomorrow, six more will be closed down. This will end the most flagrant of our current airwave problems.

"As to the future," Hoover pushed back a white wisp of hair that had fallen over his forehead, "tomorrow I will begin meetings with representatives of the Republic of Mexico and see what can be done about establishing frequencies for their use. They were summarily ignored when Canada and the United States divided the airwaves in 1924."

The station manager leaned forward intently.

"If this means another division and realignment of the frequencies of existing stations, so be it," said Hoover.

The station manager slapped his hand to his forehead and shook it from side to side.

"Furthermore," said Hoover, "under powers given to me, I am ready to issue commercial radiovision/radio movie/ television licenses to any applicant who will conform to the seventy line, thirty frame format for monochrome . . ."

"He's gone *meshuggah*!" said the engineer. "*Nobody* uses that format!"

"Quiet," said Carmody. "Mr. Hoover's talking."

". . . or the one-forty line, sixty frame format for color transmission and reception, with the visual portion on the shortwave and the audio portion on the newly opened frequency modulated bandwidths."

"Aaiiii!!" yelled the station manager, running out of the booth toward the desk phone in the next office.

"He's *crazy*! Everybody's got a different system!" said the director.

"No doubt Mr. Hoover's in for some heat," said Mallory.

"To those who say radio-television is too primitive and experimental to allow regular commercial broadcasting, I say, *you're* the ones holding up progress. The time for review is *after* new and better methods are developed, not before. This or that rival concern have been for years trying to persuade the government to adopt *their* particular formats and methods."

He looked into the whirling lights, put down his papers. "I will say to the people of those concerns: Here is your format, like it or lump it."

Then he smiled. "For a wholesome and progressive future in America, dedicated to better broadcasting for the public

good, this is the head of your nation's Federal Radio Agency,
Herbert Hoover, saying goodnight. Good Night."

The STAND BY sign came back on. The blinding lights
went down and the disk slowed and stopped, then the whole
assembly was pulled back into the ceiling.

In the outer office the station manager was crying.

Mr. Hoover was still shaking hands when Carmody and
Mallory left.

Early tomorrow they had to take off for upstate New York.
There was a radio station there with an experimental-only license that was doing regular commercial broadcasts. It would
be a quiet shut-down, not at all like this evening's.

As they walked to the radio car, two cabs and a limo
swerved up to the curbing, missing them and each other by
inches. Doors swung open. Sarnoff jumped out of the NBC
Studebaker limo. He was in evening clothes. The head of
CBS was white as a sheet as he piled out of the cab throwing
money behind him. One of the vice-presidents of the Mutual
System got to the door before they did. There was almost a
fistfight.

There was a sound in the air like that of a small fan on a
nice spring day. Overhead the airship *Ticonderoga* was getting
a late start on its three-day journey to Los Angeles.

Mallory pulled away from the curb heading back to the hotel where Dalmas and the other agents were already asleep.
He reached forward to the dashboard, twisted a knob. A
glowing yellow light came on.

"Geez, I'm beat," said Carmody. "See if you can't get
something decent on the thing, okay?"

Nine years later, after his second heart attack and retire-
ment, Carmody was in his apartment. He was watching his favorite program, *The Clark Gable—Carole Lombard Show* on
his new Philco console color television set with the big 9″ ×
12″ screen.

He punched open the top of a Rhinegold with a church key,
foam running over onto his favorite chair. "Damn!" he said,
holding the beer up and sucking away the froth. He leaned
back. He now weighed 270 pounds.

Gable was unshaven; he'd apologized at the show's open-

ing; he'd come over from the set where they were filming
Margaret Mitchell's *Mules in Horse's Harnesses* to do the live
show. They'd just started a sketch with Lombard, carrying a
bunch of boxes marked *Anaconda Hat Co.*, asking Gable for
directions to some street.

Then the screen went black.

"Shit!" said Carmody, draining his beer.

"Ladies and Gentlemen," said an announcer, "we interrupt
our regularly-scheduled program to bring you a news bulletin
via trans-atlantic cable. Please stand by." A card saying
NEWS BULLETIN. ONE MOMENT PLEASE. came up
onscreen. Then there was a hum and a voice said "Okay!"

A face came onscreen, a reporter in a trench coat stepped
back from the camera holding a big mike in one hand.

"This morning, 3 A.M. Berlin Time, the Prime Minister of
Great Britain and the Chancellor of Germany seemed to have
reached an accord on the present crisis involving Germany's
demands in Austria." Past his shoulder there was movement,
flashbulbs went off like lightning. "Here they come," said the
newsman, turning. The cameras followed him, picking up
other television crews with their big new RCA/UFA all-
electronic cameras the size of doghouses trundling in for the
same shot.

Onscreen SA and SS men in their shiny coats and uniforms
pushed the reporters back and took up positions, machine
guns at ready, around the Chancellery steps.

Atop the steps the Prime Minister and the Führer, followed
by generals, aides and diplomats of both countries, stepped up
to a massed bank of microphones.

"Tonight," said the Prime Minister of Great Britain, "I have
been reassured, again and again, by the Chancellor, that the
document we have signed," he held up a white piece of paper
for the cameras, and more flashbulbs went off, causing him to
blink, "will be the last territorial demand of the German nation. This paper assures us of peace in our time."

Applause broke out from the massed N.S.D.A.P. crowds
with their banners, standards and pikes. The cameras slowly
focussed into a close-up view, while the crowd chanted, *Seig
Heil! Seig Heil!*, of Herr Hitler's beaming face.

"Bastid!" yelled Carmody and threw the empty beer can
ricocheting off the console cabinet.

A few minutes later, after the network assured viewers it would cover live any further late-breaking news from Berlin, they went back to the show.

There were lots of wrecked hats on the street set, and Gable was jumping up and down on one.

Lombard broke up about something, turned away from him, laughing. Then she turned back, eyes bright, back in character.

"Geez, that Gable . . ." said Carmody. "What a lucky bastid!"

DO YA, DO YA, WANNA DANCE?

AH, the Sixties.

No, they were not better than any other time to have been young. Everything that happened has now been accepted into the folk mythos (along with the Hook story and the chicken-footed Disco dancer) whether it was true or not. Something *did* happen, as surely as something happened in Europe in 1848 (I'm going to write that story eventually, too). I think there were about 15 seconds there when it could have all been different. (The Sixties started at noon on November 22, 1963 and ended at noon on August 9, 1974, for those who have forgotten.)

But I don't want to get ahead of myself.

See, at one time there was going to be an SF Rock and Roll anthology edited by Gardner Dozois. But then, nobody wanted it. (Since then, there's been a Japanese SF R 'n' R anthology and a German, for godsakes SF R 'n' R anthology—I've got two stories in each of them.) I was going to do an original for Gardner's anthology, instead of letting him pick up one of the four or five other rock and roll SF stories I've done.

Is *this* it? I don't know, because there's no anthology, yet there's this story. My other rock and roll SF stories aren't *about* the Sixties (or Fifties), but this one is. If there are other rock and roll stories in my future, they won't be about the Sixties, either, they'll be about rock and roll.

(And while we're at it, someone really should publish Brad Denton's *Buddy Holly is Alive and Well on Ganymede*.)

This is my final word on the Sixties.

All I remember about the writing was borrowing Pat Cadigan's room key at Armadillocon in 1987, and going up

151

there between other panels, and writing the last half like a silly fool in the three hours before I *had* to read it at 3 P.M.

Well, I read it and everybody went apeshit. That's about as good as criticism gets.

Both Gardner and Ellen Datlow wanted it on the spot; it was too long for *Omni*, so Gardner got it, and it appeared in *Asimov*'s less than seven months after it was written.

Yow.

It was reprinted in the *Best SF of the Year*. It was up for the usual awards, plus some others, and it lost them all. This story means a lot more to me than the length of this intro makes it seem, so I'll leave it at that.

If you want more about the Sixties, go bug somebody else.

DO YA, DO YA,
WANNA DANCE?

THE light was so bad in the bar that everyone there looked like they had been painted by Thomas Hart Benton, or carved from dirty bars of soap with rusty spoons.

"Frank! Frank!" the patrons yelled, like for Norm on *Cheers* before they canceled it.

"No need to stand," I said. I went to the table where Barb, Bob, and Penny sat. Carole the waitress brought over a Ballantine Ale in a can, no glass.

"How y'all?" I asked my three friends. I seemed *not* to have interrupted a conversation.

"I feel like six pounds of monkey shit," said Bob, who had once been tall and thin and was now tall and fat.

"My mother's at it again," said Penny. Her nails looked like they had been done by Mungo of Hollywood, her eyes were like pissholes in a snowbank.

"Jim went back to Angela," said Barb.

I stared down at the table with them for five or six minutes. The music over the speakers was "Wonderful World, Beautiful People" by Johnny Nash. We usually came to this bar because it had a good jukebox that livelied us up.

"So," said Barb, looking up at me. "I hear you're going to be a tour guide for the reunion."

There are terrible disasters in history, and there are always great catastrophes just waiting to happen.

But the greatest one of all, the thing time's been holding its breath for, the *capo de tutti capo* of impending disasters, was going to happen this coming weekend.

Like the *Titanic* steaming for its chunk of polar ice, like the *Hindenberg* looking for its Lakehurst, like the guy at

153

Chernobyl wondering what *that* switch would do, it was inevitable, inexorable, a psychic juggernaut.

The Class of '69 was having its twentieth high school reunion.

And what they were coming back to was no longer even a high school—it had been phased out in a magnet school program in '74. The building had been taken over by the community college.

The most radical graduating class in the history of American secondary education, had, like all the ideals it once held, no real place to go.

Things were to start Saturday morning with a tour of the old building, then a picnic in the afternoon in the city park where everyone used to get stoned and lie around all weekend, then a dance that night in what used to be the fanciest downtown hotel a few blocks from the state capitol.

That was the reunion Barb was talking about.

"I found the concept of the high school no longer being there so existential that I offered to help out," I said. "Olin Sweetwater called me a couple of months ago—"

"Olin Sweetwater? Olin *Sweetwater*!" said Penny. "Geez! I haven't heard that name in the whole damn twenty years." She held onto the table with both hands. "I think I'm having a drug flashback!"

"Yeah, Olin. Lives in Dallas now. Runs an insurance agency. He got my name from somebody I built some bookcases for a couple of years ago. Anyway, asked if I'd be one of the guides on the tour Saturday morning—you know, point out stuff to husbands and wives and kids, people who weren't there."

I didn't know if I should go on.

Bob was looking at me, waiting.

"Well, Olin got me in touch with Jamie Lee Johnson—Jamie Lee Something hyphen Something now, none of them Johnson. She's the entertainment chairman, in charge of the dance. I made a couple of tapes for her."

I don't have much, but I do have a huge bunch of Original Oldies, Greatest Hits albums and other garage sale wonders. Lots of people know it and call me once or twice a year to make dance tapes for their parties.

"Oh, you'll like this," I said, waving to Carole to bring me another Ballantine Ale. "She said, 'Spring for some Maxell tapes, not the usual four for eighty-nine cents kind I hear you buy at Revco.' Where you think she could have heard about that?"

"From me," said Barb. "She called me a month ago, too." She smiled a little.

"Come on, Barb," I said. "Spill it."

"Well, I wanted to—"

"I'm not going," said Penny.

We all looked at her.

"Okay. Your protest has been noted and filed. Now start looking for your granny dress and your walnut shell beads," I said.

"Why should I go back?" said Penny. "High school was shit. None of *us* had any fun there, we were all toads. Sure, things got a little exciting, but you could have been on top of Mount Baldy in Colorado in the late Sixties and it would have been exciting. Why should I go see a bunch of jerks making fools of themselves trying to recapture some, some *image* of themselves another whole time and place?"

"Oh," said Bob, readjusting his gimme hat, "you really should hang around jerks more often."

"And why's that, Bob?" asked Penny, peeling the label from her Lone Star.

" 'Cause if you watch them long enough," said Bob, "you'll realize that jerks are capable of *anything*."

Bob's the kind of guy who holds people's destinies in his hands and they never realize it. When someone does something especially stupid and life-threatening in traffic, Bob doesn't honk his horn or scream or shake his fist.

He follows them. Either to where they're going, or the city limits, whichever comes first. If they go to work, or shopping, he makes his move then. If they go to a residence, he jots down the make, model and license plate of the car on a notepad he keeps on his dashboard, and comes back later that night.

Bob has two stacks of bumper stickers in the glove compartment of his truck. He takes one from each.

He goes to the vehicle of the person who has put his life

personally in jeopardy, and he slaps one of the stickers on the left front bumper and one on the right rear.

The one on the back says SPICS AND NIGGERS OUT OF THE U.S.!

The one he puts on the front reads KILL A COP TODAY!

He goes through about fifty pairs of stickers a year. He's self-employed, so he writes the printing costs off on his Schedule A as "Depreciation."

Penny looked at Bob a little longer. "Okay. You've convinced me," she said. "Are you happy?"

"No," said Bob, turning in his chair. "Tell us whatever it is that'll make us happy, Barb."

"The guys are going to play."

Just *the guys*. No names. No *what guys*? We all knew. I had never before in my life seen Bob's jaw drop. Now I have.

The guys.

Craig Beausoliel. Morey Morkheim. Abram Cassuth. Andru Esposito. Or, taking them in order of their various band names from junior high on: Four Guys in a Dodge. Two Jews, A Wop and A Frog. The Hurtz Bros. (Pervo, Devo, Sado, and Twisto). The Bug-Eyed Weasels. Those were when they were local, when they played Yud's, the Vulcan Gas Company, Tod's Hi-Spot. Then they got a record label and went national just after high school.

You knew them as *Distressed Flag Sale*.

That was the title of their first album (subtitled *For Sale Cheap One Country Inquire 1600 Pennsylvania Avenue*). You probably knew it as the blue-cake-with-the-white-stars-on-the-table-with-the-red-stripes-formed-on-the-white-floor-by-the-blood-running-in-seven-rivulets-from-the-dead-G.I." album.

Their second and last was *NEXT!* with the famous photo of the Saigon police chief blowing the brains out of the suspected VC in the checked shirt during the Tet Offensive of 1968, only over the general's face they'd substituted Nixon's, and over the VC's, Howdy Doody's.

Then of course came the seclusion for six months, then the famous concert/riot/bust in Miami in 1970 that put an end to the band pretty much as a functioning human organization.

Morey Morkheim tried a comeback after his time in the
juzgado, in the mid-Seventies, as Moe in Moe and the Mean-
ies' *Suck My Buttons*, but it wasn't a very good album and the
times were *already* wrong.

"I can't believe it," said Penny. "None of them have played
in what, fifteen years? They probably'll sound like shit."
"Well, I'll tell you what I know," said Barb. "Jamie Lee—
Younts-Fulton is the name, Frank—said after his jail term and
the try at the comeback, Morey threw it all over and moved
down to Corpus where his aunt was in the hotel business or
something, and he opened a souvenir shop, a whole bunch of
'em eventually, called Morey's Mementoes. Got pretty rich at
it supposedly, though you can never tell, especially from
Jamie Lee—I mean, anyone, *anyone* who'd take as part of her
second married name a hyphenated name from her *first* husband that was later convicted of mail fraud just because
Younts is more sophisticated than Johnson—Johnson-Fulton
sounds like an 1830 politician from Tennessee, know what I
mean?— you just can't trust about things like who's rich and
who's not. Anyway, Morey was at some convention for sea-
shell brokers or something—Jamie says about half the shells
and junk sold in Corpus come from Japan and Taiwan—he
ran into Andru, of all people, who was in the freight business!
Like, Morey had been getting shells from this shipping company for ten years and it turns out to belong to Andru's uncle
or brother-in-law or something! So they start writing to each
other, then somehow (maybe it was from Bridget, you remember Bridget? From UT? Yeah.) she knew where Abram
was, and about that time the people putting all this reunion together got ahold of Andru. So the only thing left to do was
find Craig."
She looked around. It was the longest I'd ever heard Barb
talk in my life.
"You know where he was?"
"No. Where?" we all three said.
"Ever eat any Dr. Healthy's Nut-Crunch Bread?"
"A loaf a day," said Bob, patting his stomach.
"Craig is Dr. Healthy."
"Shit!" said Bob. "Isn't that stuff baked in Georgetown?"
"Yeah. He's been like thirty miles away for fifteen years,

baking bread and sweet rolls. Jamie said, like some modern-day Cactus Jack Garner, he vowed never to go south of the San Gabriel River again."

"But now he is?"

"Yep. Supposedly. Andru's gonna fly down to Morey's in Corpus this week and they're going to practice before they come up here. Abram always was the quickest study and the only real musical genius, so he'll be okay."

"That only leaves one question," said Penny, speaking for us all. "Can Craig still sing? Can Craig still *play*? I mean, look what happened after the Miami thing."

"Good question," said Bob. "I suppose we'll all find out in a big hurry Saturday night. Besides," he said, looking over at me, "we always got your tapes."

The name's Frank Bledsoe. I'm pushing forty, which is exercise enough.

I do lots of odd stuff for a living—a little woodwork and carpentry, mostly speakers and bookcases. I help people move a lot. In Austin, if you have a pickup, you have friends for life.

What I mostly do is build flyrods. I make two kinds—a 7′ one for a #5 line and an 8′ 2″ one for a #6 line. I get the fiberglass blanks from a place in Ohio, and the components like cork grips, reel seats, guides, tips and ferrules, from whoever's having a sale around the country.

I sell a few to a fishing tackle store downtown. The seven-footer retails for $22, the other for $27.50. Each rod takes about three hours of work, a day for the drying time on the varnish on the wraps. So you can see my hourly rate isn't too swell.

I live in a place about the size of your average bathroom in a real person's house. But it's quiet, it's on a cul-de-sac, and there's a converted horse stable out back I use for my workshop.

What keeps me in business is that people around the country order a few custom made rods each year, for which I charge a little more.

Here's a dichotomy: as flyfishing becomes more popular, my business falls off.

That's because, like everything else in these postmodernist

times, the Yups ruined it. As with every other recreation, they confuse the sport with the equipment.

Flyfishing is growing with them because it's a very status thing. When the Yups found it, all they wanted to do was be seen on the rivers and lakes with a six hundred dollar split-bamboo rod, a pair of two hundred dollar waders, a hundred dollar vest, shirts with a million zippers on them, a seventy-five dollar tweed hat, and a patch from a flyfishing school that showed they'd paid one thousand dollars to learn how to put out enough fly line to reach across the average K-Mart parking lot.

What I make is cheap fiberglass rods, not even boron or graphite. No glamour. And the real fact is that in flyfishing, most fish are caught within twenty feet of your boots. No glory there, either.

So the sport grows, and money comes in more and more slowly.

All this talk about the reunion has made me positively reflective. So let me put 1969 in perspective for you.

Richard Milhous Nixon was in his first year in office. He'd inherited all the good things from Lyndon Johnson—the social programs—and was dismantling them, and going ahead with all the bad ones, like the War in Nam. The Viet Cong and NVA were killing one hundred Americans a week, according to the Pentagon, and we were killing two thousand of them, regular as clockwork, as announced at the 5 P.M. press briefing in Saigon every Friday. The draft call was fifty thousand a month.

The Beatles released *Abbey Road* late in the year. At the end of the summer we graduated there was something called the Woodstock Festival of Peace and Music; in December there would be the disaster at the Altamont racetrack (in which, if you saw the movie that came out the next year, you could see a Hell's Angel with a knife kill a black man with a gun on camera while all around people were freaking out on bad acid and Mick Jagger, up there trying to sing, was saying, "Brothers and sisters, why are we fighting each other?"). On the nights of August 8 and 9 were the Tate-LaBianca murders in L.A. (Charles Manson had said to his people "Kill everybody at Terry Melcher's house," not knowing Terry had moved. Terry Melcher was Doris Day's son. Chuck thought Terry owed him some money or had reneged on a recording deal or something. When he realized what he'd done, he had them go out and kill some total strangers to make the murders at the Tate household look like the work of a kill-the-rich cult.) On December 17, Tiny Tim married Miss Vickie on the *Tonight Show*, with Johnny Carson as best man.

The Weathermen, the Black Panthers and, according to agents' reports, "frizzy-haired women of a radical organization called NOW," were disturbing the increasingly senile sleep of J. Edgar Hoover of the FBI. He longed for the days when you could shoot criminals down in the streets like dogs and have them buried in handcuffs, when all the issues were clear-cut. Spirotis T. Agnew, the vice-president, was gearing up to make his "nattering nabobs of negativism" speech, and to coin the term Silent Majority. This was four years before he made the most moving and eloquent speech in his life which went: *"Nolo contendere."*

We were reading Vonnegut's *Slaughterhouse-Five*, or re-reading *The Hobbit* for the zillionth time, or Brautigan's *In Watermelon Sugar*. And on everybody's lips were the words of Nietzsche's Zarathustra: That which does not kill us makes us stronger. (Nixon was working on that, too.)

There were weeks when you thought nothing was ever going to change, there was no wonderment anymore, just new horrors about the War, government repression, drugs. (They were handing out life sentences for the possession of a single joint in some places that year.)

Then, in three days, from three total strangers, you'd hear the Alaska vacation—Flannel Shirt—last man killed by an active volcano story, all the people *swearing* they'd heard the story from the kid in the flannel shirt himself, and you'd say, yeah, the world is *still* magic....

I'll really put 1969 in a nutshell for you. There are six of you sharing a three-bedroom house that fall, and you're splitting rent you think is exorbitant, $89.75 a month. Minimum wage was $1.35 an hour, and none of you even has any of *that*.

Somebody gets some money from somewhere, God knows, and you're all going to pile into the VW Microbus which is painted green, orange, and fuschia, and going to the H.E.B. to score some food. But first, since there are usually hassles, you all decide to smoke all the grass in the house, about three lids' worth.

When you get to the store you split up to get food, and are to meet at checkout lane number three in twenty minutes. An hour later you pool the five shopping carts and here's what you have:

Seven two-pound bags of lemon drops. Three bags of orange marsh-mallow goobers. A Hostess Ding-Dong assortment pack. A twelve-pound bag of Kokuho Rose New Variety Rice. A two-pound can of Beer-Nuts. A fifty-foot length of black shoestring licorice. Three six-packs of Barq's Root Beer. Two quarts of fresh strawberries and a pint of Half and Half. A Kellogg's Snak-Pak (heavy on the Frosted Flakes). A five-pound bag of turbinado sugar. Two one-pound bags of Bazooka Joe bubble gum (with double comics.) A blue 75-watt light bulb.

It fills up three dubl/bags and the bill comes to $8.39, the last seventy-four cents of which you pay the clerk in pennies.

Later, when somebody finally cooks again, everybody yells, "Shit! Rice again? Didn't we just go to the grocery store?"

PS: On July 20 that year we landed on the Moon.

Now I'll tell you about this year, 1989.

The Republicans are in the tenth month of their new Presidency, naturally. After Cuomo and Iacocco refused to run, the Democrats, like always, ran two old warhorses who quit thinking along about 1962. ("If nominated, I refuse to run," said Iacocco, "if elected, I refuse to serve. And that's a promise.")

We have six thousand military advisors in Honduras and Costa Rica. All those guys who went down to the post office and signed their Selective Service postcards are beginning to look a little grey around the gills.

There are 1,800,000 cases of AIDS in America, and 120,000 have died of it.

On Wall Street the Dow Jones just passed the 2000 mark after its near-suicide in '87. "Things are looking just great!" says the new President.

Congress is voting on the new two trillion dollar debt ceiling limit.

Things are much like they have been forever. The rich are richer, the poor poorer, the middle class has no choices. The cities are taxing them to death, the suburbs can't hold them. Every state but those in the Bible-belt South has horse *and* dog racing, a lottery, legalized parimutuel Bingo *and* a state income tax, and they're still going broke.

Everything is wrong everywhere. The only good thing I've noticed is that MTV is off the air.

You go to the grocery store and get a pound of bananas, a six foot electric extension cord, a can of powder scent air freshener, a tube of store-brand toothpaste and a loaf of bread. It fits in the smallest plastic sack they have and costs $7.82.

Let me put 1989 in another nutshell for you:

A friend of mine keeps his record albums (his CDs are elsewhere) in what looks like a haphazard stack of orange crates in one corner of his living room.

They're not orange crates. What he did was get a sculptor friend of his to make them. He got some lengths of stainless steel, welded and shaped them to look like a haphazard stack of crates. Then with punches and chisels and embossing tools the sculptor made the metal look like grained unseasoned wood, and then painted them, labels and all, to look like crates.

You can't tell them from the real things, and my friend only paid three thousand dollars for them.

Or to put it another way: And Zarathustra came down from the hills unto the cities of men. And Zarathustra spake unto them, and what he said to them was: "Yo!"

PS: Nobody's been to the Moon in sixteen years.

MY TRIP TO THE POST OFFICE
by FRANK BLEDSOE, AGE 38

I'd finished three rods for a guy in Colorado the day before. I put the clothes back on I'd worn working on them, all dotted with varnish. I was building a bookcase, too, so I hit it a few licks with a block plane to get my blood going in the early morning.

It was a nice crisp fall day, so I decided to ride my bike to the post office substation to mail the rods. I was probably so covered with wood shavings I looked like a Cabbage Patch Kid that had been hit with a slug from a .45.

I brushed myself off, put the rods in their cloth bags, put the bags in the tubes with the packing paper, and put the tubes in the carrier I have on the bike. Then I rode off to the branch post office.

I'm coming out of the substation with the postage and insurance receipts in my hand when I hear a lot of brakes squealing and horns honking.

A lady in a white Volvo has managed to get past two One Way Do Not Enter signs at the exit to the parking lot and is coming in against the traffic, and all the angles of the diagonal parking places. She has a look of calm imperturbability on her face.

Nobody's looking for a car from her direction. As they back out, suddenly there she is in the rear-view mirror. They slam on their brakes and honk and yell.

"Asshole!" yells a guy who's killed his engine in a panic stop. She gets to the entrance of the lot, does a 290 degree turn, and pulls into the Reserved Handicapped spot at the front door, acing out the one-armed guy with the Disabled American Vets license plates who was waiting for the guy who was illegally parked against the yellow curbing in the entrance to move so he could get in.

She gets out of the car. She's wearing a silk blouse, a set of June Cleaver double-strand pearls and matching earrings, and a pair of those shorts that make the wearer look like they have a refrigerator stuffed down the back of them.

"Are you handicapped?" I ask.

She looks right through me. She's taking a yellow Attempt to Deliver slip out of her sharkskin purse. She has on shades.

"I said, are you handicapped? I don't see a sticker on your car."

"What business is it of yours?" she asks. "Besides, I'm only going to be in there a minute."

That's what you think. She goes inside. I shrug at the one-armed guy. With some people it was their own fault they went to Korea or Viet Nam and got their legs and stuff blown off, with others it wasn't.

He drives off down the packed lot. He probably won't find a space for a block.

I take my bike tools out of my pocket. I go to the Volvo. In deference to Bob, I undo the valve cores on the left front and right rear tires.

Then I get on my bike and ride down to the payphone at the bakery three blocks away, call the non-emergency police number, and tell them there's a lady without a handicap sticker blocking the reserve spot at the post office substation.

After mailing the rods and using the quarter for the phone, I have eighty-two cents left—just enough for coffee at the bakery. It's a chi-chi place I usually never go, but I haven't had any coffee this morning and I know they make a cup of Brazilian stuff that would bring Dwight D. Eisenhower back to life.

I go in. They've got one of those European doorchimes that sets poor people's nerves on edge and lets those with a heavy wallet know they're in a place where they can really drop a chunk of money.

The clerk is Indian or Paki; he's on the phone talking to someone. I start tapping my change on the counter looking around. Maybe ten people in the place. He hangs up and starts towards me.

"Large cuppa—" I start to say.

The chime jingles and the smell hits me at the same time as their voices; a mixture of Jovan Musk for Men and Sassoon styling mousse.

"—game," says a voice. "How many croissants you still got?" says the voice over my shoulder to the clerk.

The counterman has one hand on the coffee spigot and a sixteen ounce styrofoam cup in the other.

"Oh, very many, I think," he says to the voice behind me.

"Give us about—oh, what, John?—say, twenty-five assorted fruit-filled, no lemon, okay?"

The clerk starts to put down the styrofoam cup. In ambiguous situations, people always move toward the voice that sounds most like money.

"My coffee?" I say.

The clerk looks back and forth like he's just been dropped on the planet.

"Could you sort of hurry?" says the voice behind me. "We're double-parked."

I turn around then. There are three of them in warmup

outfits—gold and green, blue and orange, blue and silver. They look maybe twenty-five. Sure enough, there's a blue Renault blocking three cars parked at the laundromat next door. The handles of squash racquets stick up out of the blue and orange, blue and silver, gold and green duffles in the back seat.

"No lemon," says the blond-haired guy on the left. "Make sure there's no lemon, huh?"

"You gonna fill our order?" asks the first guy, who looks like he was raised in a meatloaf mold.

"No," I say. "First he's going to get my coffee, then he'll get your order."

They notice me for the first time then, suspicion dawning on them this wasn't covered in their Executive Assertiveness Training program.

The clerk is turning his head back and forth like a radar antenna.

"I thought they gave *free* coffee at the Salvation Army," says the blond guy, looking me up and down.

"Très, très amusant," I said.

"Are you going to fill our $35 order, or are you going to give him his big fifty cent cup of coffee?" asked the first guy.

The ten other people in the place were all frozen in whatever attitude they had been in when all this started. One woman actually had a donut halfway to her mouth and was watching, her eyes growing wider.

"My big seventy-five cent order," I said, letting the change clink on the glass countertop. "Any time you come in *any* place," I went on, "you should look around the room and you should ask yourself, who's the only *only* possible one here who could have taken Taiwanese mercenaries into Laos in 1968? And you should act accordingly."

"Who the fuck do you think *you* are?" asked the middle one, who hadn't spoken before and looked like he'd taken tae-kwon-do since he was four.

"Practically nobody," I said. "But if any of you say *one more word* before I get my coffee, I'm going out to the saddlebag on my bike, and I'm going to take out a product backed by 132 years of Connecticut Yankee know-how and fine American craftsmanship and I'm coming back in here and showing you *exactly* how the rat chews the cheese."

Then I gave them the Thousand Yard Stare, focusing on something about a half mile past the left shoulder of the guy in the middle.

They backed up, jangling the doorbell, out onto the sidewalk, bumping into a lady coming in with a load of wash.

"Crazy fuck," I heard one of them say as he climbed into the car. The tae-kwon-do guy kept looking at me as the driver cranked the car up. He said something to him, jumped around the car and started kicking the shit out of the back tire of the twelve-speed white Concord leaning against the telephone pole out front.

I heard people sucking in their breaths in the bakery.

The guy kicked the bike three times, watching me, breaking out the spokes in a half moon, laughing.

"My bike!" yelled a woman on one of the stools. "That's my bike! You assholes! Get their license number!" She ran outside.

I turned to the clerk, who had my cup of coffee ready. I plunked down eighty cents in nickels, dimes and pennies, and put two cents in the TIPS cup. Then I put saccharine and cream in the coffee.

Out on the sidewalk, the woman was screaming at the tae-kwon-do-looking guy, and she was crying. His two friends were talking to him in low voices and reaching for their billfolds. He looked like a little kid who'd broken a window in a sandlot ball game. People had come out of the grocery store across the street and were watching.

I got on my bike and rode to the corner unnoticed.

A cop car, lights flashing but with the siren off, turned toward the bakery as I turned out into the street.

It was only 9:15 A.M. It was looking to be a nice day.

I got two-and-three-fourths stars in the 1977 *Career Woman's Guide to Austin Men*. Here's the entry: "Working-class bozo, well-read. Great for a rainy Tuesday night when your regular feller is out of town. PS: You'll have to pick up all the tabs."

I'm still friends with about two-thirds of the women I've ever gone with, which I'm as proud of as anything else in my life, I guess. I care a lot, I'm fairly intelligent, and I have a sense of humor. You know, the doormat personality.

At one time, in those days before herpes and AIDS, when everybody was trying to figure out just who and what they were, I was sort of a Last Station of the Way for women who, in Bob's words, "were trying to decide whether to go nelly or not." They usually did anyway, more often than not with another old girlfriend of mine.

(It all started when I was dating the ex-wife of the guy that was then living with my ex-girlfriend. The lady who was then the ex-wife now lives with a nice lady who used to be married to another friend of mine. They each have tattoos on their left shoulders. One of them has a portrait of Karl Marx and under it the words *Hot to Trotsky*.

The other has the Harley-Davidson symbol but instead of the usual legend it says *Born to Read Hegel*.)

No one set out an agenda or anything for me to be their Last Guy on Earth. It just happened, and expanded outward like ripples on a pond.

About two months ago at a party some young kid was listening to a bunch of us old farts talk, and he asked me, "If the Sixties were so great, and the Eighties suck so bad, then what happened in the Seventies?"

"Well," I said. "Richard Nixon resigned, and then, and then . . . gee, I don't know."

Another woman I dated for a while had only one goal in life: to plant the red flag on the rubble of several prominent landmarks between Virginia and Maryland.

We used to be coming home from the dollar midnight flicks on campus (*Our Daily Bread, Sweet Movie, China Is Near*) and we would pass this neat old four-story hundred year old house, and every time, she would look up at it and say, "That's where I'm going to live after the Revolution."

I'm talking 1976 here, folks.

We'd gone out together five or six times, and we went back to her place and were going to bed together for the first time. We were necking, and she got up to go to the bathroom. "Get undressed," she said.

When she came back in, taking her sweater off over her head, I was naked in the bed with the sheets pulled up to my neck. I was wearing a Mao Tse Tung mask.

It was *wonderful*.

Friday. Reunion Eve.

It was one of those days when everything is wrong. All the work I started I messed up in some particularly stupid way. I started everything over twice. I gave up at 3 P.M.

Things didn't get any better. I tried TV. A blur of talking heads. Nothing interested me for more than thirty seconds.

Outside the sun was setting past Mt. Bonnell and Lake Austin. Over on Cat Mountain the red winks of the lights on the TV towers came on. A Continental 737 went over, heading towards California's golden climes.

I put on a music tape I'd made and tried to read a book. I got up and turned the noise off. It was too Sixties. I'd hear enough of that tomorrow night. No use setting myself up for a wallow in the good times and peaking too early. I drank a beer that tasted like kerosene. It was going to be a cool clear October night. I closed the windows and watched the moon come up over Manor, Texas.

The book was Leslie Fielder's *Love and Death in the American Novel*. I tried to read it some more and it began to go *yammer yammer yibble yibble* Twain, *yammer yibble* Hemingway. Enough.

I turned the music back on, put on the headphones and lay down on the only rug in the house, looking up at the cracks in the plaster and listening to the Moody Blues. What a loss of a day, but I was tired anyway. I went to bed at 9 P.M.

It was one of those nights when every change in the wind brings an erection, when every time you close your eyes you see penises and vulvas, a lot of them ones you haven't seen before. After staring up at the ceiling for an hour, I got up, got another beer, went into the living room and sat naked in the dark.

I had one of those feelings like I hadn't had in years. The kind your aunt told you she'd had the day your grandfather died, before anybody knew it yet. She told you at the funeral that three days before she'd felt wrong and irritable all day and didn't know why, until the phone rang with the news. The kind of feeling Phil Collins gets on "In the Air Tonight," a mood that builds and builds with no discernible cause.

It was a feeling like in a Raymond Chandler novel, the kind he blames on the Santa Ana winds, when all the dogs bark, when people get pissed off for no reason, when yelling at someone you love is easier than going on silently with the mood you have inside.

Only there were no howling dogs, no sound of fights from next door. Maybe it was just me. Maybe this reunion thing was getting to me more than I wanted it to.

Maybe it was just horniness. I went to the VCR, an old Beta II, second one they ever made, no scan, no timer, all metal, weighs 150 pounds, bought at Big State Pawn for fifty bucks, sometimes works and sometimes doesn't. I put in *Cum Shot Revue #1* and settled back in my favorite easy chair.

The TV going *kskksssss* woke me up at 4:32 A.M. I turned everything off. So this is what me and my whole generation came down to, people sleeping naked in front of their TVs with empty beer cans in their laps. It was too depressing to think about.

I made my way to bed, lay down, and had dreams. I don't remember anything about them, except that I didn't like them.

I've known three women that the latter part of the twentieth century has driven slapdab crazy.

For one, it was through no fault of her own. Certain chemicals were missing in her body. She broke up with me quietly after six months and checked herself into the MHMR. That was the last time I saw her.

She evidently came back through town about three years ago, *after* she quit taking her lithium. I got strange phone calls from old friends who had seen her. Her vision, and that of the one we call reality, no longer intersected. Having destroyed her present, she had begun to work on the past and the future also.

Last I heard she had run off with a cook she met at a Halfway House; they were rumored to be working Exxon barges together on the Mississippi River.

The second, after affairs with five real jerks in a row in six months, began to lose weight. She'd only been 111 pounds to begin with. People whispered about leukemia, cancer, some wasting disease. Of course it wasn't—in the rest of the world, dying by not getting enough to eat is a right, in America, it's a privilege. She began to look like sticks held together with a pair of kid's blue-jeans and a shirt, with only two brightly-glowing eyes watching you from the head to show she was still alive. She was fainting a lot by then.

One day Bob, who had been her lover six years before, went over to her house. (By then she was forgetting to do things like close and lock the doors, or turn on the lights at night.)

Bob picked her up by her shirt collar (it was easy, she only weighed 83 pounds by then) and slapped her, like in the movies, five times as hard as he could.

It was only on the fifth slap that her eyes came to life and filled with fear.

"Stop it, Gabriella," said Bob. "You're killing yourself." Then he kissed her on her bloody, swelling lips, set her down blinking, and walked out her door and her life, and hasn't seen her since.

He saved her. She met another nice woman at the eating disorder clinic. They now live in Westlake Hills, raising the other woman's two boys by her first marriage.

The third one's cat ran away one morning. She went back upstairs, wrote a long apologetic note to her mother, dialed 911 and told them where she was, hung up and drank most of an eleven-ounce can of Crystal Drano.

She lived on for six days in the hospital in a coma with no insides and a raging 107° fever.

Her friends kept checking, but the cat never came back.

"Yo!" said Olin Sweetwater. He and two or three others were standing outside the community college on the cool Saturday morning. He had on a sweatshirt, done up in the old school colors, that said Bull Goose Tour Guide. We shook hands (thumbs locked, sawing our arms back and forth). He was balding; what hair he had left had a white plume across the left side.

The two women, Angela Pardo and Rita Jones when I'd

known them, were nervous. Olin handed us sweatshirts that said Tour Guide. We thanked him.

I looked at the brick façade. The school had been an ugly dump in 1969; it was still a dump, but with a charm all its own.

(One of the reasons Olin asked me to help with the tour is that I'd lived with a lady artist for a year who had worked part-time as a clerk in the admissions office of the community college. I guess he thought that qualified me as an Expert.)

The tours were supposed to start at 10 A.M. Sleepy college students who had Saturday labs were wandering in and out of the two-and-a-half story building or some of the other out-buildings the college leased. Olin had pulled lots of strings to let us guide people without any interference, or so he kept telling us.

Around 9:45 people started wandering up, trailing kids, shy husbands, wives, lovers. God, I thought recognizing a few here and there. We're so fucking normal looking. We look like our mothers and fathers did in 1969.

(Remember in 1973 when you saw *American Graffiti* for the first time and everybody laughed at the short haircuts and long skirts, then when you went back to see it in 1981 those parts didn't seem so strange anymore?)

I was talking to one of the few women who'd been nice to me in high school, a quiet girl named Sharon, whose front teeth then had reminded me, sweetly and not at all unpleas-antly, of Rocket J. Squirrel's. She was now, I learned, on her second divorce. She introduced me to her kids—Seth and Jason—who looked like they'd rather be on Mars than here.

Sharon stopped talking and stared behind me. I saw other people turning and followed their gaze toward the street. "Je-sus," I said. A pink flowered VW Beetle pulled up to the curb as a student drove away. Out of it came something from Mr. Natural—the guy had hair down to his butthole (a wig, it turned out), headband, walnut shell beads, elephant bell pants with neon green flash panels, a khaki shirt and wool vest, Ben Franklin specs tinted Vick's Salve blue. There was a B-52 peace symbol button big as a dinner plate on his left abdo-men, and the vest had a leather stash pocket at the bottom snaps.

Something in the way he moves . . .

Seth and Jason were pointing and laughing, other people were looking embarrassed.

"Peace, Love, and Brotherhood," he said, flashing us the peace sign.

The voice. I knew it after twenty years. Hoyt Lawton.

Hoyt Lawton had been president of the fucking Key Club in 1969! He'd worn three-piece suits to school even on the days when he didn't *have* to go eat with the Rotarians! His hair was never more than three-eighths of an inch off his skull—we said he never got it cut, it just never grew. He won a bunch of money from something like the DAR for a speech he made at a Young Republicans convention on how all the hippies needed was a good stiff tour of duty in Vietnam that would show them what America was all about. Hoyt Lawton, what an asshole!

And yet, there he was, the only one with enough *chutzpah* to show up like we were all supposed to feel. Okay, I'm older and more tolerant now. Hoyt, you're still an asshole, but with a little style.

By about 10:10 there were a hundred people there. Excluding husbands, wives, Significant Others and kids, maybe sixty of the Class of '69 had taken the trouble to show up.

Olin divided us up so we wouldn't run into each other. I started my group of twenty or so (Hoyt was in Olin's group thank god) on the second floor. We climbed the stairs.

"You'll notice they have air-conditioning now?" I said. There were laughs. Austin hits ninety-five by April 20 most years. We'd sweltered through Septembers and died in Mays here, to the hum of ineffectual floor fans. The ceilings were twenty feet high and the ceiling fans might as well have been heat pumps.

"How many of you spent most of the last semester here?" I said, pointing. Two or three held up their hands. "This used to be the principal's office; now it's the copy center. Over there was Mr. Dix's office itself." Lots of people laughed then, probably hadn't thought of the carrot-headed principal since graduation day. He'd had it bad enough before someone heard him referred to as "Red" by the Superintendent of Schools one day.

"That used to be the only office that was air-conditioned,

remember? At least you could get cool while waiting to be yelled at." I pointed to the air-conditioning units.

That there air duct I didn't say *is the one that Morey Morkheim got into and took a big dump in one night after they'd expelled him one of those times*. Only in America is the penalty for skipping school expulsion for three days.

Mr. Dix had yelled at him after the absence. "What are you going to do with your life? You'll never amount to anything without an education!"

In seven months Morey was pulling in more money in a weekend than Dix would make in ten years, legally too.

We moved through the halls, getting curious stares from students in classrooms with closed glass doors.

"Down here was where the student newspaper office was. Over there was the library, which the community college is using as a library." We went down to the first floor.

"Ah, the cafeteria!" It was now the study room, full of chairs and tables and vending machines. "Remember tomato surprise! Remember macaroni and cheese!" "Fish lumps on Friday!" said someone.

Half the student body in those days had come from the parochial junior highs around town. In 1969, parochial was the way you spelled Catholic. Nobody in the school administration ever read a paper, evidently, so they hadn't learned that the Pope had done away with "going to hell on a meat rap" back in 1964. So you still had fish lumps on Friday when we were there. The only good thing about having all those Catholic kids there was that we got to hear their jokes for the first time, like what's God's phone number? ETcumspiri 220!

"Down there, way off to the left," I said, "was the band hall. You remember Mr. Stoat?" There were groans. "I thought so. Only musician I ever met who had *absolutely* no sense of rhythm."

Ah, the band hall. Where one morning a bunch of guys locked themselves in just before graduation, wired the intercom up to broadcast all over school, and played "Louie, Louie" on tubas, instead of the National Anthem, during home room period. It was too close to the end of school to expel them, so they didn't let them come to the commencement exercise. In protest of which, when they played "Pomp and Circumstance," about three hundred of us Did the Freddy down the aisles of the municipal auditorium in our graduation gowns.

We passed a door leading to the boiler room, where all the teachers popped in for a smoke between classes, it being forbidden for them to take a puff anywhere on school grounds but in the Teachers' Lounge during their off-hour.

I stopped and opened it—sure enough it was there, dimmed by twenty years and several attempts to paint over it, but in the remains of smudged-over day-glo orange paint on the top inside of the door it still said: *Ginny and Ray's Motel.*

Ginny Balducci and Ray Petro had come to school one morning ripped on acid and had wandered down to the boiler room and had taken their clothes off. My theory is that it was warm and nice and they wanted to feel the totality of the sensuous space. The school's theory, after they were interrupted by Coach Smetters, was that they had been Fornicating During Home Room Period, and without hall passes, too!

After Ginny came down, and while her father was screaming at Ray's parents across Dix's desk, she said to her father, "Leave them alone. They didn't have *their* clothes off!"

"Young lady," said Dix. "You don't seem to realize what serious trouble you're in."

"What are you going to do?" asked Ginny, looking the principal square in the eyes. "Castrate me?"

I answered some questions about the fire escape that used to be on the south side of the building. "They fell on a community college student one day four years ago," I said. "Good thing we never *had* to use them." We were outside again.

"Over there was the gym. World's worst dance floor, second worst basketball court. Enough sweat was spilled there over the years to float the *Big Mo*. We can't go in, though, they now use it to store visual aids for the Parks and Rec department."

There was the morning when Dix had us all go to the gym for Assembly. His purpose, it went on to appear after he had talked for ten minutes, was to try to explain why the Armed Forces recruiters would be there on Career Day, along with the realtors and college reps and Rotarians who would come to tell you about the wonders of their profession in the Great Big World Out There. (Some nasty posters had appeared on every bare inch of wall in the building that morning questioning not only their presence on Career Day but also their continuing existence on the third rock from the sun.)

He was going on about how they had been there, draft or no draft, war or no war, every Career Day when a small sound started at the back of the ranked bleachers. The sound of two stiffened index fingers drumming slowly but very deliberately dum-dum-thump dum-dum-thump. Then a few other sets of fingers joined in *dum-dum-thump dum-dum-thump*, at first background, then rising, louder and more insistent, then feet took it up, and it spread from section to section, while the teachers looked around wildly. Dum-Dum-Thump Dum-Dum-Thump.

Dix stopped in mid-sentence, mouth open, while the sound grew. He saw half the student body—the other half was silent, or like the jocks led by Hoyt Lawton, beginning to boo and hiss—rise to its feet clapping its hands and stamping its feet in time—

DUM DUM THUMP DUM DUM THUMP

He yelled at people and pointed, then he quit and his shoulders sagged. And on a hidden passed signal, everybody quit on the same beat and it was deathly silent in the gym. Then everybody sat back down.

I think Dix had seen the future that morning—Kent State, the Cambodian incursion, the cease fire, the end of Nixon, the fall of Saigon.

He dismissed us. The recruiters were there on Career Day, anyway.

I'd almost finished my tour. "One more place, not on the official stops," I said. I took them across the side street and down half a block.

"Oh wow!" said someone halfway there. "The Grindstone!"

We got there. It was a one-story place with real glass bricks across the whole front that would cost $80 a pop these days. The place was full of tools and cars.

"Oh, gee," said the people.

"It's now the Skill Shop," I said. "Went out of business in 1974, bought up by the city, leased by the community college."

Ah, The Grindstone! A real old-fashioned café/soda fountain. You were forbidden on pain of death to leave the school grounds except at lunch, so three thousand people tried to get in every day between 11:30 and 12:30.

One noon the place was packed. There was the usual riot going on over at UT ten blocks away. All morning you could hear sirens and dull *whoomps* as the increasingly senile police commissioner, who had been in office for thirty-four years, tried dealing with the increasingly complex late twentieth century. *Why, the children have gone mad,* he once said in a TV interview.

Anyway, we were all stuffing our faces in the Grindstone when this guy comes running in the front door and out the back at 200 miles an hour. Somebody made the obvious stoned joke—"Man, I thought he'd *never* leave!"—and then a patrol car slammed up to the curb, and a cop jumped out. You could see his mind work.

A. Rioter turns into the Grindstone. B. Grindstone is full of people. Therefore: C. Grindstone is full of rioters.

He opened the door, fired a tear-gas grenade right at the lunch counter, turned, got in his car and drove away.

People were barfing and gagging all over the place. There were screams, tears, rage. The Grindstone was closed for a week so they could rent some industrial fans and air it out. The city refused to pick up the tab. "The officer was in hot pursuit," said the police commissioner, "and acted within the confines of departmental guidelines." Case closed.

"Ah, The Grindstone," I said to the tour group. "What a *nice* place." A wave of nostalgia swept over me. "Today, shakes and fries. Tomorrow, a lube job and tune-up."

I was so filled with *mono no aware* that I skipped the picnic that afternoon.

The Wolfskill Hotel! Scene of a thousand-and-one nights' entertainments and more senior proms than there are fire ants in all the fields in Texas.

A friend of mine named Karen once said people were divided into two classes: those who went to their senior proms and went on to live fairly normal lives, and those who didn't, who became perverts, mass murderers or romance novelists.

If you were a guy you got maybe your first blow job after the prom, or if a girl a quick boff in the back seat of some immemorial Dodge convertible out at Lake Travis. The hotel meant excitement, adventure, magic.

I hadn't gone to my senior prom. A lot of us hadn't, looking on it as one more corrupt way to suck money from the working classes so that orchids could die all over the vast American night.

There were some street singers outside the hotel, playing jug band music without a jug—two guitars, a flute, tambourine and harmonica. They were fairly quiet. The cops wouldn't hassle them until after 11 P.M. They were pretty good. I dropped a quarter into their cigar box.

You could hear the strains of the Byrds' "Turn! Turn! Turn!" before you got through the lobby. The entertainment committee must have dropped a ton o'bucks on this—they had a bulletin board out front just past the registration table with everybody's pictures from the yearbook blown up, six to a sheet.

It was weird seeing all those people's names and faces—the beginnings of mustaches and beards on the guys, we'd fought tooth and nail for facial hair—long straight hair on the women—names that hadn't been used, or gone back to three or four times, in the last twenty years.

I paid my $10.00 fee (like in the old days. Dance Tonight! Guys fifty cents Girls Free!).

Inside the ballroom people were already dancing, maybe a hundred, with that many more standing around talking and laughing in knots and clumps, being polite to each other, sizing up what Time's Heedless Claws had done to each other's bodies and outlooks.

Bob and Penny were already there. He was in a bluejean jacket and pants and wore a clear plastic tie. Penny was stunning, in a green velour thing, beautiful as she always is early in the evenings, before alcohol turns her into a person I don't know.

I was real spiffed out, for me: a nice sport coat, black slacks, a red silk tie with painted roses wide as the racing stripe on a Corvette.

There were people there in $500 gowns, $300 suits, tuxes, jeans, coveralls. Several were in period costumes; Hoyt had on another, much better than this morning's nightmare, but still what I describe as Early Neil Young. He was, of course, with a slim blonde who had once been a Houston cheerleader, I'm sure.

I saw some faculty members there. They had all been invited, of course. Ten or so, with their husbands or wives, had come. Even Mr. Stoat was there. It hit me as I looked at them that most of them had been in their twenties and thirties when they were trying to deal with us on a daily basis, much younger than we were now. God, what a thankless job they must have had—going off everyday like going back up to the Front of WWI, trying to teach kids who viewed you as The Enemy, following along behind everything you did with the efficient erasers in their minds! Maybe I'm getting too mellow—they had it easier with us than teachers do now—at least most of us *could* read, and music was more important than TV to us. Later, I told myself, I'll go over and talk to Ms. Nugent who was always my favorite and who had been a good teacher in spite of the chaos around her.

There were two guys working the tapes and CDs up on the raised stage. I didn't recognize the order of the songs so knew they weren't playing one of my tapes. On the front part of the stage were a guitar and bass, a drum set and keyboards.

So it was true, and seemed the main topic of conversation, although as I passed one bunch of people I heard someone say, "Those assholes? Them?"

Barb showed up, without a date, of course. She took my hand and led me toward the dance floor. "Let's dance until our shoulders bleed," she said.

"Yes, ma'am!" I said.

I don't know about you, but I've been hypnotized on dance floors before. Sometimes it seems as if the tune stretches out to accommodate how long and hard you want to dance, or think you can. The guys working the decks were switching back and forth between two cassette players and the music never stopped—occasionally songs *only* I could have recorded showed up. I didn't care. I was dancing.

(I've seen some strange things on dance floors in my life— the strangest was people forming a conga line to a song by the band Reptilikus called "After Today, You Got One Less Day To Live.")

"Ginny's here," I said to Barb. Barb looked over toward the door where Ginny Balducci's wheelchair had rolled in. One weekend in 1973 Ginny had gone off for a ski weekend with an intern, and had come back out of the hospital six months later with a whole different life. "I'll say hi in a minute," said Barb.

We danced to the only Dylan song you can dance to, "I Want You," "Back in the U.S.S.R.," Buffalo Springfield, Blue Cheer, Sam and Dave, slow tunes by Jackie Wilson and Sam Cooke, then Barb went over to talk to Ginny. I was a sweating wreck by then, and the ugly feeling from the night before was all gone.

I started for the *whizzoir*.

"You won't like it," said a guy coming out of the men's room.

The smell hit me like a hammer. Someone had yelled New York into one of the five washbasins. It was half full. It appeared the person had lived exclusively for the last week on Dinty Moore Beef Stew and Fighting Cock Bourbon.

A janitor came in cursing as I was washing my hands.

I went back out to the ballroom. Mouse and the Trapps' "Public Execution" was playing—someone who doesn't *dance* recorded that. Then came Jackie Wilson's "Higher and Higher."

"Dance with me?" asked someone behind me. I turned. It was Sharon. She must have Gone Borneo that afternoon. She'd been somewhere where they do things to you, wonderful things. She had on a blue dress and seamed silk stockings, and now she had an Aunt Peg haircut.

"You bet your ass!" I said.

About halfway through the next dance, I suffered a real sense of loss. I missed my butthole-length hair for the first time in ten years. The song, of course, was "Hair" off the original Broadway cast recording, Diane Keaton and all, and Joe Morton's wife Patricia, who had never cut hers, it grew within inches of the floor, suddenly grabbed it near her skull with one hand and whipped it around and around her head, the ends fanning out like a giant hand across the colored lights above the stage. Joe continued his Avalon-ballroom-no-sweat dancing, oblivious to the applause his wife was getting.

Then, they played the Fish Cheer and we all sang and danced along with "I-Feel-Like-I'm-Fixin'-To-Die-Rag."

Then the lights came up and the entertainment director, Jamie Younts-Fulton came to the mike and treated us to twenty minutes of nostalgic boredom and forced yoks. The tension was building.

"Now," she said, "for those of you who don't know, we've got them together again for the first time in nineteen years, here they are, Craig Beausoliel, Morey Morkheim, Abram Cassuth and Andru Esposito, or, as you know them, *Distressed Flag Sale*!"

It was about what you'd expect—four guys in their late thirties in various pieces of clothing stretching across twenty years of fashion changes.

Morey'd put on weight and lost teeth, Andru had taken weight off. Abram, who'd been the only one without facial hair in our day, now had a full Jerry Garcia beard. Craig, who came out last, like always, and plugged in while we applauded—all four or five hundred people in the ballroom now—didn't look like the same guy at all. He looked like a businessman dressed up at Halloween to look like a rock singer.

He was a little unsteady on his feet. He was a little drunk.

"Enough of this Sixties crap!" he said. People applauded again. "Tonight, this first and last performance, we're calling ourselves *Lizard Level*!"

Then Abram hit the keyboard in the opening trill of "In-a-Gadda-da-Vida" for emphasis, then they slammed into "Proud Mary," Creedence's version, and the place became a blur of flying bodies, drumming feet, swirling clothes. The band started a little raggedly, then got it slowly together.

They launched into the Chambers Brothers' "Time Has Come Today," always a show stopper, a hard song for everybody *including* the Chamber Bros., if you ever saw them, and the place went really crazy, especially in the slow-motion parts. Then they did one of their own tunes, "The Moon's Your Harsh Mistress, Buddy, Not Mine," which I'd heard exactly once in two decades.

We were dancing, all kinds, pogo, no-sweat, skank, it didn't matter. I saw a few of the hotel staff standing in the doorways tapping their feet. Andru hit that screaming wail in the bass that was the band's trademark, sort of like a whale dying in your bathtub. People yelled, shook their arms over their heads.

Then they started to do "Soul Kitchen." Halfway through the opening, Craig raised his hand, shook it, stopped them.

"Awwww," we said, like when a film breaks in a theater.

Craig leaned toward the others. He was shaking his head. Morey pointed down at his playlist. They put their heads together. Craig and Abram were giving the other two chord changes or something.

"Hey! Make music!" yelled some jerk from the doorway.

Craig looked up, grabbed the mike. "Hold it right there, asshole," he said, becoming the Craig we had known twenty years ago for a second. He leaned against the mike stand in a Jim Morrison vamp pose. "You stay right here, you're going to hear the god-damnedest music you ever heard!"

They talked together for a minute now. Andru shrugged his shoulders, looked worried. Then they all nodded their heads.

Craig Beausoliel came back up front. "What we're gonna do now, what we're gonna do now, gonna do," he said in a Van Morrison post-Them chant, "is we're gonna do, gonna do, the song we were gonna do that night in Miami . . ."

"Oh, geez," said Bob, who was on the dance floor near Sharon and I.

Distressed Flag Sale had gone into seclusion early in 1970, holing up like The Band did in the *Basement Tapes* days with Dylan, or like Brian Wilson and the Beach Boys did while they were working on the never-finished *Smile* album. They were supposedly working on an album (we heard through the grapevine) called either *New Music for the After People* or *A Song to Change the World*, and there were supposedly heavy scenes there, lots of drugs, paranoia, jealousy, and revenge, but also great music. We never knew, because they came out of hiding to do the Miami concert to raise money for the family of a janitor blown up by mistake when somebody drove a car-bomb into an AFEES building one 4 A.M.

"It was a great song, man, a great song," said Craig. "It was going to change the world we thought." We realized for the first time how drunk Craig really was about then. "We were gonna play it that night, and the world was gonna change, but instead they got us, they *got us*, man, and we were the ones that got changed, not them. Tonight we're not Distressed Flag Sale, we're *Lizard Level*, and just once anyway, so you'll all know, tonight we're gonna do 'Life Is Like That.' "

(What changed in Miami was the next five years of their lives. The Miami cops had been holding the crowd back for three hours and looking for an excuse, anyway, and they got it, just after Distressed Flag Sale made its reeling way onstage. The crowd was already frenzied, and got up to dance when the guys started playing "Life Is Like That" and Andru took out his dong on the opening notes and started playing slide bass with it. The cops went crazy and jumped them, beat them up, planted heroin and amphetamines in their luggage in the dressing rooms, carted them off to jail and turned firehoses on the rioting fans.

Everybody knew the bust was rigged, because they charged Morey with possession of heroin, and everybody *knew* he was the speed freak.

And that was the end of Distressed Flag Sale.

It was almost literally the end of Andru, too. What the papers didn't tell you was that, as he was uncircumcised, he'd torn his frenum on the strings of the bass, and he almost lost, first, his dong, and then his life before the cops let a doctor in to see him.)

That's the history of the song we were going to hear.

Notes started from the keyboard, like it was going to be another Doors-type song, building. Then Craig moved his fingers a few times on the guitar strings, tinkling things rang up high, like birds were in the air over the stage, sort of like the opening of "Touch of Grey" by the Dead, but not like that either. Then Andru came in, and Morey, then it began to take on a shape and move on its own, like nothing else at all.

It moved. And it moved me, too. First I was swaying, then stomping my right foot. Sharon was pulling me toward the dance floor. I'd never heard anything like it. *This* was dance music. Sharon moved in large sways and swings; so did I.

The floor filled up fast. *Everybody* moved toward the music. Out of the corner of my eye I saw old Mr. Stoat asking someone to dance. Other teachers moved towards the sound.

Then I was too busy moving to notice much of anything. I was dancing, dancing not with myself but with Sharon, with Bob and Penny, with *everyone*.

All five hundred people danced. Ginny Balducci was at the corner of the floor, making her chair move in small tight graceful circles. I smiled. We all smiled.

The music got louder; not faster, but more insistent. The playing was superb, immaculate. *Lizard Level*'s hands moved like they were a bar band that had been playing together every night for twenty years. They seemed oblivious to everything, too, eyes closed, feet shuffling.

Something was happening on the floor, people were moving in little groups and circles, couples breaking off and shimmying down between the lines of the others, in little waggling dance steps. It was happening all over the place. Then *I* was doing it—like Sharon and I had choreographed every move. People were clapping their hands in time to the music. It sounded like steamrollers were being thrown around in the ballroom.

Above it the music kept building and building in an impossible spiral.

Now the hotel staff joined in, busboys clapping hands, maids and waitresses turning in circles.

Then the pattern of the dance changed, magically, instantly, it split the room right down the middle, and we were in two long interlocking linked chains of people, crossing through each other, one line moving up the room, the other down it, like it was choreographed.

And the guys kept playing, and more people were coming into the ballroom. People in pajamas or naked from their rooms, the night manager and the bellboys. And as they joined in and the lines got more unwieldy, the two lines of people broke into four, and we began to move toward the doors of the ballroom, clapping our hands, stomping, dancing, making our own music, the same music, more people and more people.

At some point they walked away from the stage, joining us, left their amps, acoustic now. Morey had a single drum and was beating it, you could hear Andru and Craig on bass and guitar, Cassuth was still playing the keyboard on the batteries, his speaker held under one arm.

The street musicians had come into the hotel and joined in, people were picking up trash cans from the lobby, garbage cans from the streets, honking the horns of their stopped cars in time to the beat of the music.

We were on the streets now. Windows in buildings opened, people climbed down from second stories to join in. The whole city jumped in time to the song, like in an old Fleischer cartoon; Betty Boop, Koko, Bimbo, the buses, the buildings, the moon swaying, the stars spinning on their centers like pinwheels.

Chains of bodies formed on every street, each block. At a certain beat they all broke and reformed into smaller ones that grew larger, interlocking helical ropes of dancers.

I was happy, happier than ever. We moved down one jumping chain of people. I saw mammoths, saber-toothed tigers, dinosaurs, salamanders, fish, insects, jellies in loops and swirls. Then came the beat and we were in the other chain, moving up the street, lost in the music, up the line of dancing people, beautiful fields, comets, nebulae, rockets and galaxies of calm light.

I smiled into Sharon's face, she smiled into mine.

Louder now the music, stronger, pulling at us like a wind. The cops joined in the dance.

Up Congress Avenue the legislators and government workers in special sessions came streaming out of their building like beautiful ants from a shining mound.

Louder now and happier, stronger, dancing, clapping, singing.

We will find our children or they will find us, before the dance is over, we can feel it. Or afterwards we will responsibly make more.

The chain broke again, and up the jumping streets we go,

joyous now, joy all over the place, twenty, thirty thousand people, more every second.

As we swirled and grew, we would sometimes pass someone who was staring, not dancing, feet not moving; they would be crying in uncontrollable sobs and shakes, and occasionally committing suicide.

INTRODUCTION TO

WILD, WILD HORSES

IF you've read my other collections (and, if I were Isaac Asimov, I would add here "and who has not?") you'll know I think introductions to each story are something nice you do for people who buy your short story collections even though they may have already read most of the stories (that's also why I try to put an original in every collection; even if they've read everything else, they ain't read *that*).

There's also the obverse of the coin, best summed up in the old phrase, "I suffered for my art, now it's *your* turn . . ." Especially when the story, as printed, gives no idea of the six or eight months of grief, screaming, black nights of the soul, pain and what Norman Mailer refers to as "marches on the liver" that writing a story can bring.

The genesis of this is easy enough: I was reading in the *Handbook to Latin Literature*, researching another whole topic (on the as-yet unwritten thing you may hear referred to in the coming years as "the Roman Playwright story") when I came across a sentence that stopped me dead.

Like with "He-We-Await" (the original in the previous Ursus collection), the story came to me in a flash; like it, I knew undoubtedly it would take me into areas I absolutely did not want to travel.

Usually when writers say that, they're referring to dark personal things, or late toilet training, or something. Not me, Boss. What I didn't want to do was deal with one of the most pernicious publishing marvels of this benighted age:

187

Fantasy.

I don't know what it is I write anymore than *you*, but I know what I *don't* write, and what I don't write (at least not since I was fifteen or sixteen) is Fantasy.

I'm talkin' 'bout elves and demons and orcs and sea-sprites and griffons and lost swords and rings and kelpies and harpies and all that shit. Fuck a leprechaun. How many times can people rewrite Tolkien? How many amnesiac princes do you want? How many puns can you put in a book? Who cares anymore?

(Evidently, the answer to these is: A lot!)

I get review books. Ninety-seven out of a hundred go *immédiatement* to the used bookstore where I trade 'em for books I *can* use. Because there's like three words I look for on the jacket—two of them are "kingdom" and "Empire"— that tell me all I need to know. I read the best of this stuff 30 years ago—that was all I needed.

Anyway, now here I am with an idea that needs one of the trappings of—gasp!—fantasy to work.

Luckily, coming with the idea was the time of its setting, which was an advantage, because I knew a lot about that.

So what did I try to do? I tried to approach this like I would have one I was writing about truck drivers (if I wrote about truck drivers), if you know what I mean.

In the original draft (as in the Jetboy story) there were six pages of stuff showing you just how weird the reign of Julian the Apostate was (the protagonist watches a fight between a Greek-speaking Monophysite and a Latin-speaking Nestorian broken up by a pagan ædile and two German Christian reservists, or whatever it is I say in the hurried version).

Everybody said it was brilliant; everybody said it didn't belong in the story. Okay, okay. *Chu Hoy!* Ellen Datlow bought it for *Omni*. I took out the six pages for Ellen. Now I'm putting them back in. Here they are. Tough beans.

A couple of things I know that you don't: one of the characters in here is Bob Hoskins. I'm built like Bob Hoskins. All the men in my family are. Any year that's good for Bob Hoskins is good for us.

And all the names, with the exception of the two main characters, are from the glossary to *Winnie Ille Pu*, Alexander Lenard's Latin version of the Milne book.

WILD, WILD HORSES

UP on the platform, Ambrose was preaching against the heathen, in Latin, to a crowd largely pagan who spoke only Greek.

The spectacle of a man wailing, cajoling, pleading and crying in another tongue had drawn a large gathering. "Go it, Roman!" some yelled encouragingly.

The man on the raised boards at the edge of the marketplace redoubled his efforts, becoming a fountain of tears, a blur of gesticulations, now here, now there. Such preaching they hadn't seen since the old days when the Christians had been an outlawed sect.

Then another man in the crowd yelled at the onlookers in Greek. "Listen not to him!" he said. "He's a patripassionist. He believes God Himself came down and took part in the suffering of Jesus Christ on the Cross! He denies the accepted Trinity of Father, Son, Holy Ghost! Come across the creek and hear the True Word, spoken by followers of the True Church. And in a language you can understand!"

With a snarl, Ambrose flung himself over the railing and onto the other Christian. There was a great flurry of dust, growling and coughs as they tore at each other's faces and clothing. The crowd egged them on; this was better than preaching anytime.

"What's all this, then?" asked an aedile, on his morning inspection of the roadways. He began beating with his staff of office at the center of the struggle until, with yelps of pain, the two men separated.

"Heretic!" shouted the second Christian.

"Whining Nicean dog!" yelled Ambrose.

With his staff the ædile rapped Ambrose smartly on the

head and poked the second man in the ribs in one smooth motion. Two of the local military reservists hurried up through the crowd.

"What's this, your honor?" they asked, grabbing the two panting men.

"Christians," he said. "Since the new emperor Julian let all the exiles and fragmented bishops return, there's been nothing but trouble, trouble, trouble with them. It would be fine if they killed each other in private, but they endanger decent gods-fearing folk with their idiotic schisms. They cause commotion in the reopened temples and trouble at public ceremonies."

"Quite right," said the reservists, who both wore fish symbols on chains around their necks. They each punched and slapped the man they held a few times for effect.

"Don't think it doesn't do my heart glad to see officers carrying out their civic duties in spite of their personal convictions," said the aedile. "There's hope for this empire yet."

"Sorry you had to deal with this, sir. We'll take care of them," said one of the reservists, saluting with his forearm across his chest.

The crowd, grumbling, dispersed. The minor official continued on his way toward the rededicated Temple of Mars.

The four talked among themselves a moment, then the two policemen and the second Christian grabbed Ambrose and frogwalked him up a narrow alleyway.

The marketplace returned to its deadly dull normality.

P. Renatus Vegetius had been on his way to the house of his retired military friend Aurem Præbens when the fight had broken out just in front of him.

He shook his head. Surely the new emperor knew what would happen when he allowed all the exiled misfits and disgruntled Christians back. There was already talk that Julian was helping the Jews rebuild their temple in Jerusalem, that he would take state funds away from the Christian churches, that he would renew the imperial office of Pontifex Maximus.

This small town, Smyrnea, fifty miles from Constantinople where the new emperor sat after his march from Germany, was supposed to have the Emperor's ear. It was in this town he had spent his childhood and youth in exile, watched over by the old emperor's spies, before going to Rome and Athens to study in his young manhood. Well, only time would tell what would happen with Julian's plans to revitalize the increasingly disparate eastern and western provinces.

Statecraft for the statesmen, thought Vegetius. He was on his way to Præbens' house to consult manuscripts in the library there so he could put the finishing touches on his work, *de re militaria*, a training manual to be read to officers in the army. It lacked only a section on impedimenta and baggage-train convoy duties, of which Præbens had once written copious notes while accompanying Constantine on one of his eastward marches.

P. Renatus Vegetius had himself never been in the army. He had held minor offices (he had once been aedile of this very town, twenty years before, but that was when the job consisted of little more than seeing that the streets were swept; the Christians, after their big meeting at Nicea having brought pressure on Constantine and his sons to close down all the temples and call off public spectacles). Not like today where an aedile got real respect; a broad-shouldered job fitting for a man. Still, Vegetius was glad the present troubles hadn't happened in his times.

Across the street, hurrying toward him, was Decius Muccinus, nomenclator to his friend Præbens. He was moving faster than Vegetius had ever seen him do, almost at a flat run. Unseemly in a slave, even one his master had promised freedom in six months. He was a young man with a beard of the Greek cut.

"Salve, Muccinus!" said Vegetius.

The slave jerked to a stop. "Sir," he said, "forgive me. I was hurrying to your house, sent by my master to fetch you. Astonishing news, if true, which I am forbidden to tell."

"Well, well," said Renatus Vegetius, hurrying with the young man toward Præbens' town home. "Surely you can tell me something?"

"Only that you will be highly pleased." He leaned toward Vegetius, whispering. "Approaching: Singultus Correptus and Sternuus Maximus. Correptus' wife is Livia, Maximus' son is due for a promotion in the army."

"Salve, Singultus! Sternuus!" said Vegetius, stopping to shake their wrists. "How's the lovely Livia, Singultus? And

Sternuus, that son of yours has done alright for himself, hasn't he?"

After a further exchange of pleasantries they hurried on. "Thank you, Muccinus," said Vegetius. "You needn't have done that for me."

"Old habits die hard," said the slave.

"Great news, great news!" said Aurem Præbens. "One of your dreams came true! (And I'm not talking about that damned book of veterinary you want to write.) Sharpen up your javelin, you old fart! A lion's been seen here in Thracia itself. Less than twenty miles away!" He waved a letter around. "Someone, anonymous, says I and my friends should know before the news becomes general!"

There had supposedly been no lions this side of the Pontus Euxinus since the end of the Republic four hundred years before. One of Vegetius' secret wishes was to hunt lions from a chariot in the old style and to write a treatise on the subject. He had been planning a trip to Libya the year after next (gods willing) once he had finished this book, and the one on the diseases of mules and horses, to engage in such a hunt. But here, now, in Thracia!

"I've called on Morus Matutinus (who served in Africa) and Phœbus Siccus (who owns an old hunting chariot) and have sent for three teams of swift coursers for our use!" said Præbens. "How does that grab your testicles?"

Aurem Præbens was beaming. Vegetius was beside himself. Sometimes the gods were kind.

Sometimes they weren't. The party had been out for two days; thirty men and slaves, twenty horses, two impedimenta wagons and fifty yelping, fighting dogs.

As a scent they had brought with them a lion's skin that had hung on one wall of Morus Matutinus' atrium. By the second day of the dogs milling around and biting each other in uncontained excitement, the slaves were betting among themselves that the hounds would soon strike a trail and follow it the twenty miles straight back to Matutinus' house.

Phœbus Siccus, an old, old wrinkled man, was decked out in his armor from fifty years before. He could turn completely around in the worn leather and metal breastplate before it began to move with him.

"Either these are the sorriest dogs I've ever seen, or there's no lion closer than Mesopotamia. Who the Dis' idea was this, anyway?" asked Siccus through his lips which looked like two broken flints.

The dogs had run up a wisent, two scrawny deer and an ass in forty-eight hours. Each time the houndsmen would kick them howling away from the cornered animals and then stick their noses back in the lion's skin.

"I'm going over to the brook yonder," said Renatus Vegetius. He mounted his horse.

"May I go with him, master?" asked Decius Muccinus. "I should like a swim."

"The last thing I need out here," said Præbens, "is a nomenclator. The guys who own these hounds all answer to 'Hey, shithead!' " He turned to Vegetius. "Sorry. I wanted this hunt for you. We'll take the dogs back north, then home. Follow the wagon tracks. If you miss the lion, though, you'll hate yourself."

"If I don't cool off, I will die," said Vegetius. "Good hunting."

"Hah! I'm going to find out who sent that letter and turn the dogs on *his* butt," said Præbens.

It was a stream straight out of Hesiod, pure, pebbled and cold. Vegetius sat on a rock with his swollen feet in the gurgling water. Muccinus, who had stripped naked and swam back and forth a few times, was now asleep on the grass. Upstream tall rushes grew; to each side of the stream, banks lifted up and hung over, shading the western side of the waters in this early afternoon.

Their two horses stopped their grazing. One backed up whinnying, its eyes growing wider.

"What is it?" he asked the horse, reaching out to calm it. Then his blood froze. *Oh gods,* he thought, looking upstream and scrambling for his javelin, *what if the lion's found us?*

He kicked Muccinus with his bare foot.

"Mmmph?" asked the slave, rolling over. Then he jumped up, seeing Vegetius trying to put his sandals on over his head. He pulled a dagger from his lump of clothing on the ground.

"What? What?"

They looked upstream. Something moved along the tall rushes. The green fronds parted.

The oldest man they had ever seen stood at the edge of the reeds, naked from the waist up. He might as well have been clothed; his hair and beard were pure white and hung in waves down his back and chest. He looked like a white hay-stack from which a face stuck out. They couldn't tell if the hair reached the ground as the reeds covered all below his waist.

In his hand he held a thin tapered pole to which was at-tached a light line, gossamer in the sun, probably of plaited horsehair. At the end of the line was a hook with a tuft of red and white yarn tied to it. He waved the pole back and forth a few times and flipped the line into the water.

There was a splash as something rose to the lure. The line tightened, the pole bent, and the old man heaved up and back.

A two-pound grayling, blue and purple-spotted in the sun-light, its dorsal fin like a battle flag, flew out of the water at the end of the line and landed flapping back in the reeds.

The old man bent out of sight to pick it up.

"Well done, sir," said Vegetius. The old man looked up. "I'd be careful, though. There's supposed to be a lion about!"

The old man looked at them, his face breaking out into a smile. He flipped the line back out; soon he was fast to an-other grayling, this one larger, and pulled it in.

"I said, there's a lion about!" yelled Vegetius, cupping his hands.

"Nonchalant bastard," said Muccinus. "Or maybe deaf as a post."

The old man shouldered the pole and the brace of grayling and went through the reeds on his way upstream.

"I saw no houses about," said Muccinus. "Wonder where he came from?"

"Who knows?" said Vegetius.

The sun was still hot, so they followed the shady side of the brook upstream for a mile or so.

They came upon the cave around a bend. Outside were hung drying wild onions, radishes, garlics. There was a rack

out in the sun on which split fish curled. Fungi and mush-
rooms grew in the shady spots.

"Quite homey," said Muccinus. "Hello the cave!"

There was no answer.

"He has frequent visitors," said Renatus Vegetius, pointing
to the ground outside the cave opening. It was churned with
innumerable hoofprints. "Either he's a companionable old
man, or he's popular because those aren't regular mush-
rooms."

"Hello," Renatus continued, dismounting. He tied his
horse's reins to a root which grew from the cliff wall. The
horse was nervous again.

Inside, the cave was cluttered with thousands and thousands of scrolls, book boxes, clay tablets and slates.

"Muccinus," he said. "Look at *this*!"

They walked in. Amid the clutter was a chest-high table; at
one corner of the room a pile of mashed-down straw. There
were no chairs, only piles and piles of scrolls and books in a
dozen languages.

Decius Muccinus poked around in the stacks. "Greek. The
curved writing of Ind. Latin. The old triangle writing. Who
could read this stuff? What's it doing *here*?"

Renatus Vegetius went to the high table. There were several
closed scroll tubes there. One was open. On the table, by itself, was a single page, cut evidently from a lengthy work,
headed, as it was, Book 19 in Greek, and at the top, the title . . .

If Iupiter Ammon had pulled P. Renatus Vegetius up to the
top of Mount Olympus and said to him: *Go anywhere, mortal,
and get your heart's content; anywhere in time and anywhere
in the world: it is yours,* Vegetius would have in the next instant been back in this cave with his hand on this piece of
paper.

It was the *Hippiatrika,* the lost book of veterinary medicine. It was as old as time, older than Homer. When he had
read Pelagonius' *Ars Veterinaria*, Vegetius remembered the
author's railing at the fates which had lost the book to the ken
of man since the Trojan War. Pelagonius wailed for the lost
knowledge it was supposed to contain.

And here Vegetius had in his hand a page of it. He read the

first paragraph and knew, with all his mind and heart, that this was *it*.

Their horses whickered outside. Then their hooves clattered. The horses ran by, blurs. Vegetius had only his short sword with him—the javelin had been in the saddle boot. Muccinus once again drew the dagger forbidden to slaves.

They heard another clatter of hooves. At least it wasn't the lion. "Hello! Hello!" they both shouted.

"I know you're in there. No need to yell," said a voice, an old man's voice, older even than that of Phœbus Siccus.

Then the old man came into the cave followed by the horse.

No.

The old man and the horse came in together.

No.

The old man was the horse.

"Finding anything interesting to read?" he asked, looking from one to the other, then settling his gaze on Vegetius.

Somewhere down his back his hair turned into a brittle white mane. He was white and grey from the top of his head to his hooves. A back leg lifted, clacked to the floor.

It was easier, thought Vegetius, if you only looked at the front half.

"The *Hippiatrika*?" he asked. "Where did you get it?"

The centaur looked toward the table. A mixture of warm animal and human body odor came to Vegetius' nose, like sweaty men on a wet horsehide triclinium. More than anything it convinced him that the encounter he was having was real.

"I wrote it," said the centaur.

Vegetius nearly fainted.

"I think your master needs some water," said the centaur to Muccinus. "There's a cup outside. And please don't run away."

"He's . . . he's not . . . my master," said Muccinus. "And I need some too."

Vegetius held onto a table leg until the slave returned with the cup. As he stood woozily, he noticed that the hooves of the centaur were in bad shape. One leg, the right front, was thinner than the others, with a knot in it as if it had been broken once. What chest Renatus could see through the drapery of white hair looked thin and mottled. Vegetius took the cup and drank.

"Chiron," he said to the centaur. Chiron, the teacher of Hercules and Asclepius, the only centaur able to read and write. The only one ever to be married to a human woman; the only centaur able to drink wine without becoming a raging animal. Chiron, author of the *Hippiatrika*.

"You must be P. Renatus Vegetius," said the horse-man.

"How did you know my name?"

The centaur laughed, his long hair flying.

"How goes the lion hunt?"

"The letter was your doing?"

"Somewhat. I wanted to meet you. I read a copy of your *Histories*."

"And you knew I would come to hunt a lion?"

"After your rhapsody on lion-hunting in the chapter on Egypt? And in your argument, you said you would someday write a treatise on warfare, and a book amplifying Pelagonius' *Ars Veterinaria*? To read a man is sometimes to know all you need," said Chiron.

"Vegetius," said Decius Muccinus. "You're ... talking literature ... with ... a ... centaur."

"One with a purpose," said Chiron.

"What's that?" asked Vegetius.

"I have something you desire. The *Hippiatrika*. The whole manuscript." Vegetius looked wildly around. "It's in a safe place. Don't worry. Help me, and it, and all these other works, are yours."

"What do you wish?"

"I'm old. I want to return to my homeland to die. You can help me."

"Your homeland? Scythia? Ind? Africa?" asked Vegetius, following the best authorities as to the homeland of the centaurs.

"Take me to the Pillars of Hercules," said Chiron. "Then I can be home in a few days."

"The Pillars of Hercules! That's at the western edge of the Empire! That's where the Greeks once sent an expedition to see if the sun hissed as it went down in the ocean! We're in

the East! How am I supposed to get a centaur from one end
of the civilized world to the other?"

"You're an intelligent man," said Chiron. "If you can't
conceive of getting me across the empire, think what it would
be like for me, alone. When I was young and strong, I might
have done it. I could outrun any horse when I had to. But no
longer. I wouldn't be gone fifty miles before some rich man
would have me hunted down for his ménagerie. The fact that
I'm a rational being, and can think and speak, would appeal
to him not at all. I'd end my days in a cage, in Thracia."

He looked at Vegetius.

"I can't believe this," said Decius Muccinus.

"I'm the last one," said Chiron. "And you get the
Hippiatrika. It *is* all you think it to be. Just get me home,
Renatus Vegetius. I ask no more."

"I wouldn't know how to begin," said Vegetius.

"Nemo Prorsus," said Muccinus.

"What?"

"Nemo Prorsus. A very clever man in Cyzicus. If you want
to go through with this, I mean," said Muccinus. "He's done
everything, been everywhere. All it takes is money. Vast
amounts."

Chiron turned his eyes to Vegetius. "Please?"

"Done," said Vegetius, crossing his wrists three times and
spitting, "and done!"

In the week following, after he had sent for Prorsus,
Vegetius went to Aurem Præbens. He found him dictating to
Muccinus.

"I'd like to buy Decius from you," said Vegetius.

"What!?" screamed Muccinus. "After what I've gone
through! I'm to be freed in—"

"Quiet, slave," said Aurem.

"I—"

"Just what did you have in mind?" asked Præbens.

"You're to free him in six months. Sell him to me, now. I'll
free him when I return from my—researches in Alexandria."
(This was the cover story.) "You know everyone in this one-
horse town, anyway. I'll need someone quick with me, a nomenclator, one who can read and write. And I trust no one
more than your Decius Muccinus."

Decius was glowering at him.

"Besides," said Vegetius, "sell him to *me*, and it won't be *you* who has to pay the five per cent manumission tax!"

"Decius, you've been like a son to me, but business is business," said Præbens to the slave. Then to Vegetius. "3000 sesterces."

"3000? I'm going to have him read to me, not sleep with me!"

"I'm worth 4000 if I'm worth a talent," said Decius, his feelings hurt.

"3500," said Præbens.

"35? Can he fly, too?"

"3800 and not a denarius less!"

"What, does a whole family come with him, eight strong boys?" asked Vegetius.

"4000," said Præbens.

"Done!"

"Done," said Præbens, crossing his wrists three times and spitting, "and done!"

Decius was smiling as they had him write up his own bill of sale.

They decided to move Chiron nearer town as they received word Nemo Prorsus was on his way across the Hellespont. Vegetius and Muccinus went out to help him close up his cave, stacking stones across the entrance all one afternoon.

He was to stay in one of the outbuildings in an olive grove owned by Vegetius' uncle, Verbius Mellarius the rhetorician.

"Excuse me," said Chiron. He backed up, lifting his tail, and dropped a pile of road apples on the path. "I usually don't do that so close to home, but I'm leaving. And my stomach's not what it used to be."

After they sealed the cavern off fairly well, they began to ride downstream as the sun went down. Chiron took a long last look back.

"If these were the olden days," he said, "I'd ask one of the Cyclops to keep an eye on the place for me."

A few minutes later, Decius Muccinus looked at Chiron and began to laugh.

"So this is the famous Mr. Chiron, eh?" said Nemo Prorsus,

a squat thick man with a Greek beard. He wore trousers in the eastern fashion and a leather tunic covered with brass spikes. He was bald as a melon. "Glad to meet a real centaur. I once fixed up a mermaid and sold it to the Prince of Parsi, but this is the closest I ever come to a real mythical creature."

"I'm no myth," said Chiron.

"Think you can do it, Nemo?" asked Decius.

"That's *Mister* Nemo to you, slave boy!" He studied a moment. "Yeah. But it's gonna take all your master's money. Have him give it all to me."

"Why are you talking about me in the third person?" asked Vegetius.

"I didn't start this," said Nemo Prorsus. "Yeah, gov, I can do it, but you'll have to give me near all your money and go along with everything I say. Whatever's left over we can split. Bargain?"

"Done," said Vegetius, sighing.

"Done," said Prorsus, crossing his wrists three times and spitting, "and done!"

"It'll take about three days to get everything cooking. I suggest we all lay pretty low," said Prorsus.

"There's one thing I'd like to do before we leave. If Vegetius is paying," said Chiron.

"I suppose I am," said Vegetius, sighing again.

"I'd like to visit a lupercalia."

"Sonofabitch!" said Prorsus. "You're what, a million years old or somethin'? A lupercalia, no less!"

"I used to go all five ways when I was young," said Chiron. "But that was long, long ago. I'd like to go, just once, again."

"Sonofabitch!" said Nemo Prorsus. "Come on, Mr. Vegetius! Let's give the old guy a real treat. I know a place, way out in the sticks, where nobody cares what comes and goes. No offense, Mr. Chiron!"

"None taken."

So in the early morning hours they took him to a brothel by the back ways, and then into a stable by the front door, then back to the brothel again. Several of the women had several rides. Everyone became drunk and agreeable, the night became a warm blur. The women covered Chiron with flowers and sequins; one, a Greek girl name Chiote, poured libations of wine and perfumed oils on his hair and mane.

The next day no one at the lupercalia remembered much of what had happened, or whether it had or that they had only dreamed it; some illusion caused by the edicts of the new emperor, perhaps some psychic slippage to an earlier, simpler time.

"Well," said Prorsus, when he woke up with matted eyebrows and a dry mouth in the olive grove the next evening. "Time to get to work. Shell out the loot."

First he bought sixteen horses.

Then he found eight old men, solitary worshippers of Bacchus, and asked them if they could ride a horse in a straight line. Then he made them prove it. He promised them all the wine they could drink each night as long as they could ride the next morning, and free passage back to Byzantium, if they chose it, or could remember where they were from, or why they should go back whenever they got wherever it was.

"But . . . but . . ." said Vegetius. "The money!"

"An empty purse contains nothing but the seeds of failure," said Prorsus. "We made a bargain. Your centaur wants home. He's giving you something in return. You're giving me something—your complete trust and your cash. True?"

"Well, yes."

"Then let me do my job," said Prorsus, and pulled more sesterces out of the bag.

Then he went out and bought an elephant with one tusk.

He had draped two white blankets over the pachyderm's sides, tied on with rope. Prorsus took a paint brush, and in a fairly good hand painted:
                    VIDE ELEPHANTOS HANNIBALENSIS
on each side with an arrow pointing backwards.

"Not very good Latin," said Vegetius.

"Good enough for these garlic-eating yahoos!" said Prorsus. "The first rule is, when you're hiding a marvel, give them something else to gawk at!" He put down the paintbrush.

"Besides," he said. "Anyone who thinks he's going to see

some 600-year-old elephants deserves to miss a centaur or two."

He winked and left to see about the Imperial Post Road permits.

"Here goes nothing," said Muccinus, naked and sitting on the elephant's head. It was the first morning of the westward trip. They were nearing the first village on the road toward Phillipi and Dyrrhachium.

"Put your lungs in it, you old farts!" yelled Prorsus from his blue-painted horse up ahead.

The eight old men sat up as straight as they could on their horses. Two of them had bagpipes, two had trumpets, two serpentines which curved around them to rest on the backs of their saddles, and the other two flailed away at drums.

It wasn't music, it was an atrocious noise. The elephant almost ran off the road. Muccinus steered it back by kicking it behind its right ear.

Vegetius, wincing, could imagine Apollo, Orpheus, Harmonia throwing themselves off Olympus in suicide at what was being done in their names.

All the people ran out of their houses, stood in the road, made way for them.

They began to cheer and yell as the blatting entourage came even with them. Prorsus, wearing a headdress of purple ostrich feather, gave them a sweeping blessing with his arms.

All eyes were on the elephant. It trumpeted, drowning out the cacophony ahead of it for a second or two. It drew even with the middle of the village. Heads turned back toward Byzantium, peering. Most of the villagers were still looking that way when the noisy column drew out of sight around a curve in the post road.

None had noticed that in the middle of the eight old mounted men was another old man, his hair and beard now cut short, his hair combed to hide his pointed ears, who played no instrument and looked neither left nor right.

At one town, Vegetius saw Prorsus proved right. It happened on the edge of a large crowd where he rode. As they drew even with the applause, a child pointed to the mounted musicians.

"Look, mater," said the girl, "that man in the middle is half-horsey!"

The woman picked the child up by the hair and shook her.

"Learn not to lie, Portia," said her mother, never taking her eyes off the elephant.

"I can't believe it," said Vegetius. "Two and a half months gone by, halfway to the Pillars, and no troubles!"

"These is strange times," said Prorsus, putting more wood on the fire. "Nobody knows what to expect with a new emperor sittin' on the throne like it was a pot. They don't know which way to jump. They're all just waiting for the other caliga to drop." They were camped off the road near Aquilia in Noricum. The old men were already drunk or asleep. Chiron lay nearby, his human part asleep over a flat rock, his equine body folded under him. Now and then a long low sound came from his chest.

"This trip's been pretty easy. Company's better, anyway," said Prorsus. "I've had some tough jobs, with real scuzzes to work with. I once stole a quinquireme from Ephesus and sold it a week later in Sardis, and nobody ever saw it."

"Wait a minute," said Decius. "Sardis is overland from Ephesus. There aren't any rivers or canals connecting them!"

"It was for a bet," said Prorsus. "Some jobs is just easier than others, I guess."

So it went through Mutina and Trebia in Gallo Cisalpina, Dertona in Liguria, where the roads often became crowded, and missing entirely the dead backwater of Italia itself, through Augusta Taurinorem, Massilia and Narbo Martius in Narbonensis, down the long chest of Tarraconensis, past Novo Carthago on the shore of the Mare Internum, and along the coast roads, passing south of Hispalia in Bætica to the Gates of Hercules.

They were on a hill overlooking a small seaport. Across to the southwest was Mauretania, emblazoned with the sunset.

"We're here," said Vegetius to Chiron. "Now let's get you home."

"We'll have to hire a ship."

"So it is Africa we go to!" said Decius Muccinus.

"Not really," said Chiron.

"Then for the gods' sakes, where?" asked Vegetius.

"Out there," said Chiron, pointing to the sunset.

"What! There's nothing out there!"

"There's another land. The land centaurs come from. And horses."

"How the Dis did you get here?! You didn't have ships?!"

"We walked. It was colder then. The ocean was lower then, and more land stuck out. Of course, we came the other way, through Asia. I'm taking you by a short cut."

Whistling a tune, Prorsus started down the hill.

"Where are you going?" asked Vegetius, beside himself.

"To find passage back for the drunks and to find a boat that'll get him home," he said, jerking his thumb toward the centaur.

"What! What!"

"He hasn't lied to you yet, has he?" asked Prorsus, over his shoulder.

Vegetius ran down to a cork tree and gnawed at the bark, tears streaming down his face. After awhile, he felt better.

"Sorry," he said to Chiron. "It's been such a long trip. I thought it almost over."

Chiron put his hands on Vegetius' shoulders. "Soon," he said. "Soon, you'll have the book. Soon, I'll be home. It had to be this way. If I would have told you in Smyrnea, you would not have come. And you would have remained a bitter old man the rest of your life. And I would die in Thracia, so far from my homeland."

"I'm just tired."

"I, too," said Chiron. "More than you know. Let's make camp. No more masquerades. No more processions. Let the world gape. I'm going home."

They boarded a ship next midnight and set sail westward. Prorsus had sold the elephant to a merchantman captain returning to Byzantium in exchange for passage for the old men. They had said their goodbyes the evening before boarding.

When dawn broke on the ship in the Mare Atlanticum, it became very quiet. The crew saw the centaur and kept its distance.

"When do we put north or south?" asked the bosun, ex-

pecting a turn starboard toward Hibernia, or port to the Wild
Dog Islands.

"We don't," said the captain. "The course is west by northwest."

"How long?" asked the bosun.

"As long as it takes," said the captain. He reached into the
poop cabin and pulled out a bag half his size.

He kicked at it.

It jangled.

"Hear that?" asked the captain. "The bag talks!"

"That it does," said the bosun.

"What does it say?"

"It says west by northwest by the stars, sir!"

"Just what it said to me."

For two weeks the sea had been still and flat as a sheet of
lead, without a cloud in the sky.

The sail was furled. The sailors' hands were raw with rowing toward the westering sun.

"It used to be much easier to sail there for a while, or so
I'm told," said Chiron. "There used to be a big island out here
in the middle, though they charged an arm and a leg for a port
call."

During the last week they had lightened the load as much
as possible. Now there was nothing left but food, water, the
money bags and some extra canvas on board. Still the hours
of flat calm dragged by.

Vegetius, Prorsus and Muccinus took turns at the oars, and
Chiron stood helm though there was very little need to steer.

The sun came up abaft them every morning, and set before
them each evening, and it seemed they had moved not at all.

They awoke to find themselves, the captain and bosun at
one end of the vessel and the crew at the other. No one was
rowing. The oars were shipped.

"Well," said the captain. "What is it?"

One of the men stepped forward. "We've been without
wind for seventeen days now. We row all day and night. We
get nowhere."

"There's nothing for it but to put our backs on it and hope
for wind," said the captain.

"We could turn back." There were grumbles behind him from the others.

There was a consultation with the passengers. "Out of the question," said the captain. "We're more than halfway there."

"Says who?" yelled someone.

"Say I, and I'm the captain."

"Well, then," said the crew's leader. "We could lighten the load."

"What's that?" asked Prorsus, suddenly taking an interest in the proceedings.

"You know what I mean, governor," said the crewman, nodding his head sideways. "Why don't we put the horsey over the side?"

"Quite right!" said Prorsus. He grabbed the sailor by crotch and tunic and pitched him over the railing. The man coughed and floundered in the glassy water.

"Next!" said Prorsus. "I figure three more make up for my friend Chiron here." He opened his arms in a wrestler's invitation. "Weight's weight."

No one came forward.

"Toss him a line," said Prorsus.

They pulled the wet and strangling sailor back aboard.

"Do we understand each other?" Prorsus asked the assembled sailors.

"Aye, aye!" they said in one voice.

As if by some propitiatory magic, a dancing line of water moved toward them from the east. It caught up to and passed the ship. The frill of mane on Chiron's back fluttered and a cool breeze blew into Vegetius' right ear.

"Well, hell and damn!" yelled the captain to the crew. "Don't you know wind when you feel it? Unfurl the fonkin' sail!"

The canvas came down and filled, the ship groaned and jerked ahead, bearing them away from the morning sun. The sailors, among them the wet one, joined in "Old Neptune's Song."

They lowered the gangplank, and Chiron went down into the surf and onto the sandbar in the river estuary.

The shoreline was broken by trees and clearings. Here and there shaggy humped shapes grazed, some few stopping to watch, then returning to their forage. They looked like wisents only they had smaller horns.

Chiron turned to the ship.

"Fishing should be good all up the shore," he said. "Won't take long to replenish your stores. Good water, too. Follow the warm water north, then follow east when it turns. You'll end up in Brittania or Hibernia. You know them, Captain?"

"I'm half tindigger," he said. "I paint myself blue once a year when the mood overcomes me."

Chiron laughed, then coughed, a hard wracking series of them. He leaned the upper half of his body against a tree, steadying himself with his right hand. Then he straightened and turned to walk away.

"Goodbye. Goodbye horsey. So long, Mr. Chiron," they all yelled from the ship.

"Wait! Wait! The *Hippiatrika*?!" yelled Vegetius.

Chiron turned. "In the cave. On the table. The two unopened scroll tubes. Thank you, Renatus Vegetius. I will remember you always."

He then turned, lifted his tail, his regrown hair and beard streaming in the wind like a white banner, and broke, for a few paces, into a canter, and disappeared through the nearest stand of trees, heading westward.

A yell of exultation and homecoming, of surrender and defiance rose up, startling some of the browsing creatures. Then it, too, like the drumming hoofbeats, echoed and died away westward.

"Back water and up sail, you sea hogs!" hollered the captain.

In the three yeas of life remaining to him, P. Renatus Vegetius returned home, retrieved the books in the cave, and incorporated the *Hippiatrika* into his great work on the diseases of mules, horses and cattle, the *Mulomedicina*.

Decius Muccinus, free and married, had twin sons whom they named Aurem and Renatus.

Nemo Prorsus became the Christian Bishop of Sardis.

On his deathbed, Renatus Vegetius looked around his room at his sisters and their husbands and children, at his newly-freed slaves, and at what few friends as had not preceded him in death.

About the only thing he regretted was never getting to hunt lions from a chariot in the wet marshlands of Libya.

He remembered one sunny day on a far shore half a world away, and the cry of happiness that had drifted back to him out of those woods.

What was killing a few old lions compared to what he had done?

He had helped a tired old friend get home.

Vegetius was still smiling when they put the coins on his eyes.

INTRODUCTION TO

FIN DE CYCLÉ

THIS is the original to this book. The one I've referred to over the years as "the velocipede story" or "the bicycle story."

(In college, I wrote a real-life article about my first and best bicycle, detailing all the neat, terrifying things we did as kids on our bikes. It's a wonder any of us reached dating age with all our parts. It was called "Hodiak, Son of Battle.")

I'm not much of a predictor, but I've got two about the 1990s:

1. You'll see a lot more stories about the 1890s than this one.

2. If you think the end of the *last* century was something, wait'll you see *this* one.

This is the hardest story I've had to write in the last ten years. If you don't like it, you have my permission to put your opinion where the monkey puts the nuts.

Every country on the face of the earth has to go through a crisis that changes its very nature, that decides whether it will live and grow, or die, or become a tourist trap.

Sometimes—in the case of England, the U.S. and Russia, you get a couple: the Reform bill and WWI for the Brits; the Civil War and Vietnam for America; the Revolution and Afghanistan for the Soviet Union. Something snapped twice in each case: clean up the country politically, lose a generation and an Empire; hold the country together in spite of itself, decide to quit being World Cop or kill all your children; get rid of a thousand years of bad history, *then* get rid of the 70 bad years *since* then.

The list goes on and on. One country had its own Revolution, then, at the height of its creative, engineering, cultural and political life, it all came down to a question about a minor military prisoner on an out-of-the-way rock. It, of course, didn't happen the way I said it did, but it wouldn't have taken much.

And what does all this have to do with high-wheelers and velocipedes?

Heap plenty.

FIN DE CYCLÉ

I. HUMORS IN UNIFORM

A. Gentlemen, Start Your Stilts!

There was clanking and singing as the company came back from maneuvers.

Pa-chinka Pa-chinka, a familiar and comforting sound. The first of the two scouts came into view five meters in the air atop the new steam stilts. He storked his way into the battalion area, then paused.

Behind him came the second scout, then the cyclists in columns of three. They rode high-wheeled ordinaries, dusty now from the day's ride. Their officer rode before them on one of the new safety bicycles, dwarfed by those who followed behind.

At the headquarters he stopped, jumped off his cycle.

"Company! ..." he yelled, and the order was passed back along by NCOs, "... company ... company ... company! ..."

"Halt!" Again the order ran back. The cyclists put on their spoonbrakes, reached out and grabbed the handlebars of the man to the side. The high-wheelers stood immobile in place, 210 of them, with the two scouts standing to the fore, steam slowly escaping from the legs of their stilts.

"Company ..." again the call and echoes, "Dis—" at the command, the leftward soldier placed his left foot on the step halfway down the spine of the bicycle above its small back wheel. The others shifted their weight backwards, still holding to the other man's handlebars.

"—mount!" The left-hand soldier dropped back to the

213

ground, reached through to grab the spine of the ordinary
next to him; the rider of that repeated the first man's motions,
until all three men were on the ground beside their high-
wheels.

At the same time the two scouts pulled the levers beside
the knees of their metal stilts. The columns began to telescope
down into themselves with a hiss of steam until the men were
close enough to the ground to step off and back.

"Company C, 3^d Battalion, 11th Bicycle Infantry, Attention!" said the lieutenant. As he did so, the major appeared on
the headquarters' porch. Like the others, he was dressed in
the red baggy pants, blue coat and black cap with a white kepi
on the back. Unlike them, he wore white gloves, sword and
pistol.

"Another mission well done," he said. "Tomorrow—a
training half-holiday, for day after tomorrow, Bastille Day, the
99th of the Republic—we ride to Paris and then we roll
smartly down the Champs-Élysées, to the general appreciation
of the civilians and the wonder of the children."

A low groan went through the bicycle infantrymen.

"Ah, I see you are filled with enthusiasm! Remember—you
are the finest Army in France—the Bicycle Infantry! A short
ride of 70 kilometers holds no terrors for you! A mere 10
kilometers within the city. An invigorating 70 kilometers
back! Where else can a man get such exercise? And such
meals! And be paid besides? Ah, were I a younger man, I
should never have become an officer, but joined as a private
and spent a life of earnest bodybuilding upon two fine
wheels!"

Most of the 11th were conscripts doing their one year
of service, so the finer points of his speech were lost on
them.

A bugle sounded somewhere off in the fort.

"Gentlemen: Retreat."

Two clerks came out of headquarters and went to the flagpole.

From left and right bands struck up the Retreat. All came
to attention facing the flagpole, as the few sparse notes
echoed through the quadrangles of the garrison.

From the corner of his eye the major saw Private Jarry, already placed on Permanent Latrine Orderly, come from out of

the far row of toilets set halfway out toward the drill course.
The major could tell Private Jarry was disheveled from this
far away—even with such a job one should be neat. His coat
was buttoned sideways by the wrong buttons, one pants leg in
his boots, one out. His hat was on front-to-back with the kepi
tied up above his forehead.

He had his toilet brush in his hand.

The back of the major's neck reddened.

Then the bands struck up "To the Colors"—the company
area was filled with the sound of salutes snapping against cap
brims.

The clerks brought the tricolor down its lanyard.

Private Jarry saluted the flag with his toilet brush.

The major almost exploded; stood shaking, hand frozen in
salute.

The notes went on; the major calmed himself. This man is
a loser. He does not belong in the Army; he doesn't deserve
the Army! Conscription is a privilege. Nothing I can do to
this man will *ever* be enough; you cannot kill a man for being a bad soldier; you can only inconvenience him; make
him miserable in his resolve; the result will be the same. You
will both go through one year of hell; at the end you will
still be a major, and he will become a civilian again, though
with a bad discharge. His kind never amount to anything.
Calm yourself—he is not worth a stroke—he is not insulting France, he is insulting *you*. And he is beneath your notice.

At the last note the major turned on his heel with a nod to
the lieutenant and went back inside, followed by the clerks
with the folded tricolors.

The lieutenant called off odd numbers for cycle-washing
detail; evens were put to work cleaning personal equipment
and rifles.

Private Jarry turned with military smartness and went back
in to his world of strong disinfectant soap and *merde*.

After chow that evening, Private Jarry retired behind the bicycle shop and injected more picric acid beneath the skin of
his arms and legs.

In three more months, only five after being drafted, he

would be released, with a medical discharge, for "chronic jaundice."

B. Cannons In The Rain

Cadet Marcel Proust walked into the company orderly room. He had been putting together his belongings; today was his last full day in the Artillery. Tomorrow he would leave active duty after a year at Orleans.

"Attention," shouted the corporal clerk as he came in. "At ease," said Marcel, nodding to the enlisted men who copied orders by hand at their desks. He went to the commanding officer's door, knocked. *"Entre,"* said a voice and he went in.

"Cadet Proust reporting, *mon capitaine*," said Marcel, saluting.

"Oh, there's really no need to salute in here, Proust," said Captain Dreyfus.

"Perhaps, sir, it will be my last."

"Yes, yes," said Captain Dreyfus. "Tea? Sugar?" The captain indicated the kettle. "Serve yourself." He looked through some papers absent-mindedly. "Sorry to bring you in on your last day—sure we cannot talk you into joining the officers corps? France has need of bright young men like you!—No, I thought not. Cookies? Over there, Madame Dreyfus baked them this morning." Marcel retrieved a couple, while stirring the hot tea in his cup.

"Sit, sit. Please!" Dreyfus indicated the chair. Marcel slouched into it.

"You were saying?" he asked.

"Ah! Yes. Inspections coming up, records, all that," said the captain. "You remember, some three months ago, August 19th to be exact, we were moving files from the old headquarters across the two quadrangles to this building? You were staff duty officer that day?"

"I remember the move, *mon capitaine*. That was the day we received the Maxim gun tricycles, also. It was—yes—a day of unseasonable rain."

"Oh? Yes?" said Dreyfus. "That *is* correct. Do you remember, perhaps, the clerks having to take an alternate route here, until we procured canvas to protect the records?"

"They took several. Or am I confusing that with the day we

exchanged barracks with the 91st Artillery? That also was rainy. What is the matter?"

"Some records evidently did not make it here. Nothing important, but they must be in the files for the inspection, else we shall get a very black mark indeed."

Marcel thought. Some of the men used the corridors of the instruction rooms carrying files, some went through the repair shops. There were four groups of three clerks to each set of cabinets. . . .

"Which files?"

"Gunnery practice, instruction records. The boxes which used to be—"

"—on top of the second set of wooden files," said Marcel. "I remember them there. I do not remember seeing them *here*. . . . I am at a total loss as to how they could not have made it to the orderly room, *mon capitaine*."

"They were checked off as leaving, in your hand, but evidently, we have never seen them again."

Proust wracked his brain. The stables? The instruction corridor; surely they would have been found by now. . . .

"Oh, we'll just have to search and search, get the 91st involved. They're probably in *their* files. This army runs on paperwork—soon clerks will outnumber the generals, eh, Proust?"

Marcel laughed. He drank at his tea—it was lemon tea, pleasant but slightly weak. He dipped one of the cookies—the kind called a madeline—in it and took a bite.

Instantly a chill and an aching familiarity came over him—he saw his Grandmother's house in Balbec, an identical cookie, the same kind of tea, the room cluttered with furniture, the sound of his brother coughing upstairs, the feel of the wrought iron dinner table chair against the back of his bare leg, his father looking out the far kitchen window into the rain, the man putting down the burden, heard his mother hum a tune, a raincoat falling, felt the patter of raindrops on the toolshed roof, smelled the tea and cookie in a second overpowering rush, saw a scab on the back of his hand from eleven years before . . .

"*Mon capitaine!*" said Marcel, rocking forward, slapping his hand against his forehead. "Now I remember where the box was left!"

II. BOTH HANDS

Rousseau was painting a tiger.

It was not just any tiger. It was the essence of tiger, the apotheosis of *felis horribilis*. It looked out from the canvas with yellow-green eyes through which a cold emerald light shone. Its face was beginning to curve into a snarl. Individual quills of whiskers stood out from the black and gold jaws in rippling lines. The edge of the tongue showed around lips with a faint edge of white. A single flower, its stem bent, was the only thing between the face of the tiger and the viewer.

Henri Rousseau put down his brush. He stepped back from the huge canvas. To left and right, birds flew in fright from the charging tiger. The back end of a water buffalo disappeared through the rank jungle at the rear of the canvas. Blobs of grey and tan indicated where the rhinoceros and impala would be painted in later. A huge patch of bamboo was just a swatch of green-gold; a neutral tan stood in for the unstarted blue sky.

A pearl-disk of pure white canvas, with tree limbs silhouetted before it, would later be a red-ocher sun.

At the far back edge of the sky, partially eclipsed by a yellow riot of bananas, rose the newly-completed Eiffel Tower.

Rousseau wiped his hand against his Rembrandt beret. His eyes above his greying spade beard and mustache moved back and forth, taking in the wet paint.

Pinned to one leg of the easel was a yellowed newspaper clipping he kept there (its duplicate lay in a thick scrapbook at the corner of the room in the clutter away from the north light). He no longer read it; he knew the words by heart. It was from a review of the showing at the Salon des Refusés two years before.

"The canvases of Monsieur Rousseau are something to be seen (then again, they're not!). One viewer was so bold as to wonder with which hand the artist had painted this scene, and someone else was heard to reply: 'Both, sir! Both hands! And both feet!'"

Rousseau walked back to the painting, gobbed his brush three times across the palette, and made a two centimeter dot on the face of the tiger.

Now the broken flower seemed to bend from the foul breath of the animal; it swayed in the hot mammal wind.

Rousseau moved on to another section of the painting.

The tiger was done.

III. SUPPER FOR FOUR

Three young men walked quickly through the traffic of Paris on streets aclank with the sound of pedals, sprockets and chains. They talked excitedly. Quadricycles and tricycles passed, ridden by women, older men, couples having quiet conversations as they pedalled.

High above them all, their heads three meters in the air, came young men bent over their gigantic wheels. They sailed placidly along, each pump of their legs covering six meters of ground, their trailing wheels like afterthoughts. They were aloof and intent; the act of riding was their life.

Occasionally a horse and wagon came by the three young men, awash in a sea of cyclists. A teamster kept pace with a postman on a hens-and-chickens pentacycle for a few meters, then fell behind.

There was a ringing of bells ahead and the traffic parted to each side; pedalling furiously came a police tricycle, a man to the front on the seat ringing the bell, another to the rear standing on the back pedals. Between them an abject-looking individual was strapped to the reclining seat, handcuffed and foot-manacled to the tricycle frame.

The ringing died away behind them, and the three young men turned a corner down toward the Seine. At a certain address they turned in, climbed to the third landing-and-a-half, and knocked loudly on the door.

"Enter Our Royal Chasublerie!" came the answer.

Blinking, the three tumbled into the dark room. The walls were covered with paintings and prints, woodcuts, stuffed weasels and hawks, books, papers, fishing gear and bottles. It was an apartment built from half a landing. Their heads scraped the ceiling. A huge ordinary lay on its side, taking up the whole center of the room.

"Alfred," said one of the young men. "Great news of Pierre and Jean-Paul!"

"They arrived in the Middle Orient on their world tour!" said the second.

"They've been sighted in Gaza and bombed in Gilead!" said the third.

"More bulletins soon!" said the first. "We have brought a bottle of wine to celebrate their joyous voyage."

The meter-and-a-quarter tall Jarry brushed his butt-length hair back from his face. When they had knocked, he had just finished a bottle of absinthe.

"Then we must furnish a royal feast—that will be four in all for supper?" he asked. "Excuse our royal pardon."

He put on his bicycling cap with an emblem from the far-off League of American Wheelmen. He walked to the mantel-piece, where he took down a glass of water in which he had earlier placed 200 drops of laudanum, and ate the remains of a hashish cookie. Then he picked up his fly rod and fish basket and left, sticking his head back in to say, "Pray give us a few moments."

Two of the students began teasing one of Jarry's chameleons, putting it through an astonishing array of clashing color schemes, and then tossing one of his stuffed owls around like a football while the living one jumped back and forth from one side of its perch to the other, hooting wildly.

The second student watched through the single window.

This is what the student saw:

Jarry went through the traffic of bicycles and wheeled conveyances on the street, disappeared down the steps to the river, rigged up and made four casts—*Bip bap bim bom*—and came up with a fish on each one—a tench, a gudgeon, a pickerel and a trout, threw them in the basket, and walked back across the street, waving as he came.

What Jarry saw:

He was carrying a coffin as he left the dungeon and went into the roadway filled with elephants, and pigs on stilts. A bicycle ridden by a skeleton rose into the sky, the bony cyclist laughing, the sound echoing off itself, getting louder the further away it got.

He took a week getting down the twenty-seven kilometer

abyss of the steps, each step a block of antediluvian marble a hundred meters wide.

Overhead, the sun was alternate bands of green and brown, moving like a newly electric powered barber shop sign. The words "raspberry jam teapot" whispered themselves over and over somewhere just behind his right ear.

He looked into the thousand kilometer width of the river of boiling ether. The fumes were staggering—sweet and nausea-producing at the same time. A bird with the head of a Pekingese lap-dog flew by the now purple and black orb of the sun.

Jarry pulled out his whip-coach made of pure silver with its lapis-lazuli guides and its skull of reel. The line was an anchor chain of pure gold. He had a bitch of a time getting the links of chain through the eye of his fly. It was a two-meter-long, four-winged stained glass and pewter dragonfly made by Alphonse Mucha.

Jarry false-cast into the ether, lost sight of his fly in the roiling fumes, saw a geyser of water rise slowly into the golden air. The tug pulled his arm from its socket. He set the hook.

Good! He had hooked a kraken. Arms writhing, parrot beak clacking, it fought for an hour before he regained line and pulled it to the cobbles, smashing it and its ugly eyes and arms beneath his foot. Getting it into the steamer trunk behind him, he cast again.

There were so many geysers exploding into the sky he wasn't sure which one was his. He set the hook anyway and was rewarded with a Breughel monster; human head and frog arms with flippers, it turned into a jug halfway back and ended in a horse. As he fought it he tried to remember which painting it was from; *The Temptation of St. Anthony*, most likely.

The landing accomplished, he cast again just as the planet Saturn, orange and bloated like a pumpkin, its rings whirring and making a noise like a mill-saw, fell and flattened everything from Notre Dame to the Champ de Mars. Luckily, no one was killed.

Another strike. For a second, the river became a river, the fly rod a fly rod, and he pulled in a fish, a pickerel. Only this one had hands, and every time he tried to unhook it, it grabbed the hook and stuck it back in its own jaw, pulling itself toward Jarry with plaintive mewling sounds.

"*Merde!*" he said, taking out his fishing knife and cutting away the hands. More grew back. He cut them away, too, and tossed the fish into the mausoleum behind him.

Better. The ether-river was back. His cast was long. It made no sound as it disappeared. There was the gentlest tug of something taking the dragonfly—Jarry struck like a man possessed.

Something huge, brown and smoking stood up in the ether fumes, bent down and stared at Jarry. It had shoulders and legs. It was the Colossus of Rhodes. A fire burned through vents in the top of its head, the flames shone out the eyes. It could have reached from bank to bank; its first stride would take it to Montmarte.

Alfred gave another huge tug. The chain going from his rod to the lip of the Colossus pulled taut. There was a pause and a groan, the sound of a ship on a reef. With a boom and rattle, the bronze man tottered, tried to regain its balance, then fell, shattering itself on the bridges and quays, the fires turning to steam. The tidal wave engulfed the Île de la Cité and would no doubt wipe out everything all the way to the sea.

Painfully, Jarry gathered up the tons of bronze shards and put them in the wheelless stagecoach and dragged it up the attic stairs to the roadway.

The bicyclists and wolverines seemed unconcerned. Saturn had buried itself below its equator. Its rings still ran, but much more slowly; they would stop by nightfall. Pieces of the bronze Colossus were strewn all over the cityscape.

Jarry looked toward the Walls of Troy before him as he struggled with the sarcophagus. At one portal he saw his friends Hannibal, Hamilcar and Odoacer waiting for him. If the meal weren't to their satisfaction, they were to kill and eat *him*. He put up his hand in acknowledgement of doom.

The sky was pink and hummed a phrase from Wagner, a bad phrase. The Eiffel Tower swayed to its own music, a gavotte of some kind. Jarry got behind the broken-down asphalt wagon and pushed it toward the drawbridge of despair that was the door of his building.

He hoped he could find the matches and cook supper without burning down the whole fucking city.

IV. ARTFULLY ARRANGED SCENES

Georges Méliès rose at dawn in Montreuil, bathed, break-fasted, and went out to his home-office. By messenger, last night's accounts from the Théâtre Robert-Houdin would have arrived. He would look over those, take care of correspond-ence, and then go back to the greenhouse glass building that was his Star Films studio.

At ten, the workmen would arrive. They and Méliès would finish the sets, painting scenery in shades of grey, black and white, each scene of which bore, at some place, the Star Films trademark to discourage film footage piracy. The me-chanics would rig the stage machinery, which was Méliès' forte.

At eleven the actors would appear, usually from the Folies Bergère, and Méliès would discuss with them the film to be made, block out the movements, and with them improvise the stage business. Then there would be a jolly lunch, and a free time while Méliès and his technicians prepared the huge cam-era.

It was fixed on a track perpendicular to the stage, and could be moved from a position, at its nearest point, which would show the actors full-length upon the screen, back into the T-shaped section of the greenhouse to give a view encom-passing the entire acting area. Today, the camera was to be moved and then locked down for use twice during the film-ing.

At two, filming began after the actors were costumed. The film was a retelling of Little Red Riding Hood. The first scene, of the girl's house, was rolled in, accessory wings and flies dropped, and the establishing scene filmed. The actresses playing the girl and her mother were exceptionally fine. Then the next scene, of the forest path, was dropped down; the camera moved back and locked in place.

The scene opened with fairies and forest animals dancing, then the Wolf (a tumbler from the Folies) came on in a very hideous costume, and hid behind a painted tree.

The forest creatures try to warn the approaching girl, who walks on the path toward the camera, then leave. She and the Wolf converse. The Wolf leaves.

The second scene requires eleven takes, minor annoyances growing into larger ones as filming progresses. A trap door needed for a later scene comes open at one point while the animals romp, causing a painted stump to fall into it.

The camera is moved once more, and the scenery for the grandmother's house is put in place, the house interior with an open window at the back. The Wolf comes in, chases the grandmother away, in continuous action, goes to the wardrobe, dresses, climbs in bed. Only then is the action stopped.

When filming begins again, with the same camera location, Red Riding Hood enters. The action is filmed continuously from this point to when the Wolf jumps from the bed. Then the Wolf chases the girl around the room, a passing hunter appears at the window, watches the action a second, runs in the door, shoots the Wolf (there is a flash powder explosion and the Wolf-actor drops through the trap door).

The grandmother appears at the window, comes in; she, the hunter and Red Riding Hood embrace. *Fin.*

Méliès thanks the actors and pays them. The last of the film is unloaded from the camera (for such a bulky object it only holds 16 meters of film per magazine) and taken to the laboratory building to be developed, then viewed and assembled by Méliès tomorrow morning.

Now 5 P.M., Méliès returns to the house, has early supper with his wife and children. Then he reads to them, and at 7 P.M. performs for them the magic tricks he is trying out, shows new magic lantern transition-transfigurations to be incorporated into his stage act, gives them a puppet show or some other entertainment. He bids goodnight to his children, then returns to the parlor where he and his wife talk for an hour, perhaps while they talk he sketches her, or doodles scene designs for his films. He tells her amusing stories of the day's filming, perhaps jokes or anecdotes from the Folies the actors have told him at lunch.

He accompanies his wife upstairs, undresses her, opens the coverlet, inviting her in. She climbs into bed.

He kisses her sweetly goodnight.

Then he goes downstairs, puts on his hat, and goes to the home of his mistress.

V. WE GROW BORED

The banquet was in honor of Lugné-Poe, the manager of the Théâtre de l'Oeuvre.

Jarry, in his red canvas suit and paper shirt with a fish painted on it for a tie, was late. The soup was already being served.

There were 300 people, all male, attending. Alfred went to his seat; a bowl of soup, swimming with fish eyes, was placed before him. He finished it at once, as he had forgotten to eat for the last two days.

He looked left and right; to the right was a man known vaguely to him as a pederast and a *frotteur*, but whose social station was such that he would rather have swallowed the national tricolor, base, standard and spike, than to have spoken to Jarry. To the left was a shabby man, with large spade beard and mustache, wearing an artist's beret and workman's clothes. He slowly spooned his soup while deftly putting all the bread and condiments within reach into the pockets of his worn jacket.

Then Jarry looked across the table and found himself staring into the eyes of a journalist for one of the right-wing nationalist Catholic cycling weeklies.

"Are you not Jarry?" asked the man, with narrowed eyes.

"We are," said Alfred. "Unfortunately, our royal personage does not converse with those who have forsaken the One True Means of Transportation."

"Ha. A recidivist!" said the reporter. "It is we who are of the future, while you remain behind in the lost past."

"Our conversation is finished," said Jarry. "You, and Monsieur Norpois have lost our true salvation of the Wheel."

"Bi-cycle means two wheels," said the journalist. "When you and your kind realize that true speed, true meaning, and true patriotism depend on equal size and mighty gearing, this degenerate country will become strong once more."

The man to Jarry's left was looking back and forth from one to the other; he had stopped eating, but his left hand brought another roll to his pocket.

"Does not the First Citizen of our Royal Lands and Possessions to the East, the Lord Amida Buddha himself, speak of the Greater and Lesser Wheels?" asked Jarry. "Put *that* in your ghost-benighted, superstition-ridden censer and try to smoke it. Our Royal Patience becomes stretched. We have nothing against those grown weary, old, effete who go to three, four wheels or more; they have given up. Those, however, with equal wheels, riders of crocodiles and spiders, with false mechanical aids, we deem repugnant, unworthy; one would almost say, but would never, ever, that they have given in to . . . *German* ideas."

The conversation at the long table stopped dead. The man to Jarry's left put down his spoon and eased his chair back from the table ever so slightly.

The face of the reporter across the table went through so many color changes that Jarry's chameleon, at the height of mating season, would be shamed. The journalist reached under the table, lifted his heavy-headed cane, pushed it up through the fingers of his right hand with his left, caught it by the tip.

"Prepare yourself for a caning," said the turnip-faced man. No challenge to the field of honor, no further exchange of unpleasantries. He lifted his cane back, pushing back his sleeve.

"Monsieur," said Jarry, turning to the man on his left, "do us the honor of standing us upon our throne, here." He indicated his chair.

The man scooted back, picked up the one-and-a-quarter-meter high Jarry and stood him on the seat of his chair in a very smooth motion. Then the man grabbed his soup bowl and stood away.

"I will hammer you down much farther before I am done," said the reporter, looking Jarry up and down. People from the banquet committee rushed toward them; Lugné-Poe was yelling who was the asshole who made the seating arrangements?

"By your red suit I take you for an anarchist. Very well, no rules," said the reporter. The cane whistled.

"By our Red Suit you should take us for a man whose Magenta Suit is being cleaned," said Jarry. "This grows tedious. We grow bored." He pulled his Navy Colt Model .41 from his waistband, cocked it and fired a great roaring blank which caught the reporter's pomaded hair on fire. The man went down yelling and rolling while others helpfully poured pitchers of water on him.

The committee members had stopped at the gun's report.

Jarry held up his finger to the nearest waiter. "Check, please!" he said.

He left the hall out the front door as the reporter, swearing great oaths of vengeance and destruction, was carried back into the kitchen for butter to be applied to his burns.

Jarry felt a hand on his shoulder, swung his arm up, came around with the Colt out again. It was the man who had stood him on the chair.

"You talk with the accent of Laval," said the man.

"Bred, born, raised and bored *merdeless* there," said Jarry.

"I, too," said the man.

"We find Laval an excellent place to be *from*, if you get our royal meaning," said Jarry.

"Mr. Henri-Jules Rousseau," said the man.

"Mr. Alfred-Henri Jarry." They shook hands.

"I paint," said Rousseau.

"We set people's hair afire," said Jarry.

"You must look me up; my studio is on the Boulevard du Port-Royal."

"We will be happy if a fellow Lavalese accompanies us immediately to drink, do drugs, visit the brothels and become fast friends for life."

"Are you kidding?" said Rousseau. "They're getting ready to serve the cabbage back in there. Do look me up, though," he said, heading back in toward the banquet hall and putting his napkin back under his chin.

"We shall," said Jarry, and mounted his high-wheeler and was gone into the darkness.

VI. NEWS FROM ALL OVER

January 14, 1895 *Le Cycliste Français*

TRAITOR ON THE GENERAL STAFF!

ARREST AND TRIAL OF THE JEW CAPTAIN DREYFUS

DEGRADATION AND STRIPPING OF RANK

DEPORTATION TO GUIANA FOR LIFE

"Secrets vital to the Nation," says a General, "from which our Enemy will profit and France never recover. It is only the new lenient Jew-inspired law which kept the Tribunal from sentencing the human rat to Death!"

VII. LIKE THE SPOKES OF A LUMINOUS WHEEL

The reporter Norpois rode a crocodile velocipede of singular aspect. Its frame was low and elongated. The seat was at the absolute center of the bicycle's length, making it appear as if its rider were disincorporated.

Though extremely modern in that respect, its wheels were anachronisms, heavily spoked and rimmed to the uncaring eye. On a close examination it was revealed the spokes were ironwork, eight to each wheel, and over them were wrought two overlapping semicircles, one of a happy, the other of a sad, aspect of the human face.

In unison, front and back, the wheels first smiled, then frowned at the world around them as they whirled their rider along the newly macadamized roads and streets.

In his sporty cap and black knickers, Norpois seemed almost to lean between the wheels of strife and fortune. Other bicyclists paused to watch him go spoking silently by, with an almost inaudible whisper of iron rim on asphalt. The crocodile frame seemed far too graceful and quiet for the heavy wheels on which it rode.

Norpois worked for *Le Cycliste Français*. His assignments took him to many *arrondissements* and the outlying parts of the city.

He was returning from interviewing a retired general before sunset one evening, when, preparatory to stopping to light his carbide handlebar-lamp, he felt a tickle of heat at his face, then a dull throbbing at his right temple. To his left, the coming sunset seemed preternaturally bright, and he turned his head to look at it.

His next conscious thought was of picking himself and his velocipede up from the side of the road where he had evidently fallen. He noticed he was several meters down the road from where he had turned to look at the sunset. His heart hammered in his chest. The knees of his knickers were dusty, his left hand was scraped, with two small pieces of gravel embedded in the skin, and he had bitten his lip, which was beginning to swell. He absently dug the gravel from his hand. He had no time for small aches and pains. He had to talk to someone.

"Jules," he said to the reporter who shared the three-room apartment with him. As he spoke he filled a large glass with half a bottle of cognac and began sipping at it between his sentences. "I must tell you what life will be like in twenty years."

"You, Robida, and every other frustrated engineer," said Jules, putting down his evening paper.

"Tonight I have had an authentic vision of the next century. It came to me not at first as a visual illusion, a pattern on my eyes, some ecstatic vision. It came to me first through my nose, Jules. An overpowering, oppressive odor. Do you know what the coming years smell like, Jules? They smell of burning flesh. It was the first thing to come to me, and the last to leave. Think of the worst fire you ever covered. Remember the charred bodies, the popped bones? Multiply it by a city, a nation, a hemisphere! It was like that.

"The smell came, then I saw in the reddened clouds a line of ditches, miles, kilometers upon thousands of kilometers of ditches in churned earth, men like troglodytes killing each other as far as the eye could see, smoke everywhere, the sky raining death, the sky filled with aerial machines dropping explosives; detonations coming and going like giant brown trees which sprout, leaf and die in an instant. Death everywhere, from the air, from guns, shells falling on all beneath them, the aerial machines pausing in their rain of death below only to shoot each other down. Patterns above the ditches, like vines, curling vines covered with thorns—over all a pattern formed on my retina—always the incessant chatter of machinery, screams, fire, death-agonies, men stomping each other in mud and earth. I could see it all, hear it all, above all else, smell it all, Jules, and . . ."

"Yes?"

"Jules, it was the most beautiful thing I have ever experienced."

He stared at his roommate.

"There's some cold mutton on the table," said Jules. "And

half a bottle of beer." He looked back down at his paper. After a few minutes he looked up. Norpois stood, looking out the window at the last glow of twilight, still smiling.

VIII. ONE ORDINARY DAY, WITH ANARCHISTS

Alfred Jarry sailed along the boulevard, passing people and other cyclists right and left. Two and a half meters up, he bent over his handlebars, his cap at a rakish angle, his hair a black flame behind his head. He was the very essence of speed and grace, no longer a dwarfish man of slight build. A novice rider on a safety bicycle took a spill ahead of him. Jarry used his spoon-brake to stop a few centimeters short of the wide-eyed man who feared broken ribs, death, a mangled vehicle.

Then Jarry jumped up and down on his seat, his feet on the locked pedals, jerking the ordinary in small jumps a meter to the left until his path was clear, then he was gone down the road as if nothing had happened.

Riders who drew even with him dropped back—Jarry had a carbine slung across his back, carried bandoliers of cartridges for it on his chest, had two Colt pistols sticking from the waistband of his pants, the legs of which were tucked into his socks, knicker-fashion. Jarry was fond of saying firearms, openly displayed, were signs of peaceableness and good intentions, and wholly legal. He turned down a side street and did not hear the noise from the Chamber of Deputies.

A man named Vaillant, out of work, with a wife and children, at the end of his tether, had gone to the Chamber carrying with him a huge sandwich made from a whole loaf of bread. He sat quietly watching a debate on taxes, opened the sandwich to reveal a device made of five sticks of the new dynamite, a fuse and blasting cap, covered with one and a half kilos of #4 nails. He lit it in one smooth motion, jumped to the edge of the gallery balcony and tossed it high into the air.

It arced, stopped, and fell directly toward the center of the Chamber. Some heard the commotion, some saw it; Dreyfussards sensed it and ducked.

It exploded six meters in the air.

Three people were killed, 47 injured badly, more than 70 less so. Desks were demolished; the speaker's rostrum was turned to wood lace.

Vaillant was grabbed by alert security guards.

The first thing that happened, while people moaned and crawled out from under their splintered desks, was that the eight elected to the Chamber of Deputies on the Anarchist ticket, some of them having to pull nails from their hands and cheeks to do so, stood and began to applaud loudly. "Bravo!" they yelled, "Bravo! Encore!"

IX. THE KID FROM SPAIN

His name was Pablo, and he was a big-nosed, big-eyed Spanish kid who had first come to Paris with his mother two years before at the age of 13; now he was back on his own as an art student.

On this trip, the first thing he learned to do was fuck, the second was to learn to paint.

One day a neighbor pointed out to him the figure of Jarry tearing down the street. Pablo thought the tiny man on the huge bicycle, covered with guns and bullets, was the most romantic thing he had ever seen in his life. Pablo immediately went out and bought a pistol, a .22 single-shot, and took to wearing it in his belt.

He was sketching the River one morning when the shadow of a huge wheel fell on the ground beside him. Pablo looked up. It was Jarry, studying the sketch over his shoulder.

Pablo didn't know what to do or say, so he took out his gun and showed it to Jarry.

Jarry looked embarrassed. "We are touched," he said, laying his hand on Pablo's shoulder. "Take one of ours," he said, handing him a .38 Webley. Then he was up on his ordinary and gone.

Pablo did not remember anything until it was getting dark and he was standing on a street, sketchbook in one hand, pistol still held by the barrel in the other. He must have walked the streets all day that way, a seeming madman.

He was outside a brothel. He checked his pockets for money, smiled, and went in.

X. MORE BEANS, PLEASE

"Georges Méliès," said Rousseau, "Alfred Jarry."

"Pleased."

"We are honored."

"Erik Satie," said Méliès, "Henri Rousseau."

"Charmed."

"At last!"

"This is Pablo," said Satie. "Marcel Proust."

"Lo."

"Delighted," said Rousseau, "Mme. Méliès."

"Dinner is served," she said.

"But of course," said Marcel, "*everyone* knows evidence was introduced in secret at the first trial, evidence the defense was not allowed to see."

"Ah, but that's the military mind for you!" said Rousseau. "It was the same when I played piccolo for my country between 1864 and 1871. What matters is not the evidence, but that the charge has been brought against you in the first place. It proves you guilty."

"Out of my complete way of thinking," said Satie, taking another helping of calamari in aspic, "having been unfortunate enough to be a civilian all my life . . ."

"Here, here!" they all said.

". . . but is it not true that they asked him to copy the *bordereau*, the list found in the trash at the German Embassy and introduced *that* at the court-martial, rather than the original outline of our defenses?"

"More beans, please," said Pablo.

"That is one theory," said Marcel. "The list, of course, leaves off halfway down, because Dreyfus realized what was going to happen as they were questioning him back in December of '94."

"That's the trouble," said Rousseau. "There are too many theories, and of course, none of this will be introduced at the Court of Cassation next month. Nothing but the original evidence, and of course, the allegations brought up by Colonel Picquart, whose own trial for insubordination is scheduled month after next."

Méliès sighed. "The problem, of course, is that we shall

suffer one trial after another; the generals are all covering ass now. First they convict an innocent man on fabricated evidence. Finding the spying has not stopped with the wrongful imprisonment of Dreyfus, they listen to Colonel Picquart, no friend of anyone, who tells them it's the Alsatian Esterhazy, but Esterhazy's under the protection of someone in the War Ministry, so they send Picquart off to Fort Zinderneuf, hoping he will be killed by the Rifs; when he returns covered with scars and medals, they throw him in jail on trumped-up charges of daring to question the findings of the court-martial. Meanwhile the public outcry becomes so great that the only way things can be kept at status quo is to say questioning Dreyfus' guilt is to question France itself. We can all hope, but of course, there can probably be only one verdict of the court of review."

"More turkey, please," said Pablo.

"The problem, of course," said Satie, "is that France needs to be questioned if it breeds such monsters of arrogance and vanity."

"Excuse me, Mr. Satie," said Madame Méliès, speaking for the first time in an hour. "The problem, of course, is that Dreyfus is a Jew."

She had said the thing none of the others had yet said, the thing at base, root and crown of the Affair.

"And being so," said Jarry, "We are sure, Madame, if through our actions this wronged man is freed, he will be so thankful as to allow Our Royal Person to put him upon the nearest cross, with three nails, for whatever period we deem appropriate."

"Pass the wine, please," said Pablo.

"It is a rough time for us," said Jarry, "what with our play to go into production soon, but we shall give whatever service we can to this project."

"Agreed by all, then!" said Méliès. "Star Films takes the unprecedented step of collaborating with others! I shall set aside an *entire week*, that of Tuesday next, for the production of *The Dreyfus Affair*. Bring your pens, your brushes, your ideas! Mr. Satie, our piano at the Théâtre Robert-Houdin is at your disposal for practice and for the *première*; begin your plans now. And so, having decided the fate of France, let us visit the production facilities at the rear of the property, then return to the parlor for cigars and port!"

They sat in comfortable chairs. Satie played a medley of popular songs, those he knew by heart from his days as the relief piano player at the Black Cat; Méliès, who had a very good voice, joined Pablo and Rousseau (who was sorry he had not brought his violin) in a rousing rendition of "The Tired Workman's Song."

Jarry and Proust sat with unlit cigars in their mouths.

"Is it true you studied with Professor Bergson, at the Lycée Henri IV?" asked Marcel. "I was class of '91."

"We are found out," said Alfred. "We were class of all the early 1890s, and consider ourselves his devoted pupil still."

"Is it his views on time, on duration? His idea that character comes in instants of perception and memory? Is it his notion of memory as a flux of points in the mind that keeps you under his spell?" asked Proust.

"He makes us laugh," said Jarry.

They spent the rest of the evening, after meeting and bidding goodnight to the Méliès children, and after Madame Méliès rejoined them, playing charades, doing a quick round of Dreyfus Parcheesi, and viewing pornographic stereopticon cards, of which Georges had a truly wonderful collection.

They said their goodbyes at the front gate of the Montreuil house. Pablo had already gone, having a hot date with anyone at a certain street address, on his kangaroo bicycle; Rousseau walked the two blocks to catch an omnibus; Satie, as was his wont, strode off into the night at a brisk pace whistling an Aristide Bruant tune; he sometimes walked twenty kilometers to buy a piece of sheet music without a second thought.

Marcel's coachman waited. Jarry stood atop the Méliès wall, ready to step onto his ordinary. Georges and Madame had already gone back up the walkway.

Then Marcel made a Proposal to Alfred, which, if acted upon, would take much physical activity and some few hours of their time.

"We are touched by many things lately," said Jarry. "We fear we grow sentimental. Thank you for your kind attention,

Our Dear Marcel, but we must visit the theater, later to meet with Pablo to paint scenery, and our Royal Drug Larder runs low. We thank you, though, from the bottom of our heart, graciously."

And he was gone, silently, a blur under each gaslamp he passed.

For some reason, during the ride back to Faubourg Ste.-Germain, Marcel was not depressed as he usually was when turned down. He too, hummed a Bruant song. The coachman joined in.

Very well, very well, thought Proust. We shall give them a Dreyfus they will *never* forget.

XI. THE ENRAGED UMBRELLA

In the park, two days later, Marcel thought he was seeing a runaway carousel.

"Stop!" he yelled to the cabriolet driver. The brake squealed. Marcel leapt out, holding his top-hat in his hand. "Wait!" he called back over his shoulder.

There was a medium-sized crowd, laborers, fashionable people out for a stroll, several tricycles and velocipedes parked nearby. Attention was all directed toward an object in the center of the crowd. There was a wagon nearby, with small machines all around it.

What Marcel had at first taken for a merry-go-round was not. It *was* round, and it did go.

The most notable feature looked like a ten-meter in diameter Japanese parasol made of, Marcel guessed, fine wire struts and glued paper. Coming down from the center of this, four meters long, was a central pipe, at its bottom was a base shaped like a plumb bob. Above this base, a seat, pedals and a set of levers faced the central column. Above the seat, halfway down the pipe, parallel to the umbrella mechanism, was what appeared to be a weathervane, at the front end of which, instead of an arrow, was a spiral, two-bladed airscrew. At its back, where the iron fletching would be, was a half-circle structure, containing within it a round panel made of the same stuff as the parasol. Marcel saw that it was rotatable on two axes, obviously a steering mechanism of some sort.

Three men in coveralls worked at the base; two holding the

machine vertical while the third tightened bolts with a
wrench, occasionally giving the pedal mechanism a turn,
which caused the giant umbrella above to spin slowly.

Obviously the machine was very lightweight—what appeared to be iron must be aluminium or some other alloy, the
strutwork must be very fine, possibly piano wire.

The workman yelled. He ran the pedal around with his
hand. The paper-wire umbrella moved very fast indeed.

At the call, a man in full morning suit, like Marcel's, came
out from behind the wagon. He walked very solemnly to the
machine, handed his walking stick to a bystander, and sat
down on the seat. He produced two bicyclist's garters from
his coat and applied them to the legs of his trousers above his
spats and patent-leather shoes.

He moved a couple of levers with his hands and began to
pedal, slowly at first, then faster. The moving parasol became
a flat disk, then began to strobe, appearing to move backwards. The small airscrew began a lazy revolution.

There was a soft growing purr in the air. Marcel felt gentle
wind on his cheek.

The man nodded to the mechanics, who had been holding
the machine steady and upright. They let go. The machine
stood of its own accord. The grass beneath it waved and
shook in a streamered disk of wind.

The man doffed his top hat to the crowd. Then he threw another lever. The machine, with no strengthening of sound or
extra effort from its rider, rose three meters into the air.

The crowds gasped and cheered. *"Vive la France!"* they
yelled. Marcel, caught up in the moment, had a terrible desire
to applaud.

Looking to right and left beneath him, the aeronaut moved
a lever slightly. The lazy twirling propeller on the weathervane became a corkscrewing blur. With a very polite nod of
his head, the man pedalled a little faster.

Men threw their hats in the air, women waved their four-
meter-long scarves at him.

The machine, with a sound like the slow shaking-out of a
rug, turned and moved slowly off toward the Boulevard
Haussmann, the crowd, and children who had been running in
from all directions, following it.

While one watched, the other two mechanics loaded gear

into the wagon. Then all three mounted, turned the horses, and started off at a slow roll in the direction of the heart of the city.

Marcel's last glimpse of the flying machine was of it disappearing gracefully down the line of an avenue above the tree-tops, as if an especially interesting woman, twirling her parasol, had just left a pleasant garden party.

Proust and the cabriolet driver were the only persons left on the field. Marcel climbed back in, nodded. The driver applied the whip to the air.

It was, Marcel would read later, the third heavier-than-air machine to fly that week, the forty-ninth since the first of the year, the one-hundred-twelfth since man had entered what the weeklies referred to as the Age of the Air late year-before-last.

XII. THE PERSISTENCE OF VISION

The sound of hammering and sawing filled the workshop. Rousseau painted stripes on a life-sized tiger puppet. Pablo worked on the silhouette jungle foliage Henri had sketched. Jarry went back and forth between helping them and going to the desk to consult with Proust on the scenario. (Proust had brought in closely-written pages, copied in a fine hand, that he had done at home the first two days; after Jarry and Méliès drew circles and arrows all over them, causing Marcel visible anguish, he had taken to bringing in only hastily-worded notes. The writers were trying something new—both scenario *and* title cards were to be written by them.)

"Gentlemen," said Satie, from his piano in the corner. "The music for the degradation scene!" His left hand played heavy bass notes spare, foreboding. His right hit every other note from "La Marseillaise."

"Marvelous," they said. "Wonderful!"

They went back to their paintpots. The Star Films workmen threw themselves into the spirit wholeheartedly, taking directions from Rousseau or Proust as if they were Méliès himself. They also made suggestions, explaining the mechanisms which would, or could, be used in the filming.

"Fellow collaborators!" said Méliès, entering from the yard. "Gaze on our Dreyfus!" He gestured dramatically.

A thin balding man, dressed in cheap overalls entered, cap in hand. They looked at him, each other, shifted from one foot to another.

"Come, come, geniuses of France!" said Méliès. "You're not using your imaginations!"

He rolled his arm in a magician's flourish. A blue coat appeared in his hands. The man put it on. Better.

"Avec!" said Méliès, reaching behind his own back, producing a black army cap, placing it on the man's head. Better still.

"Voilà!" he said, placing a mustache on the man's lip.

To Proust, it was the man he had served under seven years before, grown a little older and more tired. A tear came to Marcel's eye; he began to applaud, the others joined in.

The man seemed nervous, did not know what to do with his hands. "Come, come, Mr. Poulvain, get used to applause," said Méliès. "You'll soon have to quit your job at the chicken farm to portray Captain Dreyfus on the international stage!" The man nodded and left the studio.

Marcel sat back down and wrote with redoubled fury.

"Monsieur Méliès?" asked Rousseau.

"Yes?"

"Something puzzles me."

"How can I help?"

"Well, I know nothing about the making of cinematographs, but, as I understand, you take the pictures, from beginning to the end of the scenario, in series, then choose the best ones to use after you have developed them?"

"Exactement!" said Georges.

"Well, as I understand (if only Jarry and Proust would quit diddling with the writing), we use the same prison cell both for the early arrest scenes, and for Dreyfus' cell on Devil's Island?"

"Yes?"

"Your foreman explained that we would film the early scenes, break the backdrops, shoot other scenes, and some days or hours later reassemble the prison cell again, with suitable changes. Well, it seems to me, to save time and effort, you should film the early scenes, then change the costume and the makeup on the actor, and add the properties which represent Devil's Island, and put those scenes in their proper place v hen the scenes are developed. That way, you would be through with both sets, and go on to another."

Méliès looked at him a moment. The old artist was covered with blobs of grey, white and black paint. "My dear Rousseau; we have never done it that way, since it cannot be done that way in the theater. But . . ."

Rousseau was pensive. "Also, I noticed that great care must be taken in moving the camera, and that right now the camera is to be moved many times in the filming. Why not also photograph all the scenes where the camera is in one place a certain distance from the stage, then all the others at the next, and so on? It seems more efficient that way, to me."

"Well," said Méliès. "That is surely asking too much! But your first suggestion, in the interest of saving time with the scenery. Yes. Yes, we could possibly do that! Thank you . . . as it is going now, the trial may very well be over before we even *begin* filming—if someone doesn't shoot Dreyfus as he sits in court since his return from Devil's Island even *before* that. Perhaps we shall try your idea . . ."

"Just thinking aloud," said Rousseau.

"Monsieur Director?" said Marcel.

"Yes?"

"Something puzzles me."

"Yes?"

"I've seen few Lumièreoscopes—"

"That name!" said Méliès, clamping his hands over his ears.

"Sorry . . . I've seen few films, at any rate. But in each one (and it comes up here in the proposed scenario) that we have Dreyfus sitting in his cell, on one side, the cutaway set of the hut with him therein, then the guard walks up and pounds on the door. Dreyfus gets up, goes to the door, opens it and the guard walks in and hands him the first letter he is allowed to receive from France."

"A fine scene!" said Méliès.

"Hmmm. Yes. Another thing I have seen in all Lu—in moving pictures is that the actor is always filmed as if you were watching them on stage, their whole bodies from a distance of a few meters away."

"That is the only way it is done, my dear Marcel."

"Perhaps . . . perhaps we could do it another way. We see Dreyfus in his hut, in his chair. We show only his upper body, from waist to head. We could see the ravages of the ordeal upon him, the lines in his face, the circles under his eyes, the grey in his hair."

"But . . ."

"Hear me please. Then you show a fist, as if it were in your face, pounding on the door. From inside the hut Dreyfus gets up, turns, walks to the door. Then he is handed the letter. We see the letter itself, the words of comfort and despair . . ."

Méliès was looking at him as if there were pinwheels sticking from his eye sockets.

". . . can you imagine the effects on the viewer?" finished Marcel.

"Oh yes!" said Méliès. "They would scream. Where are their legs? Where are their arms? What is this writing doing in my eye?!!!"

"But think of the impact! The drama?"

"Marcel, we are here to plead for justice, not frighten people away from the theater!"

"Think of it! What better way to show the impact on Dreyfus than by putting the impact on the spectator?"

"My head reels, Proust!"

"Well, just a suggestion. Sleep on it."

"I shall have nightmares," said Méliès.

Pablo continued to paint, eating a sandwich, drinking wine.

"Méliès?" said Jarry.

"(Sigh) Yes?"

"Enlighten us."

"In what manner?"

"Our knowledge of motio-kineto-photograms is small, but one thing is a royal poser to us."

"Continue."

"In our wonderful scene of the nightmares . . . We are led to understand that Monsieur Rousseau's fierce tigers are to be moved by wires, compressed air and frantic stagehands?"

"Yes."

"Our mind works overtime. The fierce tigers are wonderful,

but such movement will be seen, let us say, like fierce tigers moved by wires, air and stage-labor."

"A necessary convention of stage and cinematograph," said Méliès. "One the spectator accepts."

"But we are not here to have the viewer accept anything but an intolerable injustice to a man."

"True, but pity . . ."

"Méliès," said Jarry. "We understand each click of the camera takes one frame of film. Many of these frames projected at a constant rate leads to the illusion of motion. But each is of itself but a single frame of film."

"The persistence of vision," said Méliès.

"We were thinking. What if we took a single click of the camera, taking one picture of our fierce tigers . . ."

"But what would that accomplish?"

"Ah . . . then, Méliès, our royal personage moves the tiger to a slightly different posture, but the next in some action, but only one frame advanced, and took another click of the camera?"

Méliès looked at him. "Then . . ."

"Then the next and the next and the next and so on! The fierce tiger moves, roars, springs, devours! But each frame part of the movement, each frame a still."

Méliès thought a second. "An actor in the scenes would not be able to move at all. Or he would have to move at the same rate as the tiger. He would have to hold perfectly still (we already do that when stopping the camera to substitute a skeleton for a lady or somesuch) but they would have to do it endlessly. It would take weeks to get any good length of film. Also, the tigers would have to be braced, strutted to support their own weight."

"This is our *idea*, Méliès; we are not technicians."

"I shall take it under advisement."

Méliès' head began to hurt. He had a workman go to the chemists, and get some of the new Aspirin for him. He took six.

The film took three weeks to photograph. Méliès had to turn out three fairy tales in two days besides to keep his salesmen supplied with footage. Every day they worked the Court of Cassation met to rehear the Dreyfus case, every day

brought new evasions, new half-insinuations; Dreyfus' lawyer
was wounded by a gunshot while leaving court. Every day the
country was split further and further down the center: there
was no middle ground. There was talk of a *coup d'état* by the
right.

At last the footage was done.

"I hope," said Méliès to his wife that night, "I hope that after this I shall not hear the name of Dreyfus again, for the rest
of my life."

XIII. THE ELEPHANT AT THE FOOT OF THE BED

Jarry was on stage, talking in a monotone as he had been
for five minutes. The crowd, including women, had come to
the Theater of the Work to see what new horrors Lugné-Poe
had in store for them.

Alfred sat at a small folding table which had been brought
on stage, and a chair placed behind it, facing the audience.
Jarry talked, as someone said, as a nutcracker would speak.
The audience had listened but was growing restless—we have
come for a play, not for someone dressed as a bicyclist to
drone on about nothing in particular.

The last week had been a long agony for Jarry—working
on this play, which he had started in his youth, as a puppet
play satirizing a pompous teacher—it had grown to encom-
pass all mankind's foibles, all national and human delusions.
Then there had been the work on the Dreyfus film with Pablo
and Rousseau and Proust and Méliès—it had been trying and
demanding, but it was like pulling teeth, too collaborative,
with its own limitations and ideas. Give a man the freedom of
the page and boards!

Jarry ran down like a clock. He finished tiredly.

"The play takes place in Poland, which is to say, Nowhere." He picked up his papers while two stagehands took
off the table and chair. Jarry left. The lights dimmed. There
were three raps on the floor with Lugné-Poe's cane, the curtains opened in the darkness as the lights came up.

The walls were painted as a child might have—representing
sky, clouds, stars, the sun, moon, elephants, flowers, a clock
with no hands, snow falling on a cheery fireplace.

A round figure stood at one side, his face hidden by a
pointed hood on which was painted the slitted eyes and mustache of a caricature bourgeoisie. His costume was a white
canvas cassock with an immense stomach on which was
painted three concentric circles.

The audience tensed, leaned forward. The figure stepped to
the center of the stage, looked around.

"Merde!" he said.

The riot could be heard for a kilometer in all directions.

XIV. WHAT HE *REALLY* THINKS

"Today, France has left the past of Jew-traitors and degen-
eracy behind.

"Today, she has taken the final step toward greatness, a return to the True Faith, a way out of the German-Jew morass
in which she has floundered for a quarter-century.

"With the second conviction of the traitor-spy Dreyfus, she
sends a signal to all his rat-like kind that France will no
longer tolerate impurities in its body-politic, its armies, its
commerce. She has served notice that the Future is written in
the French language; Europe, indeed the world, shall one day
speak only one tongue, Française.

"The verdict of—Guilty!—even with its softening of 'With
extenuating circumstances' will end this Affair, once and for
all, the only way—short of public execution by the most ex-
cruciating means, which, unfortunately the law no longer
allows—ah! but True Frenchmen are working to change
that!—that it could be ended; with the slow passing of this
Jew-traitor to rot in the jungle of Devil's Island—a man who
should never have been allowed to don the uniform of this
country in the first place.

"Let there be no more talk of injustice! Injustice has already been served by the spectacle of a thoroughly guilty man
being given *two* trials; by a man not worth a sous causing
great agitation—surely the work of enemies of the state.

"Let every true Frenchman hold this day sacred until the
end of time. Let him turn his eyes eastward at our one Great
Enemy, against that day when we shall rise up and gain just
vengeance—let him not forget also to look around him, let
him not rest until every Christ-murdering Jew, every German-

inspired Protestant is driven from the boundaries of this country, or gotten rid of in an equally advantageous way—their
property confiscated, their businesses closed, their 'rights'—
usurped rights!—nullified.

"If this decision wakens Frenchmen to that threat, then
Dreyfus will have, in all his evil machinations, his total acqui-
escence to our enemy's plans, done one good deed: he will
have given us the reason not to rest ·until every one of his
kind is gone from the face of the earth; that in the future the
only place Hebrew will be spoken is in Hell."

—Robert Norpois

XV. TRUTH RISES FROM THE WELL

Emile Zola stared at the white sheet of paper with the British watermark.

He dipped his pen in the bottle of Pelikan ink in the well
and began to write.

As he wrote, the words became scratchier, more hurried.
All his feelings of frustration boiled over in his head and out
onto the fine paper. The complete cowardice and stultification
of the Army, the anti-Semitism of the rich *and* the poor, the
Church; the utter stupidity of the government, the treason of
the writers who refused to come to the aid of an innocent
man.

It was done sooner than he thought; six pages of his con-
tempt and utter revulsion with the people of the country he
loved more than life itself.

He put on his coat and hat and hailed a pedal cabriolet, or-
dering it to the offices of *L'Aurore*. The streets were more
empty than usual, the cafés full. The news of the second trial
verdict had driven good people to drink. He was sure there
were raucous celebrations in every Church, every fort, and the
basement drill-halls of every right-wing organization in the
city and the country. This was an artist's quarter—there was
no loud talk, no call to action. There would be slow and de-
liberate drunkenness and oblivion for all against the atrocious
verdict.

Zola sat back against the cushion, listening to the clicking
pedals of the driver. He wondered if all this would end with

the nation, half on one side of some field, half on the other, charging each other in a final bloodbath.

He paid the driver, who swerved silently around and headed back the other way. Zola stepped into the *Aurora*'s office, where Clemenceau waited for him behind his desk. Emile handed him the manuscript.

Clemenceau read the first sentence, wrote, "Page One, 360 point RED TYPE headline—'J'ACCUSE'," called "Copy boy!", said to the boy, "I shall be back for a proof in three hours," put on his coat, and arm in arm he and Zola went off to the Théâtre Robert-Houdin for the first showing of Star Films' *The Dreyfus Affair*, saying not a word to each other.

XVI. CHAMBER POTS SHALL LIGHT YOUR WAY

Zola and Clemenceau, crying tears of pride and exultation, ran back arm in arm down the Place de l'Opéra, turning into a side street toward the publisher's office.

Halfway down, they began to sing "La Marseillaise"; people who looked out their windows, not knowing the reason, assumed their elation for that of the verdict of the second trial, flung *merde* pots at them from second story windows. "Anti-Dreyfussard scum!" they yelled, shaking their fists. "Wait till I get my fowling piece!"

Emile and Georges ran into the office, astonishing the editors and reporters there.

They went to Clemenceau's desk, where the page proof of Zola's article waited, with a separate proof of the red headline.

Zola picked up the proof.

"No need of this, my dear Georges?"

"I think not, my friend Emile."

Zola shredded it, throwing the strips on the pressman who was waiting in the office for word from Clemenceau.

"Rip off the front page!" Clemenceau yelled out the door of his office. "We print a review of a moving picture there! Get Veyou out of whatever theater watching whatever piece of stage-pap he's in and hustle him over to the Robert-Houdin for the second showing!"

Emile and Georges looked at each other, remembering.

"The Awful Trip To The Island!"

"The Tigers of the Imagination!"
"First News of Home!" said Emile.
"Star Films," said Clemenceau.
"Méliès," said Zola.
"Dreyfus!" they said in unison.

Three days later, the President overturned the conviction of the second court, pardoned Dreyfus and returned him to his full rank and privileges. The Ministry of War was reorganized, and the resignations of eleven generals received.

The President was, of course, shot down like a dog on the way home from a cabinet meeting that night. Three days of mourning were declared.

Dreyfus had been released the same night, and went to the country home of his brother Mathieu; he was now a drawn, shaken man whose hair had turned completely white.

XVII. THREE FAMOUS QUOTES WHICH LED TO DUELS:

1. "The baron writes the kind of music a priest can hum while he is raping a choirboy."

2. "I see you carry the kind of cane which allows you to hit a woman eight or ten times before it breaks."

3. "Monsieur Jarry," said Norpois, "I demand satisfaction for your insults to France during the last three years."

"Captain Dreyfus is proved innocent. We have called attention to nothing that was not the action of madmen and cowards."

"You are a spineless dwarf masturbator with the ideas of a toad!" said Norpois.

"Our posture, stature and habits are known to every schoolboy in France, Mister Journalist," said Jarry. "We have come through five years of insult, spittle and outrage. Nothing you say will make Dreyfus guilty, or goad our royal person into a gratuitous display of our unerring marksmanship."

Jarry turned to walk away with Pablo.

"Then, Monsieur Jarry, your bicycle . . ." said Norpois.

Jarry stopped. "What of Our Royal Vehicle?"

"Your bicycle eats *merde* sandwiches."

XVIII. THE DOWNHILL BICYCLE RACE

A. Prelims

The anemometer barely moved behind his head. The vane at its top pointed to the south; the windsock swelled and emptied slowly.

Jarry slowly recovered his breath. Below and beyond lay the city of Paris and its environs. The Seine curved like a piece of grey silk below and out to two horizons. It was just after dawn; the sun was a fat red beet to the east.

It was still cool at the weather station atop the Eiffel Tower, 300 meters above the ground.

Jarry leaned against his high-wheeler. He had taken only the least minimum of fortifying substances, and that two hours ago on this, the morning of the duel.

Proust had acted as his second (Jarry would have chosen Pablo—good thing he hadn't, as the young painter had not shown up with the others this morning, perhaps out of fear of seeing Jarry maimed or killed—but Proust had defended himself many times, with a large variety of weapons, on many fields of honor). Second for Norpois was the journalist whose hair Alfred had set afire at the banquet more than a year ago. As the injured party, Jarry had had choice of place and weapons.

The conditions were thus: weapons, any. Place: the Eiffel Tower. Duelists *must* be mounted on their bicycles when using their weapons. Jarry would start at the weather station at the top, Norpois at the base. After Jarry was taken to the third platform, using all three sets of elevators on the way up, and the elevator man—since this was a day of mourning, the tower was closed, and the guards paid to look the other way—returned to the ground, the elevators could not be used, only the stairways. Jarry had still had to climb the spiral steps from the third platform to the weather station, from which he was now recovering.

With such an arrangement, Norpois would, of course, be waiting in ambush for him on the second observation platform by the time Jarry reached it. Such was the nature of duels.

Jarry looked down the long swell of the south leg of the

tower—it was grey, smooth and curved as an elephant's trunk, plunging down and out into the earth. Tiny dots waited there; Norpois, the journalist, Proust, a few others, perhaps by now Pablo. The Tower cast a long shadow out away from the River. The shadow of the Trocadéro almost reached to the base of the Tower in the morning sun. There was already talk of painting the Tower again, for the coming Exposition of 1900 in a year and a half.

Alfred took a deep breath, calmed himself. He was lightly armed, having only a five-shot .32 revolver in his holster and a poniard in a sheath on his hip. He would have felt almost naked except for the excruciatingly heavy but comforting weapon slung across his shoulders.

It was a double-barreled Greener 4-bore Rhino Express which could fire a 130-gram bullet at 1200 meters per second. Jarry had decided that if he *had* to kill Norpois, he might as well wipe him off the face of the earth.

He carried four extra rounds in a bandolier; they weighed more than a kilo in all.

He was confident in his weapons, in himself, in his high-wheeler. He had oiled it the night before, polished it until it shone. After all, it was the insulted party, not him, not Dreyfus.

He sighed, then leaned out and dropped the lead-weighted green handkerchief as the signal he was starting down. He had his ordinary over his shoulder opposite the Greener and had his foot on the first step before he heard the weighted handkerchief ricocheting on its way down off the curved leg of the Tower.

B. The Duel

He was out of breath before he passed the locked apartment which Gustave Eiffel had built for himself during the last phase of construction of the Tower, and which he sometimes used when aerodynamic experiments were being done on the drop-tube which ran down the exact center of the Tower.

Down around the steps he clanged, his bike brushing against the spiral railing. It was good he was not subject to vertigo. He could imagine Norpois' easy stroll to the west leg, where he would be casually walking up the broad stairs to the

first level platform with its four restaurants, arcades and
booths, and its entry to the stilled second set of elevators.
(Those between the ground and first level were the normal
counterweighted kind; hydraulic ones to the second—
American Otis had had to set up a dummy French corporation
to win the contract—no one in France had the technology, and
the charter forbade foreign manufacture; and tracked ones to
the third—passengers had to change halfway up, as no elevator could be made to go from roughly 70° to 90° halfway up
its rise.

Panting mightily, Jarry reached the third platform, less than
a third of the way down. Only 590 more steps down to sure
and certain ambush. The rifle, cartridges and high-wheeler
were grinding weights on his back. Gritting his teeth, he
started down the steep steps with landings every few dozen
meters.

His footsteps rang like gongs on the iron treads. He could
see the tops of the booths on the second level, the iron frame-
work of the Tower extending all around him like a huge narrow cage.

Norpois would be waiting at one of the corners, ready to
fire at either set of stairs. (Of course, he probably already
knew which set Jarry was using, oh devious man, or it was
possible he was truly evil and was waiting on the first level.
It would be just like a right-wing nationalist Catholic safety-
bicycle rider to do that.

Fifteen steps up from the second level, in one smooth
motion, Jarry put the ordinary down, mounted it holding
immobile the pedals with his feet, swung the Rhino Express
off his shoulder, and rode the last crashing steps down, holding back, then pedalling furiously as his giant wheel hit the
floor.

He expected shots at any second as he swerved toward a
closed souvenir booth: he swung his back wheel up and
around behind him, holding still, changing direction, the
drainpipe barrels of the 4-bore resting on the handlebars.

Over at the corner of another booth the front wheel and
handlebar of Norpois' bicycle stuck out.

With one motion Jarry brought the Greener to his cheek.
We shall shoot the front end off his bicycle—without that he

cannot be mounted and fire; ergo, he cannot duel; therefore, we have won; he is disgraced. *Quod Erat Demonstrandum.*

Jarry fired one barrel—the recoil sent him skidding backwards two meters. The forks of the crocodile went away— Fortune's smiling face wavered through the air like the phases of the Moon. The handlebars stuck in the side of another booth six meters away.

Jarry hung onto his fragile balance, waiting for Norpois to tumble forward or stagger bleeding with bicycle shrapnel from behind the booth.

He heard a noise behind him; at the corner of his eye he saw Norpois standing beside one of the planted trees—he had to have been there all along—with a look of grim satisfaction on his face.

Then the grenade landed directly between the great front and small back wheels of Jarry's bicycle.

C. High Above The City

He never felt the explosion, just a wave of heat and a flash that blinded him momentarily. There was a carnival ride sensation, a loopy feeling in his stomach. Something touched his hand; he grabbed it. Something tugged at his leg. He clenched his toes together.

His vision cleared.

He hung by one hand from the guardrail. He dangled over Paris. His rifle was gone. His clothes smelt of powder and burning hair. He looked down. The weight on his legs was his ordinary, looking the worse for wear. The rim of the huge front wheel had caught on the toe of his cycling shoe. He cupped the toe of the other one through the spokes.

His hand was losing its grip.

He reached down with the other for his pistol. The holster was still there, split up the middle, empty.

Norpois' head appeared above him, looking down, then his gun hand with a large automatic in it, pointing at Jarry's eyes.

"There are rules, Monsieur," said Jarry. He was trying to reach up with the other hand but something seemed to be wrong with it.

"Get with the coming century, dwarf," said Norpois, flipping the pistol into the air, catching it by the barrel. He brought the butt down hard on Jarry's fingers.

The second time the pain was almost too much. Once more and Alfred knew he would let go, fall, be dead.

"One request. Save our noble vehicle," said Jarry, looking into the journalist's eyes. There was a clang off somewhere on the second level.

Norpois' grin became sardonic. "You die. So does your crummy bike."

There was a small pop. A thin line of red, like a streak of paint slung off the end of a brush, stood out from Norpois' nose, went over Jarry's shoulder.

Norpois raised his automatic, then wavered, let go of it. It bounced off Alfred's useless arm, clanged once on the way down.

Norpois, still staring into Jarry's eyes, leaned over the railing and disappeared behind his head. There was silence for a few seconds, then:

Pif-Paf! Quel Bruit!

The sound of the body bouncing off the ironworks went on for longer than seemed possible.

Far away on the second level was the sound of footsteps running downstairs.

Painfully, Jarry got his left arm up next to his right, got the fingers closed, began pulling himself up off the side of the Eiffel Tower, bringing his mangled high-wheeler with him.

D. Code Duello

A small crowd had gathered, besides those concerned. Norpois' second was over by the body, with the police. There would of course be damages to pay for. Jarry carried his ordinary and the Greener which he had found miraculously lying on the floor of the second level.

Proust came forward to shake Alfred's hand. Jarry gave him the rifle and ordinary, but continued to walk past him. Several others stepped forward, but Jarry continued on, nodding.

He went to Pablo. Pablo had on a long cloak and was eating an egg sandwich. His eyes would not meet Alfred's.

Jarry stepped in front of him. Pablo tried to move away

without meeting his gaze. Alfred reached inside the cloak, felt around, ignoring the Webley strapped at Pablo's waist.

He found what he was looking for, pulled it out. It was the single-shot .22. Jarry sniffed the barrel as Pablo tried to run away, working at his sandwich.

"Asshole," said Jarry, handing it back.

XIX. *Fin de Cyclé*

The bells were still ringing in the New Century.

Satie had given up composing and had gone back to school to learn music at the age of 38. Rousseau still exhibited at the Salon des Refusés, and was now married for the second time. Proust had locked himself away in a room he'd had lined with cork and was working on a never-ending novel. Méliès was still out at Montreuil, making films about trips to the Moon and the Bureau of Incoherent Geography. Pablo was painting; but so much blue; blue here, blue there, azure, cerulean, Prussian. Dreyfus was now a commandant.

Jarry lived in a shack over the Seine which stood on four supports. He called it Our Suitable Tripod.

There was noise, noise everywhere. There were few bicycles, and all those were safeties. He had not seen another ordinary in months. He looked over where his repaired one stood in the middle of the small room. His owl and one of his crows perched on the handlebars.

The noise was deafening—the sound of bells, of crowds, sharp reports of fireworks. Above all, those of motor-cycles and motor-cars.

He looked back out the window. There was a new sound, a dark flash against the bright moonlit sky. A bat-shape went over, buzzing, trailing laughter and gunshots, the pilot banking over the River. Far up the Seine the Tower stood, bathed in floodlights, glorying in its blue, red, and white paint for the coming Exposition.

A zeppelin droned overhead, electric lights on the side spelling out the name of a hair pomade. The bat-shaped plane whizzed under it in near-collision.

Someone gunned a motor-cycle beneath his tiny window. Jarry reached back into the room, brought out his fowling piece filled with rocksalt and fired a great tongue of flame

into the night below. After a scream, the noise of the motor-
cycle raced away.

He drank from a glass filled with brandy, ether and red ink.
He took one more look around, buffeted by the noise from all
quarters and a motor-launch on the River. He said a word to
the night before slamming the window and returning to his
work on the next Ubu play.

The word was "*merde!*"